P9-DCW-844

DISCARD

A Sampler of Jewish-American Folklore

"This book encapsulates and clearly shows Jewish history in a way that makes it accessible to Jews and non-Jews alike. For those who may have felt disconnected from their roots, this is an interesting way to feel a sense of belonging through ritual and folklore that can touch upon memories of the past."

– Vara Kamin, author of
The Gold Key in the Mahogany Box and Other Fables

"This is a book that is easy to read, but difficult to put aside once started."

– Sid Abrams
Cleveland Jewish News

This title is part of the
American Folklore Series,
which also includes the
following works:

American Indians' Kitchen-Table Stories
Keith Cunningham

Midwestern Folk Humor
James P. Leary

The Oral Tradition of the American West
Adventure, Courtship, Family, and Place
in Traditional Recitation
Keith Cunningham

Mexican-American Folklore
John O. West

American Foodways
What, When, Why and How We Eat in America
Charles Camp

German-American Folklore
Mac E. Barrick

Native American Legends
The Southeastern Tribes
George E. Lankford

American Children's Folklore
Simon J. Bronner

Southern Folk Ballads, Volume I
Southern Folk Ballads, Volume II
W. K. McNeil

Ozark Mountain Humor
W. K. McNeil

A Sampler of Jewish-American Folklore

Josepha Sherman
Illustrations by Jacqueline Chwast

This volume is part of
The American Folklore Series
W.K. McNeil, General Editor

August House Publishers, Inc.
LITTLE ROCK

A Sue Katz & Associates, Inc. Book

© 1992 by Josepha Sherman
All rights reserved. This book, or parts thereof,
may not be reproduced in any form without permission.
Published by August House, Inc.,
P.O. Box 3223, Little Rock, Arkansas, 72203,
501-372-5450
A Sue Katz & Associates, Inc. Book

Printed in the United States of America
10 9 8 7 6 5 4 3 2 1

LIBRARY OF CONGRESS
CATALOGING-IN-PUBLICATION DATA

Sherman, Josepha.
A sampler of Jewish-American Folklore / Josepha Sherman.
p. cm. — (The American folklore series)
1st ed.
Includes bibliographical references (p.)
ISBN 0-87483-194-6 (hb : alk. paper) : $21.95—
ISBN 0-87483-193-8 (pb : alk. paper) : $11.95
1. Jews—United States—Folklore. 2. Jewish folk literature—United States. 3. Jews—United States—Social life and customs. I. Title. II. Series.
GR111. J48S54 1992
398'.089'924073—dc20 92-2844
CIP

First Edition, 1992

This volume is a part of the American Folklore Series
Series editor: W.K. McNeil
Acquisition editor: Liz Parkhurst
Project editor: Sue Katz
Cover and Text Illustrations: Jacqueline Chwast
Design Director: Ted Parkhurst
Cover Design: Harvill-Ross Studios
Typography: Braun-Brumfield, Inc.

This book is printed on archival-quality paper which meets
the guidelines for performance and durability of the
Committee on Production Guidelines for Book Longevity
of the Council on Library Resources.

AUGUST HOUSE, INC. PUBLISHERS LITTLE ROCK
A SUE KATZ & ASSOCIATES, INC. BOOK

For the Altschuler Family

Contents

◇ ◇ ◇

INTRODUCTION

◇ ◇ ◇

On May 5, 1887, a circular letter signed by seventeen people was sent to various parts of the United States and Canada and was followed in October by a second letter bearing one hundred and four signatures. The two letters contained a proposal to establish a folklore society in America, and, on January 4, 1888, this idea became a reality when the American Folklore Society was organized at Cambridge, Massachusetts. Officially the Society was established for two basic purposes: (1) "For the collection of the fast-vanishing remains of Folk-Lore in America" and (2) "For the study of the general subject and publication of the results of special students in this department." Specifically mentioned as being among those "fast-vanishing remains" were "relics of Old English Folk-Lore," Negro and Indian lore, and the lore "of French Canada, Mexico, etc."[1] This brief list obviously omitted most of the ethnic folklore of the New World, one of which was the folk traditions of Jewish-Americans.

Given this expressed bias, it is hardly surprising that relatively little on Jewish-American folklore appeared in the pages of the *Journal of American Folklore*. Six issues appeared before the first article on the topic found its way into the quarterly's pages. That essay, by a German scholar, Friederich S. Krauss, now best remembered for his pioneering work in erotic folklore,[2] bears the interesting title "Jewish Folk-Life in America." This brief paper is not as broad-ranging as its heading suggests, but, rather, is almost exclusively concerned with proverbs. Krauss does, however, issue a plea for Americans to collect and study the folk traditions of Jewish immigrants in their country "before it is too late." He was convinced that the "next generation of Jews will have become merged in Anglo-American folk-life" and thus their traditions would be lost forever. Krauss noted that it wasn't just Americans, but Europeans as well, who were guilty of ignoring Jewish traditions. Indeed, in listing scholars who had dealt with the subject he could come up with only three names, none an American. Yet he noted that the paucity of material was not just attributable to a lack of scholarly interest—the Jewish immigrants also were partially to blame. Many Jews, he said, did not wish to be identified as purveyors of folklore; in other words, to be viewed as old-fashioned. Also, most Jews spoke German, and because of the then growing anti-Semitic movement in German countries, there was a growing Jewish hatred and indignation against everything German, even if that included their own traditions. Simultaneously there was a growing preference among Jews for "the congenial, liberal, and truly exalted spirit of Anglo-American world-citizenship."[3]

Whether the reasons Krauss cited are the chief factors or not, it is undeniable that the situation in regard to the publishing of Jewish-American folklore has changed relatively little since 1894. Indeed, many of Krauss's complaints could be made with equal force today. Little wonder, then, that Raphael Patai asserted in 1960 "that Jewish folklore has not figured so prominently in American folklore research as have several other bodies of folklore, and that the study of American Jewish folklore has not been so integral a part of American folklore research as the study of the folklore of other nationalities in this country."[4]

When one gets to the even more specialized area of folk narratives the record is even more slender. While periodically collections of jests and anecdotes such as *Der Amerikaner Vitzling* (1926), *Arbeter Vitzen* (1927), *Royte Pomerantsen* (1947), and *Jewish Wit and Wisdom* (1969) have been issued, relatively little of a more scholarly nature has appeared. Indeed, it was 1920 before the first notice was given to the topic of Jewish-American folk narratives in an academic publication. This article, "Yiddish Folk Stories and Songs in St. Louis," by a St. Louis high school teacher, Leah Rachel Clara Yoffie, is brief indeed, consisting of only three pages and part of that given to songs.[5] Earlier, in a note in the 1916 issue of the *Journal of American Folklore,* Yoffie referred to legends current among Jewish-Americans but spent most of her space talking about various customs.[6] Yet, Yoffie's scant mention was the only reference to Jewish-American folk narrative in the *Journal of American Folklore* until Raphael Patai's 1946 survey article, "Problems and Tasks of Jewish Folklore and Ethnology," which also did little more than refer to the subject.[7] It was several more years yet before an article solely devoted to Jewish-American folk narrative appeared in the pages of America's foremost folklore publication. Outside the American Folklore Society there was a small body of published materials, but certainly far less than what one might expect considering the richness of the Jewish-American folk narrative tradition.

Despite these gaps in scholarship, the picture is not entirely bleak. In at least one area of Jewish-American folk narrative there has been a steadily growing body of publication, both popular and scholarly, over the past sixty-five years. This single area is that of folk humor: the earlier publications have consisted of collections while in recent years a number of more analytical works have appeared.

The earliest of these publications is Jacob Richman's *Laughs From Jewish Lore* (1926), which the author proudly claims is "the first attempt of its kind in the English language."[8] The book, broken down into seventeen chapters, is noteworthy for other reasons, most significantly for the inclusion of several Jewish-American anecdotes. Richman also attempts to define a Jewish story, concluding that it is one that depicts "Jewish life, Jewish character," or reflects "the Jewish habit of thought."[9] This effort is admirable but virtually useless because it assumes that Jewish culture is homogeneous and fails to take into account some important considerations. For example, an anti-Semite might relate a narrative that depicts Jewish life and character and possibly even reflects a supposed Jewish habit of thought. Would this then be an example of a Jewish story? It seems unlikely that many scholars would so categorize it.

Richman apparently did research of a sort for he speaks of "much new material, which the author has gathered for many years."[10] Unfortunately, the exact sources of this "new material" are never identified and it is even unclear whether the numerous tales included come from printed or oral sources. One suspects the former since Richman did some writing for the New York *Evening World* and New York

Sunday *World* and even says that some of the material in his book previously appeared in those pages. Even though most of the texts show evidence of being "improved" there is little doubt that some of his material came, either directly or indirectly, from oral tradition.[11] It must also be noted that Richman was not posing as a folktale scholar but intended his book primarily for a popular audience.

Many of the complaints about Richman's book apply equally well to several other compilations designed mainly for popular audiences. For example, S. Felix Mendelssohn produced four volumes—*The Jew Laughs* (1935), *Let Laughter Ring* (1941), *Here's a Good One* (1947), and *The Merry Heart* (1951)—that are similar in nature and typical of many other popular compilations. Not only does Mendelssohn omit sources: Literary and folk, translated and English texts are mixed together indiscriminately, no distinction is made between European and American tales, and the texts contain little in the way of suggestions for a worthwhile typology of Jewish-American jokelore. Also in this vein are such efforts as Elsa Teitelbaum's *An Anthology of Jewish Humor* (1946), Mark Feder's *It's a Living: A Personalized Collection of Jewish Humor* (1948), Jacob Richman's *Jewish Wit and Wisdom* (1952), and Nathan Ausubel's *Treasury of Jewish Humor* (1953). This, of course, is but a sampling of such titles and by no means exhausts the list. Neither should one think that such publications ended in the 1950s. Volumes like Henry D. Spalding's *Encyclopedia of Jewish Humor* (1969) and William Novak and Moshe Waldoks's *Big Book of Jewish Humor* (1981) sufficiently dispel that notion.

It was 1960 before a folklorist published an article of Jewish jokelore. That paper, "Jewish-American Dialect Stories on Tape," presented seventy-six texts collected by Richard M. Dorson from a large number of informants, many of them not Jewish, and dealt with a form that earlier compilers omitted, in some cases intentionally.[12] Later, in an article in *Midwest Folklore,* Dorson published sixteen more texts, all coming from a single informant, Harold Males, an Indiana University graduate student from Brooklyn.[13] Unlike earlier compilers of Jewish-American jokelore, Dorson paid attention to his informants, identifying them and giving data on their background, education, and frequently how and where they learned the jokes. His annotations, which were occasionally extensive, provided comparative data and placed the jokes in the context of folk tradition. His arrangement suggested a typology for such stories, and he also observed that these narratives are, despite the stance of the earlier commentators, told by

Jew and non-Jew alike. Indeed, his research revealed that many non-Jews got such jokes from Jews.

Dorson's ground-breaking article was soon followed by a number of other studies of Jewish-American jokelore. Naomi and Eli Katz pondered the seeming paradox of the anti-Jewish Jewish joke, i.e., the dialect story, in a *Journal of American Folklore* essay, "Tradition and Adaptation in American Jewish Humor."[14] They concluded that dialect stories represent "an adaptation to an altered set of social relations in a new country." In eastern Europe Jews were traditionally excluded from participation in the majority culture while in America "relatively complete participation" was possible if Jews would adopt the ways of the majority culture. What this meant was that a dialect story "when told by a gentile can be regarded as anti-Semitic to the degree that the repulsive Jew is meant to stand for all Jews. When told by an American Jew its point is precisely that the subject does not stand for all Jews. Rather than being anti-Semitic it is anti-greenhorn, anti-immigrant, anti-Old World, and possibly anti-poor."[15]

Ed Cray, however, has the distinction of being the first scholar to publish an article on Jewish-American jokelore in the *Journal of American Folklore.* His "The Rabbi Trickster" is an examination of both Jewish-American and urban folk narratives traditions.[16] Like Dorson, Cray identifies informants, gives details about their background, and provides annotations for his fourteen texts. Unlike Dorson, he also attempts to determine what function these jokes serve their tellers, concluding that they act as "a social cement" that serves as formal recognition of their Jewishness.[17]

The only other Jewish-American joke cycle studied by a folklorist is the Jewish-American Princess jokes popular in the late 1970s and early 1980s. This body of jokes receives detailed examination by Alan Dundes in "The J.A.P. and the J.A.M. in American Jokelore."[18] Dundes limns the characteristics assigned to J.A.P.s and J.A.M.s (Jewish-American Mother) in jokelore and contrasts them because "the J.A.P. cannot be understood in isolation from the Jewish American Mother."[19] The J.A.M. is seen as being overly concerned with her children's welfare, anxious for her daughters to marry well and for her sons to become professionals. She is overly protective, expert at creating feelings of guilt, and comfortable in the role of martyr.

The stereotype of the J.A.P. differs considerably from that of the J.A.M. though ultimately the latter is to a great extent responsible for the former's characteristics. In jokelore the J.A.P. is spoiled, overly concerned with appearance—and indifferent to sex, which Dundes says is her most notable trait. Dundes goes beyond just outlining character traits to consider such matters as whether or not the stereotypes have any basis in fact, whether the J.A.P. jokes are an example of self-hate, and why they are told by Jews. In regard to the latter he points out that they may serve a variety of functions, being told by males for one reason and by females for another. This richly layered discussion very effectively demonstrates the value of examining joke traditions. Unfortunately, such investigations remain rare because in general the joke, Jewish-American or otherwise, has been regarded as one of the relatively unimportant forms of folklore.

Other folklorists have struggled with the general concept of Jewish humor and their work is relevant to those interested specifically in Jewish-American jokelore. Heda Jason noted that much of the problem in studying Jewish jokes lies in the lack of a commonly accepted definition of the subject.[20] Dan Ben-Amos opined that Jewish humor is a "myth" in the sense that there is an inherent special relationship between Jews and humor.[21]

In "The People of the Joke: On the Conceptualization of a Jewish Humor," Elliott Oring explored the concept of Jewish humor and the Jewish joke by offering a set of four hypotheses.[22] These are: (1) Jewish humor is a relatively modern invention; (2) Jewish humor is a product of the late nineteenth century because at that time the faculty of humor was regarded as one sign of civilized humanity, and Jews wanted to demonstrate that they had participated in this humanity; (3) the conception of a Jewish humor is derived from the belief that Jewish history is one of despair; and (4) this belief allows for only three possibilities for articulating this humor—it had to be transcendent, defensive, or pathological. Oring observes that Jewish humor "is transcendent when it reflects the unwillingness of the individual to surrender to the impossible conditions of existence and attempts to achieve a measure of liberation from the social, political, economic, and even cosmic forces that remain beyond one's control."[23] Humor is defensive when it is used to mask a serious purpose—particularly a hostile or critical one—and pathological when used as self-criticism. Whether one agrees with Oring or not, it is undeniable that he has offered some tantalizing ideas that merit further consideration.

Most of the analytical works on jokelore have been done by folklorists, but two noteworthy ones have been produced by scholars from other backgrounds. In "Beyond *Kvetching* and Jiving: The Thrust of

Jewish and Black Folkhumor," an essay written for the book *Jewish Wry* (1987), historian Joseph Boskin argues that American Jews and blacks have shared the humor of the oppressed. Much of their jokelore is derived from a history of intense discrimination and is characterized by much gallows humor, i.e., jokes that call attention to and even insult a particular undesirable situation while at the same time recognizing its inevitability. Similarly, both groups have devised disguise techniques for addressing their adversaries, have utilized trickster motifs "to undermine the most insulting aspects of prejudice assigned to them," and have "relied heavily on retaliatory humor as a means of counter-aggression."[24]

Despite these similarities, he argues, the two groups have used humor differently in responding to the continuous stress they confront. Jews have relied on self-criticism but have not shied away from open attacks on their oppressors and other ethnic and racial groups. Because of historical circumstances blacks were forced to be more resourceful in disguising their jokes, "not only as a way of creating an inner world of dignity and expressiveness but also as a means of sheer physical durability."[25] In other words, only black accommodative humor was heard by outsiders; all other jokelore was virtually incomprehensible to non-black audiences. Unfortunately, Boskin does not support his ideas with material collected from oral tradition but rather illustrates his points with texts taken largely from sources that fail to properly distinguish between folk and literary materials.

The most recent volume to analyze Jewish-American jokelore is appropriately titled *What Is a Jewish Joke?* (1991). Henry Eilbirt, the author, is a former dean of the School of Business and Public Administration at Baruch College, and a self-described "humorologist." Despite his title Eilbirt is exclusively concerned with Jewish-American humor, although he readily admits there are many Old World stories in New World tradition. To his credit he usually distinguishes between the two types.

On the other hand, his book can be faulted on a number of counts. He fails to identify sources, although it is obvious that many texts are taken from earlier printed works; he often "improves" jokes, which is perhaps less problematic than it normally would be since Eilbirt is, apparently, a skillful teller of Jewish jokes noted for this activity long before writing this book; and he tends to give short shrift to those aspects of Jewish jokelore that he doesn't find appealing. For example, he dismisses jokes about Jewish-American Princesses, stating: "I'm tired of them and there are indications that they have become staples of anti-Semitism."[26] Both statements may be true, but as Alan Dundes effectively demonstrated, those jokes are part of Jewish-American tradition and therefore merit more attention in a book like Eilbirt's than he gives them.

Eilbirt does, however, go to some lengths to answer the question in his book's title, and while his conclusions may not meet with widespread approval, they are certainly more meaningful than the definition given by Jacob Richman sixty-five years earlier. According to Eilbirt, a joke must have three elements to be properly designated as Jewish. First, it comes from the conditions of Jewish life or from the experience of the Jewish people. Second, the joke or the punch line depends on the use of a Jewish language, especially Yiddish. Finally, Jewish jokes show real or supposed Jewish characteristics or stereotypes. Unlike many other commentators who dismiss dialect stories as anti-Semitic, Eilbirt readily includes them as part of Jewish tradition and perceptively notes that their usage can be seen in a positive way or a negative way depending on who is using them—and how and when. In other words, the teller is often as important as the tale. Eilbirt also attempts to show the function that jokes have, although his remarks in this regard tend towards repetition of ideas proposed by many earlier writers. Finally, in the book's four chapters Eilbirt provides some basic suggestions for classification of Jewish jokes. Unfortunately, he seems unfamiliar with prior efforts by folklorists along these lines.

The sparse record of publication of non-humorous Jewish-American narratives includes both popular and academic works. Among the former the most notable is Nathan Ausubel's massive 765-page *Treasury of Jewish Folklore* (1948). This mammoth tome was part of a series of folklore "treasuries" published in the 1940s and 1950s that provided a real mish-mash of items from both printed and oral tradition, with a greater emphasis on the former than the latter. Ausubel doesn't always identify his sources, and his concept of folklore is at best fuzzy. Despite the title, the entire spectrum of Jewish folklore is not represented, only folk narratives, proverbs, riddles, songs, and dances. Most of the volume deals with Old World folklore, but in a few instances Ausubel shows an awareness that American culture has also helped shape Jewish lore.

Of the academic works on Jewish-American folk narrative, Jerome Mintz's *Legends of the Hasidim* (1968) merits special mention. This absorbing study examines the transplanting of a European folk culture to the United States and indicates what happens to these people and their lore when moved to America. The Hasidim came to Brooklyn in the twentieth century to escape Nazi persecution in Poland and Hungary and in the New World practiced their own highly insulated religious orthodoxy, one that rejected the secular world, the gentile, even the non-Hasidic Jew. While Old World legends persist, many of the supernatural motifs, such as possession by a dybbuk, have disappeared. There are also New World tales revealing anxieties resulting from American pressures, such as living a rushed, fast-paced life rather than the more leisurely one the Hasidim were accustomed to in the Old World. The book consists of a lengthy discussion of the Hasidic people that is wisely keyed to the 271 pages of collected tales that make up the book's second part. The narratives, which are given in the words of the informants, cover a time span ranging from the Napoleonic era to the Six-Day War of 1967 and are mostly concerned with traditional belief. *Legends of the Hasidim* is the most significant treatment to date of the Jewish-American folk narrative tradition.

The preceding discussion has not listed every publication on Jewish-American folk narrative, but it has covered the types of books and articles issued to date on the subject. Given the fact that most of Jewish history has been lived in places other than the United States it is understandable that the vast majority of books on Jewish folklore in general and folk narrative in particular have concentrated on Old World rather than New World traditions. Such a focus has, however, distorted the picture of Jewish folk narrative traditions by downplaying the importance of the Jewish contact with American culture. The present collection is one of a small number of publications that correct that imbalance by showing that the Jewish-American folk narrative tradition is a blend of both Old and New World materials.

W. K. McNeil
The Ozark Folk Center
Mountain View, Arkansas

PREFACE

◇ ◇ ◇

"A Jew is composed of twenty-eight percent fear, two percent sugar, and seventy percent nerve."[1]

That the Jews have needed every bit of that nerve over centuries of persecution can hardly be denied. Scattered throughout the world, murdered for their faith or their politics, they still have managed to survive. And the vast body of Jewish folklore, influencing and influenced by the many and various cultures in which it came in contact over the ages, reflects both the struggle and the triumph of being a Jew.

The stories in this book come from many sources. Some are known to the author's own family, others have been collected by the author directly, while still others have been collected by various folklorists from Jewish immigrants from Europe, the Near East, and Central Asia. Some tales were first written down in scholarly or religious texts in Hebrew, the ancient language of the Jews; a modern form of Hebrew is the official language of Israel. Other tales were transcribed from Yiddish-speaking Jews. Yiddish, a Germanic-influence language written in the Hebrew script, is of much more recent origin than Hebrew, dating from about the thirteenth or fourteenth centuries. Although it is a slowly dying language, Yiddish is still spoken in New York City, with its high concentration of Jews, where a Yiddish theater continues to thrive.

Crosscultural contact can best be seen in the form of folklore known as "wonder tales." The Jewish variants on these classic types of fairy tale are as full of transformed princes, magical beings, and happy endings as those of any other people. But Jewish folklore, whether collected from the Ashkenazim, the Jews of Europe, or the Sephardim, the Jews of Spain and the Near East, also possesses a separate, distinct identity. This uniquely Jewish flavor can be seen most easily in the emphasis upon ethical behavior and—understandable in a people who have been so fiercely persecuted down through the ages—in the equally strong emphasis upon survival through cleverness, kindness and, above all, through humor. Humor is an essential part of the Jewish character, and Jewish tales are full of wry wit, cutting irony and, sometimes, downright belly laughs. There's a bittersweet reason for this: As many a Jew has said, "If we don't laugh, we must weep,"[2] a fact that remains sadly true even today.

NOTES

1. Known to the author. See also Shirley Kumove, *Words Like Arrows: A Collection of Yiddish Folk Sayings* (New York: Schocken Books, 1985). See also Nokhem Shtutshkof, *Der oyster fun der Yidisher Shprakh* (New York: Yiddish Scientific Institute-YIVO, 1950).
2. Known to the author, source unknown.

PART ONE
LIFE CYCLES

◇ ◇ ◇

CHAPTER ONE
LIFE AND CELEBRATIONS

◇ ◇ ◇

"Make a joyful noise unto God, all ye lands."[1]

For over four thousand years of turbulent history, Jews have lived—and continue to live—in almost every region throughout the world. But though each group of voluntary or involuntary immigrants of course picked up elements of the cultures surrounding them, and though some customs have been abandoned or altered over the centuries, the fundamental principle of Judaism remains unchanged: Judaism is first and foremost concerned with living an honest, ethical life.

YEARLY HOLIDAYS

The lunar calendar, which depends on the regular cycle of the moon, is an ancient one, very much predating the Gregorian calendar (a solar calendar, which was formulated by Pope Gregory XIII in the sixteenth century), and is, in fact, still in use in such Near Eastern countries as Saudi Arabia. Although modern American Jews follow the same Gregorian calendar in daily life as everyone else in the Western world, the traditional lunar calendar is used to mark the holidays of Judaism. As a result, the specific dates of Jewish holidays move within the Gregorian calendar from year to year (as do such lunar-based Christian holidays as Easter). But no matter in what part of a month a holiday may fall, the basic significance remains the same.

The Months

The Jewish year begins in the fall and works its way through the seasons approximately as follows:

Tishri, mid-September to mid-October
Cheshvan, mid-October to mid-November
Kislev, mid-November to mid-December
Teveth, mid-December to mid-January
Shevat, mid-January to mid-February
Adar, mid-February to mid-March
Nisan, mid-March to mid-April
Iyar, mid-April to mid-May
Sivan, mid-May to mid-June
Tamuz, mid-June to mid-July
Ab, mid-July to mid-August
Elul, mid-August to mid-September

The Holidays

All Jewish holidays are celebrated from sundown of the night before to sundown of the holiday itself. The traditional reason for this is because in the biblical story of Creation "there was evening and there was morning, one day," which is taken to mean that a day begins with sunset.[2]

The Jewish year starts in the autumn, on the first day of Tishri, which was originally the time just after the harvest was safely in, when people had a chance to rejoice or be contemplative. As with most peoples, Jews begin their year with a New Year's celebration, *Rosh Hashanah,* which literally means "the beginning of the year." But unlike the traditional American New Year, this is not a holiday for riotous eating and drinking. In addition to visiting friends and relatives, Rosh Hashanah is a time for self-examination and repentance, for paying debts, giving to the needy—*tzedakah,* or charity, is one of the basic tenets of Judaism—and cleaning one's personal slate. It is a time for puzzling out both who one is and what type of person one would like to be.[3]

Although Rosh Hashanah holds the joy of renewal within it, it also marks the beginning of the Ten Days of Repentance, or the Days of Awe, a good time for forgiveness and reconciliation. These sacred days end with the most solemn of Jewish holidays: *Yom Kippur,* the Day of Atonement, devoted entirely to contemplation, confession to God, and atonement for the sins of the past year. If Rosh Hashanah is for finding one's inner best, Yom Kippur is for coming to terms with and controlling one's inner worst. Perhaps the element of Yom Kippur best known to non-Jews is the tradition of fasting from sundown to sundown. This is more than mere mortification of the flesh; the day of fasting and contemplation also teaches self-discipline and empathy for those for whom hunger is a way of life. The meal following Yom Kippur, after the coming-to-terms with one's self and with God, is a joyous one.[4]

Tishri also holds a third holiday: the traditional harvest festival of *Sukkoth,* a Jewish celebration of thanksgiving. The name Sukkoth is taken from *sukka,* which literally means "booth." It is customary for those celebrating the holiday to build a *sukka* to commemorate the forty-year wanderings of the Jews in the desert after the escape from Egypt; the *sukka* represents the wanderers' hastily built shelters. Some families may eat or even sleep in their *sukka* for the ritual seven days of the holiday. A very old ritual takes place on the last day, *Hoshana Rabba,* which is celebrated with a ceremonial waving of willow bunches as a supplication to God for rain, a carryover from the days when rain meant life or death to desert farmers.[5]

Following the lunar calendar along, the next major Jewish holiday falls in Kislev. This is *Hannukah,* perhaps the most familiar Jewish holiday to non-Jewish Americans because such a traditional Hannukah symbol as the *menorah,* the seven-branched candlestick, is sometimes combined in civic holiday displays with Christmas crèches in the spirit of "equal time," although the two holidays have nothing in common save the season and the tradition of gift giving.

Hannukah is, at its most basic, a celebration of freedom. It commemorates the victory in 164 B.C.E.[6] of Judas Maccabee and his followers over the Greco-Syrian tyrant Antiochus Ephiphanes and the liberation and rededication of the Temple in Jerusalem. An eight-day festival was proclaimed in celebration of the Maccabees' victory. Legend has it that though there was only enough oil left in the Temple for a single day's lighting of the menorah, the oil miraculously lasted for all eight days. Nowadays, one candle is lighted on each successive sundown till all eight are burning;[7] the ever-brightening glow is a warm, vivid reminder of Jewish resistance to oppression.

Down through the centuries, special foods, particularly those fried in oil, have become Hannukah treats. Among the Ashkenazim, the "European" Jews, potato pancakes called *latkes* are well-known delicacies, while the Sephardim, "oriental" Jews, serve *sufganiyot,* or jelly doughnuts. Hannukah is also a holiday for children, who are given a new gift each day, and who play games with such special toys as the *dreidel,* a four-sided top inscribed with Hebrew letters that are a mnemonic for "a great miracle happened here."[8]

In Adar comes *Purim,* the Feast of Lots, a joyous holiday celebrating the Book of Esther. Haman, corrupt vizier to Ahasurerus, King of Persia in the fifth century B.C.E., developed a passionate hatred both for Mordecai, a Jew who refused to grovel before him, and for all Jews, and sought to have them slaughtered. The *purim,* or lots, were those used by Haman to decide the date of the fatal day. But Mordecai's cousin Esther, Ahasurerus's Queen, successfully appealed to her husband to have the vizier's order rescinded. The Jews were saved, and treacherous Haman ended up on the royal gallows.

The holiday of Purim, obviously, recalls the dangers of anti-Semitism, but it also celebrates the triumph of good over evil. During its celebration, both adults and children dress up in costume; recent costumes have reflected current events, with various modern-day political villains sometimes taking the place of Haman. Feasting is very much a part of Purim, and one of the best-known delicacies associated with those feasts are *hamantaschen,* "Haman's pockets," triangular pastries filled with poppy seeds or fruit, purportedly mimicking the corrupt vizier's bribe-stuffed pockets. Their triangular shape is supposed to imitate Haman's tricornered hat, though there is no evidence to support this tradition.[9]

Purim is considered a happy but minor holiday. But after Adar comes the month of Nisan, in which another major Jewish holiday is celebrated: *Pesach,* or Passover. This celebration of the Exodus, the Hebrew liberation from Egypt, is one of the earliest holidays mentioned in the Bible. The Exodus is one of the focal points of Judaism, symbolizing not only physical freedom and the striving for the Holy Land but also the striving towards ethical perfection.

Passover is also a celebration of springtime and new growth, *Chag Haaviv* (the Spring Festival), incorporating within its seven days two pastoral holidays, *Chag Hamatzot* (Festival of Unleavened Bread) and *Chag Hapesach* (Festival of the Pascal Lamb) as well. The first and, with some families, the second nights of Passover are marked by a special family gathering, the *seder,* which means "order." The earliest Passover service, described in the Book of Exodus, involved the offering of a lamb, which was then roasted and eaten. The first true *seder* may date to the end of the first century C.E. A modern *seder* involves the recitation of the *Haggada,* which tells the story of the Exodus, and the eating of six ritual foods:

Maror, or bitter herbs (often in the form of horseradish), symbolizes the bitter lot of the Jews in Egypt.

Karpas, a vegetable (often parsley or radishes), symbolizes the traditional opening of a first century C.E. Jewish meal.

Charzeret, a more bitter vegetable, is added in reference to a biblical quote in Numbers 9:11 referring to eating the Pesach lamb "with unleavened bread and bitter herbs." The *charzeret* is often omitted from modern seders.

Charoset, a nut, apple, and cinnamon mix, symbolizes the mortar the Jews were forced to make during their Egyptian captivity.

Zeroa, the roasted shankbone, is symbolic of the original lamb sacrifice.

Baytza, a hard-boiled egg, is also symbolic of the original Temple sacrifice.

Matzah, unleavened bread, is also a vital part of any Passover celebration, and commemorates the fact that the escaping Jews could carry only the simplest foodstuffs and were restricted to making bread strictly from flour and water. Red wine, sufficient to fill four cups for each member at the table, is also a part of the Passover *seder.*[10]

There are almost as many versions of the Haggada as there are Jews, and each variant includes local additions and deletions to suit the needs of the local communities. The Sephardic Jews of Turkey and Yemen often add legends about the Exodus, while European Jews have added poems and folksongs into their Haggadas, such as the counting-out rhyme, "Echad Mi Yodaya," or "Who Knows One," which begins:

Who knows one?
I know one.
One is our God in heaven and on earth.
Who knows two?
I know two.
Two are the Tables of the Covenant,
One is our God in heaven and on earth.

The song continues through various holy symbols up to thirteen, the thirteen attributes of God. As with "The Twelve Days of Christmas," the point of the song is for the singer to add on one more number with each repetition.[11]

The last holiday in the yearly cycle falls in Sivan, and is *Shavuoth,* the Feast of Weeks, named that because it falls seven weeks (or a week of weeks) after Passover. This is one of the three so-called Pilgrim Festivals, together with Passover and Sukkoth; originally these Pilgrim Festivals were celebrated in Jerusalem, to which Jews from all over the area travelled for the occasion. Shavuoth is also known as *Chag Habikurim,* the Festival of First Fruits, reflecting its origin as a thanksgiving holiday celebrating the harvesting of the first crop of wheat.

In the *Talmud,* the encyclopedic compilation of Rabbinical belief, thought, law, and lore that was assembled in the fifth century C.E., Shavuoth is further described as being "the time of the giving of the *Torah,*" the first five books of the Holy Scriptures, the heart of Jewish law, and so Shavuoth became a holiday celebrating the study of the Torah as well.

In modern Shavuoth services, it has become customary to read the Book of Ruth, that loyal first millennium B.C.E. Moabite woman who found love and faith in Judaism. The eating of cheese and cheese products is a Shavuoth tradition as well, possibly to symbolize the sweetness of studying the Torah—and by extension of learning—or, as one legend proposes, in memory of those Israelites who, after receiving the Torah at Mount Sinai, had no time to prepare a properly sanctified meat meal and put together a more easily assembled dairy meal instead.[12]

THE SABBATH

Perhaps more has been written about the Sabbath, the holy *Shabbat,* than about any other Jewish ceremony. As with the "daughter-faiths" of Christianity and Islam, Judaism sets one day of the week aside for prayer and rest from toil.[13] In Judaism, this day is observed from sundown of Friday night through to sundown of Saturday, which is traditionally the day God rested after creating the Universe. The celebration of the Sabbath is considered the first and greatest of all Jewish holy days, because it was the first mentioned in the Bible, prior even to the giving of the Ten Commandments. When the Jews who had escaped Egypt were gathering the mysterious, life-giving *manna* in the desert, they were told to gather a double portion on the sixth day so that they could honor the seventh day as a day of rest and as "a Sabbath to the Lord."[14] The Sabbath is thus seen as a covenant between God and the Jews: "I have given them my Sabbath to be a sign between Me and them, so they will know that I am the One that sanctifies them." The Sabbath isn't an excuse for idleness, as the bewildered and disapproving Romans thought, but a chance to "turn from the results of creation to the mystery of creation; from the world of creation to the creation of the world."[16]

To make the Sabbath celebration truly special, a home should be made as spotless as possible before sundown. The fact that no fires are permitted during the Sabbath eliminates cooking, and meals must be prepared in advance. But they should be good meals, not something hastily thrown together, because traditionally the Friday night dinner is the dining high point of the week. Some families prefer the same menu for each Sabbath celebration, but no special foods need to be prepared.

The first stage of a typical Friday night Sabbath is the putting aside of money for *tzedakah* (charity) into a special collection box or jar. The family then sings one or more of the many Hebrew songs associated with the Sabbath. One of the simplest, warmest, and best-known consists of only two repeated words, "*Shabbat Shalom,*" or "Sabbath Peace."

After the singing comes the lighting of the Sabbath candles by the wife and mother of the family in a ceremony dating back at least to the first century C.E.. At least two candles must be lit, symbolizing that life is made up of dualities, male and female, light and darkness, and so on, but how many more candles are lit is up to the individual family.[17] Once the candles are lit, the woman recites a quiet blessing, calling down Sabbath peace on the family.

A series of blessings follow: for the children, for the husband and wife, and for the wine and bread. The blessing of the bread has special significance, since "bread" and "life" are virtually synonymous in many cultures.[18] The family then settles down to enjoy the Sabbath meal. A special blessing, the *birkat hamazon,* or blessings for food, is said after everyone is finished eating. Some families follow up by attending Friday night services at their synagogue, but this isn't mandatory, and many families prefer to spend the time after dinner listening to music, reading from a Jewish text, or simply relaxing. For husband and wife, Friday night is traditionally considered the most auspicious time for conceiving a child.[19]

EVERYDAY OBSERVANCES

The Mezuzah

One religious item found in Jewish households throughout the world is the *mezuzah,* literally "doorpost." The *mezuzah* (the plural is *mezuzot*) is a little box or cylinder containing a *klaf,* a small parchment scroll on which are inscribed the *Shema,* the proclamation of God's oneness that is usually translated as "Hear O Israel, the Lord our God, the Lord is One," and the lines from Deuteronomy that command Jews to "write these words upon the doorposts of your house and on your gates."[20] *Mezuzot* cases may be of any material, from stone to metal to ceramic, and are often handsomely ornamented with painted designs or carvings, while the scroll itself is traditionally inscribed by a *sofer,* a trained scribe.

Many meanings have been assigned to the *mezuzah* over the ages, which has served as a declaration of faith, a welcome sign and—human nature being what it is—an amulet. During the Talmudic period (about 400–500 C.E.), the *mezuzah* was considered powerful enough to ward off evil spirits, and during the Middle Ages, mystical additions, including the names of various angels, were added to the scroll; these superstitious additions have long since been removed, though a lingering tradition of the *mezuzah* being an amulet remains.[21]

The *mezuzah* must be hung on the upper doorpost of the outer door, but many Jews follow the custom of placing *mezuzot* on every doorpost in the home as well. The hanging of a *mezuzah,* which should be done within thirty days of moving into a new home, is often celebrated with a small ceremony known as *hanukat habayit,* the "dedication of the home."[22] And if a Jewish family sells or rents a home to another Jew, the *mezuzot* must be left in place, so that the new owner, who may not have had time to purchase his or her own, will not have to live in a home without *mezuzot.*

The Dietary Laws

One unifying factor for the Jews, who have, after all, been scattered to the ends of the Earth, has always been the observance of the laws of *kashrut,* the kosher dietary laws that divide all food into two categories: *kosher,* which means "proper" or "fit", and *trafe,* which comes from the Hebrew word for "damaged" or "torn," unfit to eat. Not every Jew follows the entire list of dietary distinctions: the Orthodox always do, Conservatives usually do to varying degrees, and Reform Jews usually do not, but every Jew knows at least something about what is and is not kosher.

Down through the ages there has been much debate over the reasons behind the laws of *kashrut.* Rabbi Moses ben Maimon, the great twelfth century philosopher better known as Maimonides, theorized that the dietary laws trained Jews to master their appetites, to avoid falling into the trap of gluttony.[23] Earlier Rabbis believed that following the laws kept the Jews a people apart, helping them retain a separate religious identity. In more modern times, health has been cited as one justification for the establishment of the *kashrut* laws. Although the good sense in avoiding such potentially risky foods as pork and shellfish, particularly in a hot climate where food spoiled quickly, undoubtedly did play a part in some of the laws,[24] and others might have been political in origin,[25] many can only be classified as *chukim,* mandatory statutes to be obeyed even though there doesn't always seem to be logic behind them.

The dietary laws place no bans on fruits and vegetables, other than the very practical one that fruit must come from a tree at least three years old; trees were and are highly valuable in arid Israel, and no farmer would wish to endanger an immature tree. But there are many restrictions regarding food animals. All winged and creeping insects are considered *trafe,* as are all shellfish; kosher fish must have scales and fins. Only cud-chewing, cloven-hoofed mammals are considered kosher, although beasts of burden, such as the cloven-hoofed ox, are forbidden. All birds of prey or eaters of carrion are *trafe.*

One of the tenets of Judaism is a prohibition against cruelty to animals or the unjust killing of animals. Hunting for sport is forbidden, and only a licensed individual, the *Shohet,* is allowed to slaughter animals for food. Death must be as merciful and quick as possible. Once the animal is slain, the *Shohet* must then examine it for any sign of internal disease before the meat can be properly *kashered,* or made kosher by the draining of as much blood as possible; Biblical law forbids the eating of blood, for "the blood is the life."[26] Modern American meat-packing plants have separate kosher departments, headed by a special inspector, the *Mashigiach,* in addition to a *Shohet.* Some states, such as New York, have special laws to ensure that meat sold as kosher really is as advertised.[27]

Keeping a kosher home in modern America is no easy thing, because in addition to making sure that only kosher meat is prepared and eaten, the homemaker must also keep separate pots, cooking utensils, dishes, and cutlery for dairy or meat meals, which are never combined. However, the rules vary from family to family. Some prefer to carry the separation down to owning two sets of dishtowels and sponges, while others are content to use a single set of dishes. Kosher cooking need not be dull; thanks to the fact that Jews have lived in every corner of the world, books of kosher recipes reflecting this diverse heritage are easily available in bookstores and libraries.[28]

CHAPTER TWO
LOVE AND MARRIAGE

◇ ◇ ◇

"Many waters cannot quench love, nor rivers drown it."[1]

In the Holy Scriptures, God, after having created Adam, muses, "It is not good for man to be alone; I will make for him a companion."[2] In Judaism, marriage has always been seen as more than merely a way of propagating the faith. It is also pictured as an end to loneliness, a necessary aspect of a happy life.

Until this century, a good many Jewish marriages were arranged by the parents, often with the aid of the *shadhan,* or matchmaker, an honored professional who could trace his or her occupation back to Biblical times; even the Jewish Patriarch, Abraham, used an emissary to find a bride for his son, Isaac. Of course, this doesn't mean that young people weren't allowed to fall in love on their own and even to announce their desire to wed, but the final decision was in the hands of the parents.[3]

There have always been certain bans on who Jews could or could not marry; a list of prohibited marriages can be found in the Holy Scriptures,[4] and include, as is true in most societies, a ban on marriage between close kin. In addition, although most parents would no longer consider a child who weds a non-Jew as dead, intermarriage, marriage to a non-Jew, is still very much frowned upon.

ENGAGEMENT TRADITIONS

Originally, a betrothal, both in Jewish and Christian tradition, was a legal act, often more important and binding than the actual wedding. At a formal ceremony, the *eirusin,* the marriage contract was signed, and the couple was considered betrothed; the wedding was simply the actual moving of the bride from her father's house to that of her new husband, carried out with much festivity. However if the husband was poor, no shame was attached to his moving in with her family instead till his fortunes should improve.[5]

In Biblical days, a young man who proposed marriage promptly entered into negotiations with his intended's family. Because the loss of a daughter meant the loss of a useful part of a household, the family of the groom had to pay a certain amount of compensation. Later, economics changed, and a bride brought as valuable a dowry with her as her family could afford.[6]

Parties were and remain a popular way of celebrating an engagement. From about the twelfth century to the nineteenth, Ashkenazim practiced the *tena'im,* a ritualized form of celebration meaning "teams" or "conditions" and involving the reading of the document setting the date of the wedding and listing the dowry arrangements.

A dish was then smashed, possibly to recall the destruction of the Temple in Jerusalem.

In modern America, the *tena'im* is practiced only by Orthodox Jews. But nowadays, particularly in America, almost all engagements, regardless of religion, are usually celebrated with a happy engagement shower.[7]

THE WEDDING

A favorite time for most weddings is in the spring, and Jewish weddings are no exception. However, weddings on the Sabbath or on religious holidays are forbidden. If either bride or groom is mourning a death in the family, the wedding must be postponed for at least a month after the burial. Over the centuries, various superstitions and traditions have surrounded the choice of which day of the month and week to pick for the wedding. The phase of the moon was often taken into consideration, favorable phases being the new moon, marking the start of a new month and, by extension, a new undertaking, and the waxing moon, which symbolized fertility. Monday was considered unlucky for weddings, but Tuesday was particularly favorable since in the Book of Genesis the words "and God saw how good this was" are not mentioned for the second day, Monday, but are repeated twice for the third day, Tuesday. However, the modern five-day work week has led to a good many American Jewish weddings being celebrated on Sunday. But Jews in Medieval times preferred to wed on Fridays for a very practical reason: the next day being the Sabbath, they didn't have to work and could continue the wedding festivities![8]

A Jewish wedding may be held just about anywhere—anywhere a *huppah,* or bridal canopy, can be erected—but the preferred places for the actual ceremony are either at home or in a synagogue. Outdoor ceremonies in the synagogue courtyard were popular in the Middle Ages, and might have harkened back to ancient Biblical tradition.[9]

One Jewish prewedding tradition that has survived is the *mikvah,* the ritual cleansing bath taken separately by bride and groom. The Sephardic variant, however, turned the solemn *mikvah* for women into a happy party during which female family members accompanied the bride to and from the bath with music and song, while the *mikvah* for the groom was an opportunity for male family members to happily tease the husband-to-be.

In addition to the *mikvah,* another form of purification practiced by most Ashkenazi and some Sephardic families is for the bride and groom to fast on their wedding day, so that they may enter marriage cleansed of the sins of the past.

Among some Jewish brides and grooms, particularly those who have lost parents, a prewedding tradition is to visit the cemetery for a quiet prayer of remembrance.[10]

As with other peoples, the Jewish bride and groom are usually kept separate for a time before the marriage, from a day to a week, until they actually meet under the *huppah.* This time apart is seen by some Jews as a time for reflection, but it also serves as a tension breaker and a heightener of anticipation.[11]

The basic points of a Jewish wedding ceremony are simple and have not changed very much from Talmudic days: the groom gives the bride a symbolic present—in modern America, any gift worth more than a dime—and a ritual statement of agreement and consecration, both of which she accepts. These actions must take place before at least two witnesses.

Jewish weddings in America are performed before a rabbi, almost always under the *huppah,* the wedding canopy that possibly is reminiscent of the Jewish tribal desert heritage. It also symbolizes the union of bride and groom under one roof.[12]

A modern Jewish wedding includes the betrothal ceremony. It begins with an invocation by the rabbi and the betrothal benediction, recited over a cup of wine from which both bride and groom drink. This is followed by the ring ceremony. Traditionally, a wedding ring should be of plain metal, though an engraved ring is permitted. In recent days, a double-ring ceremony has been added to some Jewish weddings. The *ketubah,* the certificate of marriage—sometimes a hand-drawn work of the Jewish calligrapher's art—signed by the rabbi and the traditional two witnesses, is given to the bride and groom, but not read at the ceremony.[13]

At the end of the ceremony, the groom breaks a glass by stepping on it. This is a very old custom, one shrouded in mystery. One theory has it that it symbolizes the destruction of the Temple. At Sephardic weddings, a definite link with the longing for Jerusalem is included as verses from Psalm 137 are recited: "If I forget thee, O Jerusalem, let my right hand forget her cunning." Another theory on the reason behind the breaking of the glass quotes the Talmudic story of Mar bar Rabina, who smashed a precious glass goblet during his son's wedding to stun a too-rowdy party into quiet. One thing the custom definitely is not is a good luck charm or a demonstration of the groom's dominance over his bride![14]

CHAPTER THREE
BIRTH AND CHILDHOOD

◇ ◇ ◇

"Each child brings his own blessing into the world."[1]

BEGINNINGS

The first commandment in the Old Testament is to "be fruitful and multiply,"[2] and the delight of a husband and wife in each other was and is considered a sacred and proper thing in Judaism. Although there are no religious dictates surrounding conception and pregnancy, there are traditions. Lovemaking is encouraged on the holy Sabbath night, when, according to the *Midrash,* a compilation of literature based on the Scriptures, the male and female aspects of God are reunited.[3] Some couples may mark their decision to become parents with a *mikvah,* the sanctifying ritual bath. Such a ritual cleansing, symbolic as well as physical, originally involved a natural body of water, a river, pool, or lake, and in Biblical times was performed by a man or woman who, for whatever reason, had become ritually impure. The *mikvah* is still used today by women at the end of their menstrual cycle and by Orthodox men prior to the Sabbath and Jewish holidays.[4]

One thing all Jewish communities have always shared is a respect for and reverence of pregnant women. And, like people everywhere, Jews down through the ages have held a multitude of superstitions surrounding pregnancy, far more than can possibly be listed here. Moroccan Jews, for example, tied and locked a belt around the belly of a pregnant woman in a symbolic protection against miscarriage; nineteenth century Jewish women in what was then Palestine used instead a silk thread that had measured the Western Wall of the Temple in Jerusalem. Ruby and coral were seen as useful in preventing miscarriage as well, as was the carrying of citron or, in Morocco, the drinking of a concoction of honey, almonds, dates, and raisins.[5] In the *shtetls,* the Jewish communities of middle and eastern Europe, pains were taken to be sure pregnant women weren't exposed to such unhappy conditions as being confronted with someone suspected of casting the *ayn horen,* the evil eye; to ward off such evil, the pregnant woman might recite the verses from Exodus that begin "Let terror and dread fall upon them."[6]

Just as with pregnancy, a vast number of superstitions surrounded the birth of a Jewish baby, again enough to make a book in themselves. Fear of the evil eye or of evil spirits harming the newborn led to some elaborate folk spells to ward off such perils, often invoking the beneficent powers of earth or the purifying powers of salt. Among various Near Eastern Jewish groups from Biblical times on, it has been the custom to salt a newborn baby as part of a protective ritual. And children down through the ages have worn a variety of amulets engraved with Hebrew letters symbolizing guardian phrases.[7]

Superstitions surrounding birth and childhood survive even in modern Jewish-American households, where it's considered the worst of luck to have a crib or other baby supplies in the house before the baby is born, and where a red ribbon is often tied around the handle of a baby carriage or about the crib, though few mothers today know the reason for the latter is that a red ribbon was an ancient protective charm against the evil eye. It is still considered unlucky to openly praise a baby, at least not without thanking God at the same time (or, more superstitiously, knocking wood or spitting three times), though no one nowadays would believe they were warding off jealous demons in the process. In some communities, Jews used to attach nuts and sweetmeats to the crib so that spirits would be attracted away from the baby. As the saying goes, "Although one should not believe in superstitions, it is better to be careful."[8]

A more modern American tradition is the baby shower, which is sometimes tied into the Jewish *Rosh Hodesh,* the celebration of the new moon, the start of a new month and, by extension, the start of a new life. There are some ancient variations on the modern theme: Persian Jews, for instance, offer the mother-to-be apples in the hope that she will have a short labor and easy delivery.[9]

The birth of any baby is generally a sign for rejoicing, and the birth of a Jewish baby was and is celebrated with a *simcha,* a party. There aren't any hard and fast rules as to the type of meal the party should be centered about, but some foods that might be served include those symbolic of fertility and new life, such as eggs, olives—which symbolize both life and, because of olive oil's ancient use in lamps, light—and green vegetables. A proper Jewish baby shower is also marked by *tzedakah,* (charity). Sephardic Jews sometimes pass around a tray, filled with candles and flowers, to which each guest makes a financial contribution. After the meal, the tray is auctioned off among the partygoers, and the winner contributes the entire sum to charity.[10]

In the past, and in some Jewish-American homes today, a ceremony known as *Shalom Zachar* welcomed a new son into the Jewish community on the first Friday night after his birth. According to legend, every baby knows the entire *Torah,* but at birth an angel presses a finger gently against the child's upper lip, banishing the knowledge; the mark of the angel's forefinger is to be seen in the indentation in the upper lip. In addition to welcoming the baby into the community, tradition said that the *Shalom Zachar* helped console him for his loss.

Modern American Jews have added a similar ceremony for baby girls, the *Shalom Nekavah.*[11]

NAMING THE BABY

Originally, a Jewish man would be given two names, one secular, reflecting the culture in which he lived, and one religious/Hebrew. A Jewish woman usually had only one, Hebrew, name. The tradition of naming children after relatives probably dates to about the sixth century B.C.E. Among the Ashkenazim and American Jews, a child is usually named after a deceased relative to perpetrate his/her memory, but Sephardic Jews often name children after living grandparents or other relations.

Superstitions about the power of names abound in all cultures. In earlier days, high infant mortality led to many desperate ruses to ward off the Angel of Death from a newborn. Ashkenazim avoided naming babies after living relatives lest the Angel of Death make a mistake and take the baby instead of the aged ancestor. A Polish Jew might go a step further by naming a baby *Alte* (Old One) or *Zaida* (Grandfather) both to confuse Death and, hopefully, to help ensure that the baby would live to old age.

The superstition of altering names to confuse supernatural forces was not uncommon among adults as well. In the early days of Judaism, husband and wife might sometimes follow the pagan custom of switching names with each other at night to fool the dark forces, a custom practiced often enough to warrant condemnation by the rabbis. However, among European Jews after the first millennium C.E., the names of the ill were often changed to confuse evil spirits; all that was necessary was that the new name be announced before a *minyan,* or quorum of ten adults, and that a prayer be said to notify heaven of the change. A protective new name might be "Life": *"Chayim"* for a man, *"Chaya"* for a woman.[12]

CIRCUMCISION

Brit or *berit* literally means "covenant," and symbolizes the covenant between God and man. The *brit milah,* the ceremony of naming and circumcising male Jewish babies, bringing those babies into the faith, is one of the oldest rituals in Jewish history: "At the age of eight days every male among you throughout the generations shall be circumcised."[13]

Circumcision, the removal of the foreskin of the penis, should be performed, wherever possible, either by a *mohel* (a trained specialist) or, should the parents prefer, a Jewish doctor and must be performed under the most sterile of medical conditions. A circumcision may, according to Jewish law, be performed even on the Sabbath, so in the early days if there was to be a Sabbath morning *brit,* the *mohel* might leave his scalpel tucked under the baby's pillow the night before for safekeeping. This custom (performed because it wasn't legal for a *mohel* to carry his scalpel about on a Sabbath) was picked up by sixteenth century mystics, who believed that any demons who might attack newborn babies would be scared off by the presence of knives, but is never practiced nowadays.[14]

The modern *brit milah* ceremony takes into account the extreme youth of the baby and is very brief, lasting no longer than ten minutes. First a blessing is given and the circumcision performed. This is followed by the *kiddush,* or blessing over wine, and a longer prayer which gives the baby his name, which in turn is followed by the *seudat mitzvah,* the meal of celebration. Some Sephardic Jews add a blessing over spices to the *kiddush.* The father may hand the *mohel* his scalpel in a symbolic act of taking responsibility, while the *sandek,* usually a family member or a close friend, has the honor of holding the baby during the circumcision. The baby also gains a godmother, the *kvatterin,* who carries the baby to the ceremony, and a godfather, the *kvatter,* who brings the baby to the chair of Elijah; according to legend, the prophet Elijah attends every *brit milah.*

While the *brit milah* is one of the oldest traditions, one of the newest is the *brit habat,* or welcoming of a new daughter, a ceremony first begun in the 1970s. Prior to this time, baby girls were brought to the synagogue to be named after the father had been honored with an *aliyah,* being called up to read from the Torah, but many families felt that the birth of a daughter ought to be celebrated more fully, and many rabbis now include welcoming ceremonies for girls as well as boys.[16]

Some Jewish groups already had their own ways of welcoming new daughters. Sephardic families held the *Seder zeved habat,* the "celebration for the gift of a daughter." Spanish Jews in particular held a special party known as *las fadas,* probably inspired by non-Jewish folkloric beliefs in good fairies.[17]

A purely superstitious celebration was formerly held among the Ashkenazim the night before a *brit milah.* It was known as *Lel Shemurim,* the night of the vigil, during which neither baby nor mother would be left alone for a moment, since they were both thought to be in peril from the demonic Lilith, Adam's first wife turned evil, and must be protected both by prayer and by a chalked circle to keep out dark forces. Sephardic Jews marked the night before a *brit milah* too, but for them it was a time of celebration and feasting, the *Zocher HaBrit,* the remembering of the *brit.*[18]

THE BAR/BAT MITZVAH

Jews have retained a "rite of passage" ceremony for the young, marking the point at which a child becomes an adult: the *Bar Mitzvah* for boys, the *Bat Mitzvah* for girls. The words mean, literally, "Son of the Divine Commandment" and "Daughter of the Divine Commandment."[19]

The origins of the Bar Mitzvah are lost in time, although the Talmud does note that it was customary during the time of the Second Temple (520 B.C.E. to 70 C.E.) for a boy who had reached the age of thirteen and who had fasted on Yom Kippur—that is, one who was adult enough to have accepted responsibility for his or her own actions—to be blessed by the sages. Thirteen is also the average age a boy undergoes puberty, becoming a man biologically, and the Talmud accepts this fact, recognizing a thirteen-year-old male as an adult even in legal matters. In addition, a father was deemed responsible for his son's acts only up to age thirteen. The *Mishnah,* the Code of Jewish Law, further states that the threshold of puberty (thirteen for a boy, twelve for a girl) marked the end of a childish acting strictly on instinct and selfishness and the beginning of moral responsibility, that is, *yetzer hatov,* or "good inclination."[20]

The Bar Mitzvah, attaching a specific ceremony to a boy's coming of age, dates back to only about the fourteenth century C.E.. The exact rules were not codified till the sixteenth century C.E.; during that period, a Bar Mitzvah was still a simple event: the boy-turned-man would receive the honor of an *aliyah,* being called up to read from and bless the Torah in the synagogue, and his father would recite: "Blessed be Thou our God, King of the Universe who has relieved me from punishment of this one," acknowledging that the boy had become an adult. Family and friends would then celebrate at home without much fuss.[21]

The modern Bar Mitzvah has become a far more elaborate affair, involving years of planning, both for the religious ceremony in the synagogue—consisting of the *aliyah* and usually followed by the *d'rash,* the Bar Mitzvah boy's speech, which is intended to show how well he has mastered the lessons of his faith— and for the celebration afterwards, which often lasts a whole weekend, from the Friday night before to the Sunday after the actual ceremony. But for all the gift giving, feasting, and festivities, acknowledging modern society doesn't really accept that a boy truly becomes a man at puberty, the basic purpose of the Bar Mitzvah remains the same: the acceptance of a boy's responsibility for his own actions and his acceptance of the tenets of Judaism.[22]

In contrast to the Bar Mitzvah, the Bat Mitzvah, the ceremony surrounding a Jewish girl's coming of age, is a very modern one, an American custom first introduced by the Reconstructionist movement (originally a branch of Conservative Judaism) in New York City and dating only to 1922. It was probably inspired by the growing movement for women's equality; women had won the vote in America only two years before. Although the Bat Mitzvah has yet to become as elaborate as the modern Bar Mitzvah, the basic concept of acceptance of adult responsibility is the same.[23]

Behind the very contemporary Bat Mitzvah ritual lie some very ancient traditions. A woman's fertility has always been vital to the survival of any people, and the coming of age of a girl has been marked with some ceremony by every culture in history. Although there are no details surrounding pre-Talmudic Jewish puberty rites for girls, there is some evidence that they did exist. By the time of the Talmud, the age of womanhood was accepted as twelve, and some families might, on the occasion of a daughter's twelfth birthday, celebrate at home, with the girl delivering a speech and her father adding his blessing. This was not, however, considered a religious celebration. Even the Bat Mitzvah ceremony was originally limited to a Friday night reading from the *haftarah,* the Books of the Prophets, rather than from the Torah itself, but the differences between the Bar and Bat Mitzvah ceremonies are beginning to fade as women take on a more active role both in Judaism and in the outside world.[24]

CHAPTER FOUR
DEATH AND MOURNING

◇ ◇ ◇

"Comfort ye, comfort ye, my people."[1]

In Jewish tradition, since the human body was created by God, it must be treated with respect even after death. Modern medical science may call for an autopsy, but such "mutilation" of a Jewish corpse can only be allowed under extraordinary circumstances, to solve a crime, for example, or to help others by adding to medical knowledge.[2] Nor can a Jewish corpse be embalmed, since embalming involves the draining of blood; under Judaism, the blood is part of the body, and cannot be removed. Making the deceased look as "lifelike" as possible is also frowned on as showing disrespect for the dead, as is viewing the remains, a fairly recent American custom originally practiced in Europe only in the event of the death of a head of state.[3]

While it is still lying in the home, a Jewish corpse should be covered by a sheet, oriented so that the feet face the doorway, and a candle placed at the head; the candle symbolizes both a special event and the human being him or herself, the wick symbolizing the body, the flame, the soul. Before being removed to the cemetery, the body should be washed and placed in a clean, plain shroud, traditionally white, the color of purity in many cultures.[4] Out of courtesy to the deceased, the body is not to be left unattended. One custom calls for friends and relatives to ask forgiveness of the deceased at this time for any injuries done during his or her lifetime. As in many other cultures, mirrors in the house of the deceased must be covered. Several reasons have been proposed for this custom, the most common being that mirrors promote personal vanity, improper during a period of mourning.[5]

In Jewish tradition, there is no long period of lying in state; burial is done swiftly, following the commandment in Deuteronomy, "Thou shalt bury him the same day."[6] One argument given for this commandment is that life is for the living; another, very practical argument takes into account the hot desert climate that, for obvious reasons of health, predicated swift burial.

Before the first millennium C.E., Jews buried their dead without coffins (though there were exceptions: Joseph, a favorite at Pharoah's court, buried his father according to Egyptian rites and was himself buried in a coffin in Egyptian style).[7] By the time of the Talmud, fashions had changed, and it was considered wrong to bury someone without a coffin, but by the Middle Ages, the custom varied from Jewish community to community. In America, the secular law insists on the use of coffins. Jewish law forbids cremation (in the Holy Scriptures God told Adam, "For dust thou art, and unto dust shall thou return"),[8] therefore, a Jewish body must be buried in earth. Although flowers were once strewn on Jewish graves,[9] floral arrangements are not a part of modern Jewish burial ceremonies.

En route to the cemetery it is customary for a funeral procession to pause periodically; this custom is interpreted as an expression of the mourners' reluctance to say farewell to the deceased.[10] The practice of pausing on leaving the cemetery, begun in the ninth century, has a more magical significance: each pause shakes off any evil spirits who may be clinging to the living.[11]

A very old custom performed at the cemetery is *keriah,* or the rending of clothing; close relations tear their clothing over their hearts, symbolizing a torn heart. Modern practicality has led to some mourners substituting a symbolic ribbon for rending rather than ruining their clothing.[12]

Upon returning from the cemetery, relatives wash their hands before entering their homes; this may possibly be a symbolic cleansing after contact with death. The *seudat havra-a,* the "meal of condolence," which has been prepared by friends or neighbors, is then eaten; it consists of such foods symbolic of eternal life as the never-ending roundness of bagels and boiled eggs.[13] The bereaved now enter the seven-day period of intense mourning known as *shivah,* during which mourners are expected to stay at home save for visits to the synagogue where they recite the *Kaddish,* the ancient Aramaic mourner's prayer, and refrain from such mundane pursuits as shaving or worrying about good grooming. Paying condolence calls to the mourners during this period is considered a lawful act of compassion, though callers must remember the solemnity of the occasion and avoid undue conversation. Traditionally these condolence calls begin on the third day of *shivah,* to allow mourners time to begin coming to grips with grief. The seven days of *shivah* are intended to balance the seven days of Jewish feasts.[14]

As with many other cultures, the usual practice is to erect gravestones over Jewish graves. This custom goes back at least to Biblical days, when Jacob "set up a pillar" over the grave of his wife, Rachel, and is considered both a sign of respect for the deceased and as a marker for family and friends. A simple headstone is best; anything ornate is considered ostentatious. No special unveiling ceremony is necessary. Friends and family visiting a grave often leave stones on the tombstone as a sign that they have not forgotten the departed.[15]

Every year in a Jewish family, the anniversary of a death within the family is commemorated with the burning of a *Yahrzeit,* or memorial candle, lit at sundown of the night before and allowed to burn for the following twenty-four hours. As with any other important occurrences, a Jewish death is also often marked by the family's giving to charity.[16]

What lies beyond death has been a subject of much discussion among Jews down through the ages, with theories ranging from the traditional Heaven and Hell to that of simply living on in the memories of others. There is no specific Jewish ruling; Judaism is above all a religion not only of leading an ethical life, but of hope and a sense of just how precious life may be.

PART TWO
FOLKLORE

◇ ◇ ◇

CHAPTER FIVE
WONDER TALES

◇ ◇ ◇

"Wonder tales" are the traditional fairy tales known to all cultures, full of magic and marvelous creatures. In their centuries-long wanderings, the Jews have picked up and transmitted wonder tales in plenty, a good many of which they brought with them to the New World.

Readers are sure to recognize certain familiar, tale types—but these are wonder tales with specifically Jewish twists.

The Weasel and the Well

A girl who was travelling alone to her father's people lost her way and found herself in a wilderness through which she walked and walked, growing ever thirstier. At last she came upon an abandoned farm. And there was a well, with a rope still hanging from it. She climbed down the rope to the water's edge and drank. Only then did the poor girl realize the rope had frayed so badly she could not climb back up. Despairing, she began to weep and cry out for help.

Now, it happened that a young man was travelling that way. He heard her calling and asked warily, since evil things often haunted such desolate places, "Are you of humankind, or are you a demon?"

"Oh, I am of humankind!" the girl called back up, and told him her story. He hurriedly pulled her to safety. And as soon as they could see each other clearly, the two young people fell deeply in love. They wished to give their troth to each other. But who could be the witness between them?

Just then a weasel passed near them. The young man said, "Heaven, that weasel and the well shall be our witnesses that we do not lie to each other."

They went their ways. The girl kept her troth, refusing all other suitors. Ah, but the young man soon forgot her. He married the woman his parents had chosen for him and thought no more of his love.

Then his wife conceived and gave birth to a son. And a weasel crept in and killed the child. His wife conceived a second time, and gave birth to a second son. And as the boy was old enough to walk, he fell into a well and drowned. Guilt-stricken, the young man remembered his love and the troth he had forsworn. Cast out by wife and family, he wandered alone till at last he found the girl and confessed his sin to her. She forgave him, and they were married and lived fruitfully and happily together.[1]

TWO MAGICAL APPRENTICES

The Sorcerer's Apprentice

Once, a poor man and his son traveled to Odessa, where they took part in a feast provided by a rich man for beggars. There, the son saw a sorcerer entertain the rich man by changing from a dog to a cat to a bird and back again, and cried to his father:

"Apprentice me to that sorcerer!"

The father was reluctant, but the sorcerer was willing, signing a contract to teach the boy sorcery for three years. "You cannot see him for those three years," he told the father. "But when the time is past, you may come for him."

Three years came and three years went, and the father traveled the long, weary way to the sorcerer's home, deep within the forest. The sorcerer told him, "I have turned your son and my daughter into two doves. Tell me which one is your son and you may take him. Otherwise, he stays with me."

The father tried, but the two doves were identical. Heartbroken, he rushed off into the forest, where he wept in despair till he slept. In a dream, an old man came to him and said, "Pluck several stalks of rye. Throw the kernels on the ground and watch. The dove that gobbles up the kernels is the sorcerer's child. The dove that eats slowly is your son, pining to be with you."

The father woke, did as he was told, and won back his son. The angry sorcerer said, "You may have him. But first you must sign a contract agreeing that he will do no magic in my lifetime."

This seemed a hard thing to the young man after all he had learned, but he agreed, his father signed, and the two left. As soon as they were safely away, the young man said, "Father, the three years haven't been kind to you. I shall turn myself into a splendid horse, and you shall sell me at market. Only be sure not to sell my bridle, or I'll be a horse forever!"

The father nervously agreed. But little did he suspect that in the marketplace at Odessa would be the sorcerer in disguise. "How much do you want for that horse?" the sorcerer asked.

"A thousand rubles."

"So much? Then let me see if he's worth it!"

With that, the sorcerer leaped onto the horse's back, tearing the reins from the man's hands. "You signed a contract and broke it!" he shouted, dug his spurs into the horse's sides, and galloped away.

The sorcerer stabled the horse in his own stable and treated it harshly indeed. Never once did he remove the horse's bridle. But then he was called away to entertain at the rich man's house. And once he was gone, his daughter, pitying the horse, removed the bridle. The horse became the young man once more, begging for water, and as soon as the sorcerer's daughter turned away, he became a dove and flew away.

The sorcerer, on his way to the rich man's home, recognized the dove for his apprentice. Turning himself into a hawk, he hurried in pursuit. Before the cruel talons could seize him, the dove turned into a ring and dropped into the sea. The hawk transformed to a duck, hunting in the water, but the ring washed safely ashore. There the king's daughter spotted it and slipped it on her finger.

Once she was home, the princess felt the ring squeeze her finger so painfully that she tugged it off. It fell to the floor and turned into the young man once more.

"Don't be afraid," he told her. "I'm as human as you, but I'm a sorcerer. I will not harm you, my word on it. But a more powerful sorcerer is coming, and he means to kill me!"

Quickly he told her what would happen. And so it was. The sorcerer appeared, promising the princess mountains of gold for the ring, swearing it was very precious to him. The princess refused. Then the sorcerer tried to grab the ring from her hand, but the princess hastily threw it to the ground. It turned into a pea, and the sorcerer became a hen trying to peck up the pea. But before the sorcerer could transform again, the pea had become a polecat, which quickly wrung the hen's neck. The hen's carcass was thrown into the street, and the young man thanked the princess for her aid. He flew back to the sorcerer's daughter, who was good where her father had been evil, and married her. Now it was the young sorcerer, not the old, who went to Odessa to perform, but he used his magic only to help the poor, not to harm, and so he prospered.[2]

The Devil's Apprentice

Once, there was a young man who loved the governor's daughter, and she loved him. But her father would not let her be wooed by a mere nobody; first this idle boy must learn a useful trade.

What could that trade be? The young man tried working for a blacksmith but managed only to hit the blacksmith with his hammer; he tried working for a cobbler but managed only to stick the cobbler with his awl. At last the young man could find no one in town to hire him. He went wandering out into the forest, where he came upon a fine palace ruled over by a devil. Now, the devil said he liked this human lad's looks and took him on as an apprentice in magic. All went well until the day the devil left the palace, warning his apprentice, "While I am away, you may wander as you will through the first six rooms of this palace—but do not dare enter the seventh room!"

As soon as the devil was gone, the young man opened the seventh room. Within, to his horror, he saw dead men suspended from ropes. Only one was still breathing, and the young man hurried to cut him free. The dying man thanked him, then warned him with his last breath:

"Do not trust the devil. First he teaches us magic, then becomes jealous of our powers and kills us."

The young man fled the palace. Knowing the devil would surely follow him, he used the magic he'd learned to turn himself into a fine horse, telling his mother as he did so to sell him to the governor but not to part with the bridle. So he safely entered the governor's estate. But that very day the devil recognized his runaway apprentice as the fine horse. The young man fled and used his magic to change himself into a beautiful mansion. But the devil again recognized him. The mansion crumbled and reformed into a riding mule, but the devil leaped on his back. The devil tried to force the mule into the ocean to drown, but the mule became a fish and leaped safely into the waves. The devil leaped after him, and the fish soared up into the sky as an eagle. The devil followed, and the eagle turned into a ring and fell into the arms of the governor's daughter. She hid the ring in her jewelry box. The devil went to the governor and bought the ring. But the ring turned into a pomegranate. The devil tried to grab it, but it burst, scattering all its seeds. The devil changed into a rooster and started gobbling the seeds. But one seed turned into a knife and killed the devil, then transformed once more into the young man himself.

The governor had to agree the young man most certainly had learned a useful trade and gave him the hand of his daughter in marriage.[3]

The Dancing Demons and the Hunchback

Once there lived two brothers, both of them, alas, hunchbacked. But where one brother was a mean and spiteful man, the other was a kindhearted soul despite his hump. Unable to stay with his quarrelsome brother any longer, he set out into the world. Night overtook him in the forest, and he found shelter in a ramshackle old hut, said his prayers, and slept. But the sound of music and merriment woke him. Creeping out of the hut, he found himself in the middle of a ring of demons, dancing and cavorting to the strains of high, wild music.

"A human!" they cried. "Come dance with us, human!"

What could he do? Run? The demons could run more swiftly than any poor hunchback. Besides, the music sounded so wild and free that he joined the demons, dancing and singing as gaily as he could until he was so weary he could hardly move. The demons were pleased with him, so pleased that they cried:

"We shall not let you go! You must return tomorrow night and dance with us again! Yes, yes, and to be sure you return, you must leave us a pledge!"

"A pledge!" repeated the hunchback. "I have nothing, save the clothes I wear—"

"No, no, we don't want them!"

"—or the hump on my back."

"Yes, yes! There is the pledge we shall take!"

The demons swarmed around him, then were gone as swiftly as smoke. And with them went the hunchback's hump. Hunchback no longer, he returned to his village, walking tall and straight. When his mean-spirited brother saw what had happened and heard the story of the dancing demons, he decided that he too would get himself a demonic reward. Off he went to dance with the demons. But, alas, demons can't tell one man from another.

"You have returned!" they cried. "You are an honorable fellow! Come, let us return your pledge."

And so the mean-spirited brother was forced to creep back to his home with not one hump, but two.[4]

The Willow Twigs

One Hoshana Rabba night, a Jew was on his way to synagogue, carrying a *heshayne,* a bunch of hallowed willow twigs, when he met a woman with a baby in her arms—or so it seemed. Because he was in a holy mood, and because he was carrying the *heshayne,* he realized that this was no woman at all, but a she-demon clutching a stolen human child.

"What is that you carry?" asked the demon.

"A sacred sheaf of willow twigs," the Jew answered.

"I think it's a broom," said the demon.

"A sacred sheaf of willow twigs," the Jew repeated.
"It is a broom!"
"Willow twigs."
"A broom!"

The demon's eyes glowed in the darkness. The Jew realized that she meant to trick him into saying he held merely a broom, for once he denied them, the willow twigs would lose their sanctity. And then the demon would kill him! She insisted and insisted that he held nothing more than a useless broom, stealing closer and ever closer to him. But as soon as the demon was within reach, the Jew lashed her across her face with the willow twigs. The demon shrieked at the touch of holiness and vanished into smoke. The baby fell to the ground, and the Jew picked it up, comforting it. He took it to town with him to find the baby's mother. At first the bewildered woman insisted that this could not be; her baby was still safe in its cradle. But when they looked, in the cradle was nothing more than a bundle of straw. Demonic power had made that straw seem alive until the demon's spell was broken by the holy willow twigs.[5]

The Magic Sheep

Once, long ago, a farmer was driving his empty wagon home when he saw a nice, fat, healthy sheep lying by the side of the road with never a mark of ownership on it. The farmer looked carefully about but saw no one. Delighted with his find, he climbed down from the wagon and bound the unresisting sheep, then tried to lift it into his wagon. It was no simple thing! That one sheep, fat though it was, seemed far heavier than it should be. At last the farmer succeeded. Now, though, the sheep seemed to grow heavier and heavier still, till the farmer's good, strong horses were straining in the traces, barely moving. Frightened, the farmer wondered what to do? Should he get out and push? Should he just dump this too-heavy sheep off his wagon?

All at once, the team bounded forward, as though the wagon had suddenly become lighter. The startled farmer glanced back over his shoulder and saw the sheep, now miraculously unbound, stand up on its hind legs and show him its backside. As he stared, the sheep turned into a tiny imp of a demon.

"What a fine trick I played on you!" it called after him, as he lashed his horses into a gallop. "What a fine, fine trick!"[6]

Fate

A rich man, very happy with his way of life, began to worry about having to leave that life. Could death possibly be avoided? He consulted astrologers, and he consulted soothsayers, and all of them told the rich man the same sad story: one day he would be killed by a horse.

"Then all I need do is avoid horses, and I will live forever!" cried the rich man.

He moved into a tent in the very heart of the desert, far from the homes of men and the stables of horses. The day the soothsayers had prophesied as his day of death came and went, and the rich man cried out:

"The day is done, and I am still alive! Why, those soothsayers cheated me! Tomorrow I'll go back to town and demand my money back from those frauds!" Even as he said this, a huge, huge eagle flapped wearily by overhead. And in its enormous talons was the body of a horse. But the horse's weight was too much even for that huge bird of prey. The eagle lost its grip, and the horse's body went plunging down and down—and so, indeed, the rich man who thought himself safe from Fate, was killed by a horse.[7]

The Deadly Libel

Years ago, in a far off land, there lived a king who was kind to the Jews in his land. But his ministers, jealous of the favor the Jews were shown, plotted to destroy them. And so one day they seized the king's own son and secretly murdered him, dumping the small, sad body within the synagogue. When the king was informed of this, he cried aloud in anguish and had the rabbi of the congregation brought before him.

"If your people have murdered my son," the king told him, "I shall slay all the Jews in the land!"

"Good King, you cannot believe us guilty of such a horror!" the rabbi exclaimed. "Give us three days to solve this crime."

The king agreed. And that night the rabbi dreamed a true dream. In it, the Prophet Elijah came to him and told him who had truly slain the child.

The next day, the rabbi returned to the palace and asked that the body of the murdered boy be brought out. In the presence of the king and the ministers, the rabbi touched the child's forehead, then his own, and lost himself in prayer.

King and ministers gasped to suddenly see the boy open his eyes.

"Tell us how you were killed," the rabbi said.

The boy's voice was strained and distant. "I was playing in the garden when these men seized me." His finger pointed, stabbing at each minister in turn, one, two, three, four, five. "They carried me to the edge of town. I begged them not to hurt me, but they stabbed me with their knives. My blood splashed a large stone beside me."

The boy's eyes closed. He lay still and lifeless once more.

The stunned king sent some guards to find the stone. Find it they did and brought it before him. He at once begged the Jews to pardon him for his accusation. But there was no pardon for the murderous ministers. They died that very day.[8]

The Moving Finger

A group of young men were walking along, jesting merrily, when they saw what looked very much like a finger sticking up out of the ground, moving back and forth. Being in a frivolous mood, one of the young men placed his ring on the finger as a wedding token. The finger disappeared into the ground. The young men went their way, and eventually forgot what had happened.

The day came for the wedding of the young man who had given away his ring. But before he could exchange vows with his bride, a woman shouted, "He cannot marry another! He already is wed to me! See, here is his ring on my hand!"

The wedding party was in an uproar. The furious father of the bride took his daughter home, leaving the young man alone with the stranger. Rabbi Isaac Luria, alone of all those there, recognized the woman for what she truly was: a demon. He took the young man aside and asked:

"Do you truly wished to be wed to this she-demon?"

"No!" the young man cried. "Who'd be fool enough to *want* to marry a demon?"

The rabbi called the she-demon to him. "Why do you want to wed this young man? He is a human. Go and wed one of your own people."

The she-demon shook an impatient head. "How can I marry anyone else after he wedded me with his ring?"

"That was an error," the rabbi told her. "He never saw your face. He didn't even know you were a demon! It was only a joke that his ring was placed on your finger."

The she-demon was stubborn. Maybe she didn't want to be a mere human's wife, but the young man had given her his ring, she was married to him, and that was that.

Rabbi Luria found a solution: he summoned a scribe and had the young man give the she-demon a legal divorce. After making sure she swore not to bring any demonic vengeance on the young man or his family, the rabbi nodded his approval. The she-demon was satisfied, the young man was relieved, and Rabbi Luria sent the she-demon on her way. The subdued young man married a second time—this time to a human bride.[9]

The Water Spirit

There was a rabbi who, alas, was not always pure of heart. In fact, that rabbi was a sinner. The reason he dared sin was this: he lived by a lake, and each time he would sin, he would simply cast that sin into the lake and be clean once more. Each year the sin he cast into the waters was darker and more foul. Each year the lake grew more and more stormy as it tried in vain to hurl back the sins, until at last it surged like the sea, waiting darkly, waiting vengeance.

Now, the rabbi and his wife had no children, and it was a sorrow tothem. So the rabbi went off to his cousin, the Baal Shem Tov, of whom it was said he could perform wonders. And the Baal Shem Tov promised him one child, a son, who would grow to be a strong, happy boy.

"But," the Baal Shem Tov added sadly, "on his thirteenth birthday, he shall go into the water and drown."

The rabbi heard these words, and cried out in despair. "Help me!" he begged.

The Baal Shem Tov shook his head. "The lake hates you for the sins with which you have befouled it. There is only one way to save your son, and that is to keep him away from the water."

The rabbi was about to run joyfully for home when the Baal Shem Tov called after him, "I will give you a sign to remind you. On the fatal day, you'll begin to dress yourself, and you'll pull both stockings onto one foot."

That seemed a strange warning to the rabbi, but he thanked the Baal Shem Tov and headed home. Soon enough, he and his wife were the parents of a fine, healthy son. They forbade him nothing—save the lake.

The years passed. The rabbi and his wife nearly forgot the dark prophesy. Their son grew and flourished like a healthy young tree. Then on the morning of the boy's thirteenth birthday, the rabbi woke and sleepily began to dress.

"My stocking," he muttered. "Where's my other stocking?"

"You have both of them on one foot," his wife answered.

The rabbi cried out in horror. "The prophesy!"

Husband and wife raced for their son's room.

"He's gone!"

The rabbi rushed outside, and saw the boy walking as though in the middle of a deep sleep—walking straight towards the lake. Barefoot, half-clad, the rabbi ran after him.

"My son, no!"

The boy started at that shout, stumbled over a tree root, and fell headlong. With the help of his wife, the rabbi dragged his struggling son back to their house and locked him within. All that day, the rabbi prayed, while his son moaned and burned as though with fever and begged to go to the lake. But no matter how much the boy pleaded, the rabbi would not release him.

Slowly the hot day passed. Just before the sun dipped below the horizon to signal the day's end, the lake waters roiled. A hand appeared, then a second hand. A creature, all of dripping green lake weed, pulled itself up out of the waters and cried:

"One is missing!"

But just then, the sun dipped below the horizon. The day was done at last, and the lake-spirit sank back below the waters and was seen no more.[10]

Blessings and Curses

Once upon a time, there lived a husband and wife, and their beautiful, kindhearted daughter. One day, the wife took ill and died, and the grieving widower, who was a merchant often on the road, not wanting his daughter to be alone or to grow up without a mother, married again.

This second wife was cruel and spiteful at heart. At first she pretended to love her new stepdaughter. But when she gave birth to a daughter of her own, as mean and spiteful as the mother herself, the cruel stepmother began to openly hate her husband's beautiful first child and to plot ways to be rid of her.

One day, when the merchant was away, she told the girl, "Take the dirty clothes down to the river outside town."

Now, that river was known to be haunted, and the girl began to weep in fright. But there was nothing she could do but obey her stepmother.

As the girl washed the clothes in the river, tears ran down her cheek and plopped into the river. All at once three water-spirits rose up out of the water.

"Why do you weep?" they asked.

"I weep because my stepmother has sent me here to be rid of me."

"Don't weep, princess," said the first water-spirit. "Go home. From now on, wondrous roses will spring up in your footsteps."

"And when you wash yourself," continued the second water-spirit, "the water in the basin will turn gold."

"And when you speak," finished the third water-spirit, "your breath will be a wonderful perfume."

The girl went home, wondering. Sure enough, roses sprang up in her footsteps. Sure enough, the water in the washing basin turned to gold. Her stepmother asked how this could be, and the girl told about the three water-spirits and their gifts.

"So!" thought the stepmother. "I'll send my daughter to the river for gifts, too!"

But when the ugly daughter came to the river, she told the water-spirits rudely, "You gave my sister gifts. I want some too!"

"Oh you do, do you?" cried the insulted water-spirits. "So be it!"

"When you walk," said the first water-spirit, "nettles will spring up in your footsteps!"

"When you wash yourself," said the second water-spirit, "frogs will fill the basin!"

"And when you talk," said the third water-spirit, "Your breath will stink!"

So it was. The ugly girl went home, leaving nettles in her wake. Frogs filled the basin every time she washed. And when she tried to tell her mother what had happened, her breath was so foul, the stepmother fled the house.

Now, in a nearby country lived a king with one son. And that son was hunting a bride. He heard about the maiden in whose footsteps roses grew and went to see her. The moment he saw her, and she saw him, they fell in love. For fear that the stepmother would try to stop her, the girl stole off in the middle of the night and married the prince.

Time passed. The evil stepmother consulted this fortune-teller and that, till at last she learned how happy the young royal couple were. Worse, she learned that her stepdaughter had given birth to a child just as charming as she.

The stepmother ranted and raved and raged. At last she went to see a sorceress. "Name your price!" she said. "Just kill that stepdaughter of mine!"

"It shall be done," said the sorceress.

Off she went to the royal palace and snuck into the bedchamber through her dark arts. There slept the princess and her baby. The sorceress drew a long, sharp knife and killed the baby, then left the knife in the princess' hand.

The prince had no choice but to believe his wife had killed their child. The sorceress' evil had even destroyed the water-spirits' gifts, so no roses grew in her footsteps, no gold shone in her basin, no perfume sprang from her breath.

The cruel law in that land demanded that the princess' eyes be put out and she be driven from the palace, her dead baby in a sack on her back. Grieving bitterly, the blinded princess found her way into a forest, sank exhausted to the ground beneath a tree, and slept. As she slept, her own mother came to her in a dream.

"Poor child, you have suffered much, and you will suffer more. But in the morning, you will wake beside a well. Bathe your eyes and your baby's body in the water."

In the morning, the princess woke to find it had been a true dream, for she was beside a well. When she bathed her eyes, her sight returned. And when she bathed her baby's body, the baby was alive and well once more. Joyfully, the princess hugged her living child to her.

Off they went, princess and baby, wandering from town to town, the princess earning a living as a singer. At last, weary of wandering, she settled in a city with her growing child and found employment as a servant in the house of wealthy folk.

It happened that the princess' employer was a friend of the king, and he gave a banquet at which the king and his son appeared. The entertainers all sang for the prince, but no one could raise his sadness.

"Ah, if only I could hear a song that reminded me of the happy days with my poor wife!"

The princess heard. She came forward in her servant's clothes and sang of their former happiness together. The prince sprang to his feet, weeping. Seeing her sparkling eyes, seeing her happy, living child, he knew she had been falsely accused. Taking her by the hand, he cried:

"This is my own true, blameless wife, and I love her dearly!"

And so they were husband and wife once more and lived happily ever after.[11]

The Vizier's Daughter

Once, a vizier and his daughter lived in a house with high, protective walls and a wide, flat roof. One day, he was forced to go off on a journey, leaving his daughter alone. Before he left, the vizier warned his daughter:

"Beware of strangers. Do not open the door to anyone."

She agreed, and off he went.

That day, the vizier's daughter refused to open the door to anyone. But that night, she heard a strange sound, not from the door, but from the roof. Snatching up a long, sharp knife, she hurried up to see what was wrong. A man attacked her in the darkness, but the vizier's daughter slashed out with her knife and cut off his head. A second bandit sprang at her, but she killed him too. At the end of the fight, forty bandits lay dead, and only the forty-first, their leader, survived. He too attacked the girl. She slashed at him with her knife but succeeded only in cutting off his ear. He ran away, shouting back over his shoulder:

"I'll get you yet!"

The vizier's daughter and her servants got rid of the dead bandits and cleaned up the roof. The servants were all sure that everything would now be well, but the vizier's daughter could not forget the bandit chief's threat.

The vizier came home. Life seemed normal. But though the bandit chief quickly forgot his dead comrades, he could not forget his missing ear, cut off by a mere girl. So he disguised himself as a merchant, opened a store next door to the vizier's house, and stocked it with his stolen merchandise. He prospered and became such a charming neighbor to the vizier that the two became fast friends. When the bandit chief asked for the hand of the vizier's daughter in marriage, the vizier and his daughter—who never suspected his true identity—agreed.

That night, when the new husband and wife were alone together, the bandit chief asked, "Don't you recognize me? Don't you know who I am?"

"No."

He tore off his turban. She saw the missing ear and cried out in horror, "But now we're husband and wife!"

"Oh you fool! Why do you think I married you? You killed my comrades and cost me my ear! Did you think I would forget my threat?"

He caught her up before she could escape and carried her off to the forest, where he tied her to a tree. "Now I shall call forth the widows of the slain thieves and let them take their revenge on you!"

Off he went, leaving the vizier's daughter alone. Fortunately for her, an old man, a dealer in oil, chanced to pass by just then. The vizier's daughter begged him for help, and when he heard her story, he cut her bonds and took her home with him, hiding her in an empty oil barrel.

Sure enough, the raging bandit chief came hunting his escaped prey. He threatened the old oil dealer, but the old man simply shrugged.

"I haven't seen any girl. I sell oil. Do you want to buy any oil?"

The bandit chief never thought to look in the barrels. He went roaring off to tell the bandits' widows, "I couldn't find her."

Meanwhile, the vizier's daughter came out of hiding. But she didn't dare go back to her father, not when the bandit chief might still be hunting her. She and the old oil dealer lived together in the forest like daughter and father. And whenever a stranger passed by, the vizier's daughter hid in the empty oil barrel.

One day, a prince went riding through the forest. He chanced to see the vizier's daughter when she didn't know he was there, and fell in love with her on the spot. But when he rode to the oil dealer's home, the vizier's daughter hid as usual.

"Old man," the prince said, "I love your daughter and wish to marry her."

"I have no daughter," the old man said, and refused to hear another word. After the prince had ridden away, he asked the vizier's daughter, "Would you like to marry him?"

"I can't!" she cried. "I am already married to the bandit chief!"

The old man assured her that a marriage made through deception was no lawful marriage at all. And the vizier's daughter, who had fallen in love with the prince, agreed to wed him.

But even through her happiness, the vizier's daughter still worried about the bandit chief. She asked her husband for a house with a high wall and a bodyguard of two huge, well-trained lions. And he, though she refused to tell him what she feared, gave her the house and the lions.

Meanwhile, the bandit chief had never given up his hunger for revenge. He kept hunting for the vizier's daughter until he heard that she had married the prince. He gathered his new gang about him and wrapped a sheepskin about himself till no one could have said he was a man, not a sheep.

"Sell me in the marketplace as a magic sheep that can dance and sing," he told his men. "Ask so high a price that only the prince will buy me."

So they did. Sure enough, the prince bought the sheep as a present, thinking it would amuse his sad wife.

That night, when all the palace was asleep, the bandit chief threw off his sheepskin disguise and crept into the chambers of the vizier's daughter. She awoke with a scream. And that woke the two lions! They pounced on the intruder and gobbled him up.

The vizier's daughter began to laugh with relief. Her husband rushed to her side, and she told him the whole story. Soon the whole palace was rejoicing.

Word was sent to the vizier, who had been mourning his lost daughter. He raced to the palace and embraced his daughter. Word was sent to the old oil dealer too. And they all lived joyfully all their days.[12]

A Jewish Cinderella

Once there lived a rabbi with three daughters. One day he took it into his head to ask them, one by one, how much they loved him.

The oldest never hesitated. "I love you as much as gold," she said.

"Very good," beamed her father.

The second daughter never hesitated either. "I love you as much as silver," she told him.

"Very good," repeated her father.

But when he asked his third daughter, "How much do you love me?" she answered: "As much as meat loves salt."

As much as meat loves salt? What manner of ungrateful reply was that? Angry, the rabbi drove his third daughter from his house.

Weeping, she went her way. Night came and day, and night again, and still she wandered on, for where had she to go? But in her path suddenly stood an old man. And though she didn't know it, this was none other than the Prophet Elijah.

"Where are you going, child?" he asked, and his voice was so kind the girl told him her whole story.

"Never fear. All may still be well. Here, child, take this stick. Stay on this path till you come to a house where you can hear someone saying the blessing over wine. Be sure to add 'Amen.' They will invite you inside, but wait until the rabbi himself asks you in before you enter. Once inside, hide the stick in the attic. Whenever you need anything, all you need do is take the stick and bid it, 'Stick, open!'"

With that, the old man disappeared, and the girl went on till she saw the house and heard a voice reciting the blessing over the wine. Three times, in the proper places, she added her "Amen."

Hearing this new voice, a girl's voice, from outside, the people in the house were surprised. The rabbi's wife came out and invited the girl to enter. But it wasn't until the rabbi himself invited her that she entered. She looked so ragged and worn from her journeyings that the people took her for nothing more than a poor beggar girl. They gave her food out of charity and a place to sleep beside the stove. That night, she crept upstairs and hid the stick in the attic as the old man had told her.

The next day, the rabbi and his family dressed in their finery and left for a splendid wedding. How the girl ached to go with them! She went up to the attic, took out her stick, and told it, "Stick, open!"

The stick opened, revealing soap and a basin of water. Once she had bathed off the grime coating her, she said again, "Stick, open!"

The stick opened, revealing a wonderful gown and dainty golden shoes. The girl dressed in this beautiful clothing and went to the wedding. There, the rabbi's son was smitten with this lovely maiden, never recognizing the shabby beggar girl who had crouched by the stove. He asked her again and again who she was, but she would never reply.

The rabbi's son was a clever young man! He spread pitch on the doorsill. And when it was time for the wedding guests to leave, the beautiful maiden tried to hurry away so she could get home before the others. But she stepped right into the pitch, and one golden shoe stuck to it. She had to run on without it. The rabbi's son lost the beautiful maiden, but he picked up the shoe.

By the time the rabbi, his wife, and his son returned home, the girl had already hidden her fine clothes. Smeared with dust, dressed in her rags, she huddled by the stove. No one suspected she had ever moved from it.

The rabbi's son searched high and wide for the owner of the shoe. But not one maiden could wear it. At last he returned home, sad and weary.

"Let me try the shoe," the girl told him.

"What, a poor little beggar girl?" he laughed.

She snatched the shoe from him, and of course it fit her perfectly.

The rabbi and his wife were dismayed, as can well be imagined. What, their son marry a dirty little beggar girl? That night, though, they both had a dream in which they were warned not to stop the wedding. In the morning, disturbed by what they had dreamed, the rabbi and his wife went out for a walk, so they could ponder what to do now. The rabbi's son was left alone with the girl.

"You aren't *really* the maiden I saw at the wedding, are you?" he asked.

The girl smiled. "Come with me," she said, "and see who I really am."

She led him up to the attic and picked up her stick.

"Stick, open."

It did, and wonderful, beautiful clothes appeared.

"You see?" she said. "There are some for you, some for me!"

Dressed as finely as a prince and princess, they went for a walk, arm in arm. The rabbi and his wife saw them and were struck with wonder. Surely this was part of their dream, their son dressed so richly and walking arm and arm with a beautiful stranger? They hurried home, but by the time they entered, the two young people had already changed back to their old clothes.

"Never mind," the rabbi's son told his parents. "I'm going to marry her, and that's that."

"What can we say?" asked the confused parents. "Then marry her, you shall."

They sent out invitations to all the countryside. And one of those who accepted the invitation was the girl's father. When she learned he had accepted, she hurried to the kitchen. There she told the cooks who were preparing the wedding feast:

"Be sure to cook one meal without any salt at all."

The wedding day came. Thanks to the magic stick, bride and groom were as splendid as a princess and prince, and the groom's parents were astonished to realize the beggar girl and the beautiful maiden were one and the same.

After the ceremony, people feasted. Only one man did not feast, and that was the girl's father. No, he sat staring sadly at his food.

The bride approached. "You don't seem to be enjoying the feast," she said.

"Alas, how can I enjoy a meal that has no salt at all?"

"Now you understand!" she said. "Father, Father, do you remember when you asked me how much I loved you? Do you remember how I told you I loved you as meat loves salt? You were so angry you drove me out of the house!"

When he heard these words, her father nearly fainted. But when he recovered, he begged his daughter's forgiveness and told everyone the whole story.

And everyone lived joyfully from then on.[13]

The Snake Son

Once, there was a good Jewish husband and wife who had everything anyone could possibly want, save for one thing: they had no child. At last, despairing, they went to a wise rabbi and asked for his help.

The rabbi, after much prayer, said to them, "With God's help, you will, indeed, have a child, a son. First, you must hold a feast to celebrate *Rosh Hodesh*. Invite everyone, rich and poor. And when a stranger arrives, you must place him at the head of the table, in the place of honor. Do this, and all will go well."

Joyously the couple went home and began to prepare their feast. And that was a splendid *Rosh Hodesh* celebration indeed, with fine food and wine and happiness. In the middle of it, a stranger appeared, a ragged old man who asked to be taken to the head of the table. Husband and wife looked at each other in dismay. What, this poor old beggar sit in the place of honor? This could never be!

So the husband took the old man gently by the arm and led him instead to one of the smaller tables, where poor folk were sitting. "You will eat and drink as well as anyone," he promised.

But the old man insisted, "Let me speak to your wife."

And what he told her was, "You have disregarded the rabbi's advice. You refused to seat the stranger at the head of the table. You shall still have your son—but he shall be not a boy, but a snake!"

With that, the old man disappeared.

Time passed, and the couple did their best to forget the old man's strange words. But how could they forget? And sure enough, nine months later, the wife gave birth not to a boy, but to a snake. Husband and wife wept for a time, then decided reluctantly that the snake, strange though it was, was still their child. Indeed, as the snake grew, it showed a human intelligence and kindness. Gradually, the couple began to accept the snake, and then to love him, treating him as their son and educating him in all the proper ways. And so the years passed.

Then one day the snake came to his parents and said, "I am now old enough to wed. Please, pick me a bride, and I will return in a month for the wedding."

What could the couple do? Who would want to marry a snake? Despairing, they went off to the wise rabbi once more.

"How can we possibly find a bride for our son?" they asked. "What woman will wed him? Who will not run from him in terror?"

After much prayer, the rabbi replied, "God has a solution to every problem. There is a town several days' travel from here. Seek out the poorest man in that town, and share the Sabbath with him. There you will find your son's bride."

Sure enough, the couple found the town and within it the hovel of the poorest man. When he heard that these two well-dressed folk wished to spend the night and share the Sabbath with him, he cried out in despair:

"I have no place for guests to sleep! And my family and I have no food for the Sabbath."

"Never mind," they told him. "We will sleep on the floor and buy your family some Sabbath food."

To the couple's puzzlement, on Friday night the poor man set out five dishes, in addition to those for himself, his wife, and his guests, and took those five dishes into another room. He did the same thing for the second Sabbath meal and the third. By this time, the couple could no longer hold back their curiosity.

"Why do you bring those five plates of food into another room?"

The poor man sighed. "I have five daughters in there. But they have no fine clothes to wear, only rags, and are ashamed to be seen by guests."

"We will buy them clothes. Have them come out so we may meet them."

The five daughters came out in their new clothes. They were all beautiful, so the couple asked each one if she would marry their son.

One by one, the daughters refused—except for the youngest daughter.

"If I leave," she said, "my father will have one less mouth to feed. Yes, I will marry your son."

The couple gave the poor family much money and left with the youngest daughter. But they were afraid to tell her about their son and would not let her see him.

The day of the wedding arrived. As the bride was dressing for her marriage, a large green snake slithered in through the window.

"Don't be afraid," he said.

"I . . . I'm not," the young woman stammered.

Suddenly the snake rose up on its tail, wriggling and writhing till its skin split open. A handsome young man stepped free. As the young woman stared, too astonished to speak, he repeated:

"Don't be afraid. Before I was born, my parents were told they would only have a son if they gave the place of honor to a beggar at a *Rosh Hodesh* celebration. They refused, and so I was born in the shape of a snake, not a boy. But now the spell has nearly run out. I'm to be your husband, if you will have me. But you must keep my secret a little longer, even if it's a snake that is with you under the wedding canopy. Will you do that?"

Speechless with wonder, she nodded. The young man turned back into a snake and quickly slithered from the room. At the wedding, everyone whispered in horror at the thought of a woman being married to a snake. Only the bride herself was calm. And sure enough, right under the wedding canopy, the *huppah,* the snake was gone, and in its place stood a fine young man, richly dressed.

There was much rejoicing at that wedding, as can well be imagined. And they all lived happily to the end of their days.[14]

The Demon's Midwife

Once, a midwife was hurrying home after having attended to a birth. The hour was late, there was no moon, and the night was very dark indeed. To the midwife's horror, her candle blew out, leaving her in total blackness.

"Dear God, now what can I do?"

Suddenly a huge white cat, glowing in the darkness, brushed against her legs, purring gently. As soon as the midwife bent to pet it, the cat moved away, stalking forward, tail up in determined cat fashion, as though trying to get the woman to follow. Deciding she had no other choice, the midwife did follow. And sure enough, the cat led her safely to her home.

The grateful midwife bent to stroke the cat. "God grant that as you saved me, I will someday be able to save you."

The cat purred once, then vanished into the night.

A year passed. One night, as the midwife sat peacefully at home, there came a wild knocking at her door. Opening it, she found herself facing a tall, dark-eyed stranger shrouded in a huge black cloak.

"I beg you, come quickly," he said. "You are needed to help a woman deliver her first child."

The midwife followed him out into the night. Whether they went a short way or a long way, she couldn't say, but all at once she was being hurried into a magnificent mansion. And within it lay her patient, a young woman who was laboring painfully. The midwife set about her work and soon had eased the young woman's pain. Soon after that, she welcomed a new baby into the world and smiled to see it nestled against his mother's breast. But the new mother drew the midwife to her and whispered:

"Do you recognize me? No? I am a demon, and all these people are demons, too. Don't be afraid, though. I was also the white cat who saw you safely home a year ago and heard you bless me. Now you have saved me, and so I offer you these warnings: when my relatives ask you to join their feast, tell them you are fasting; and when they offer you gold and silver treasures, refuse them. Since it is our custom, you must be rewarded for your work, but take nothing but the smallest rug that lies by the treasury door."

Sure enough, the demon woman's relatives asked the midwife to join their feast. Politely, she told them she could not, since she was fasting. They brought her to their treasury, full of wondrous gold and silver treasures. But the midwife remembered the demon woman's warning and asked only for the small rug that lay by the treasury door.

As the midwife was ready to leave, the new mother, in her inexperience, let the baby slide away from the breast. The baby, naturally, began to wail, and all the demons covered their ears. Because few babies are born to their kind, they didn't know that crying is quite natural to the young. And one demon exclaimed:

"Let us exchange this noisy child with a quiet human baby!"

Off the demons went to the human world and soon returned with a sleeping human baby. The midwife pretended to help them switch the babies, but as she did so, she jabbed the sole of the human child's foot so that he woke with a yell and started wailing wildly. The demons muttered:

"This baby is noisier than our own! We must return it and keep the demon child!"

The midwife agreed to help them. First she settled the demon baby back at his mother's breast. He stopped crying the moment he tasted milk; he suckled peacefully. The human child continued to wail, and the demons hurried it and the midwife back to the human world. She returned the baby to its rightful mother, warning her never to leave her child untended again, and wearily went home, leaving the small demon rug on the floor.

In the morning, she found that rug covered with gold. She shared that treasure with those in need, and lived happily all her days.[15]

GOOD LUCK AND BAD: A CYCLE OF FOLKTALES

The Sleeping Luck

Once, there lived a poor peasant who seemed to be cursed by perpetual bad fortune while his brother thrived. Things grew so bad that the only way the poor man could survive was by working as his wealthy brother's servant. But one day the poor man saw an odd little fellow carry a sack of gold into his brother's house and asked:

"Who are you?"

"Why, I am your brother's luck!" the little man replied.

Amazed, the poor man asked, "Can you tell me where to find my own luck?"

"Oh, I can, but it won't do you much good. He's a lazy fellow, out there snoring in the fields. If you go out there, you will see a hundred lucks sleeping or waking. Ignore them. Go straight to the luck who snores the loudest. He's your luck."

So the poor man went out into the fields. He saw a hundred lucks but ignored them all and went straight for the luck who was snoring the loudest.

"Ah, luck, my luck, wake up!"

The luck only continued to snore.

"Please, my luck, I need you! My family needs you! You've slept long enough! Wake up!"

At last, to the peasant's delight, he saw the luck yawn and open an eye. Without stirring more than he needed to, the luck handed the peasant a single silver coin.

"Only one coin?" asked the disappointed peasant. "Your pardon, but what good is only one coin?"

"Go to the market," the luck said gruffly. "Buy the first thing you see."

So the peasant went to the market. The first thing he saw was a hen. He hardly saw how one little hen could help him but, obeying his luck's command, the peasant bought her and took her home. In the morning, the glint of gold caught his eye. That plain little hen had laid a golden egg!

And from that day on, the poor man's luck stayed awake, and life was good![16]

Bad Luck

Once, there was a coachman who worked from sunrise to sunset hauling whatever loads he could find, without once earning enough to do more than barely feed and clothe his family. No matter what he did, bad fortune seemed to always follow him. Then one day his fortune failed altogether when his horse died. For what good is a coachman without a horse? The Jews of the town felt sorry for the hard-working coachman and took up a collection to buy him a new horse. Joyfully, he took the horse home with him. Surely his fortune had finally turned for the better!

But there in the barn he saw a small fellow, stark naked and hairy, jumping up and down in his wagon.

"Who are you?" the coachman cried.

"Why, I'm your luck!" the ugly little fellow cried. "Your own Bad Luck! Now I don't have to leave you. Now I can once more ride in your wagon like a gentleman and not have to slog about after you on foot all day!"[17]

The Luckless Young Man

Once, there was a young man who, though he was good, kind, and pious, was born with no luck at all. But he never lost heart, no matter how poorly things went with him. Remembering the saying, "Change your place and you change your luck," he set out into the world and soon found himself lost in the desert even as a blinding sandstorm swirled up. He heard what sounded like the joy of the Sabbath service, and made his way through the storm to a synagogue bright with lights. Hurrying inside, he called out, "Blessed are those who have gathered in the name of the Lord!"

To the young man's horror, harsh voices mocked him, "Blessed are those who have gathered in the name of Ashmodai!"

He had fallen into the hands of demons! They caught at his arms, tore at his clothes, forced a goblet of wine to his lips. Even though his throat ached with dryness, the young man found the courage to hurl the goblet from him and shout out with all his strength:

"Hear O Israel! The Lord is our God, the Lord is One!"

There was a wild scream, and the false synagogue went silent and dark, save for thousands of small, twinkling lights, gold, green, and brown. Then the young man heard the sound of one small demon sobbing.

"Every drop of wine you spilled," it whimpered, "became another link in this chain that binds me, and without your help, I'll never be free!"

It was such a very small and very sad-looking demon that the young man sighed. "I'll free you if you tell me what all these lights are."

"They are people's lucks."

"And which one is mine?"

The demon pointed out one that was so dark a brown it was nearly black. The young man sighed again. "I thought as much." But then his eye was caught by one luck that glowed with so pure and lovely a light that he asked the demon, "Whose luck is that?"

"That belongs to a young maiden," said the demon and told the young man where she could be found.

The young man touched the chain, and it dissolved. The freed demon disappeared and did no more harm. The young man travelled straight to the maiden's house and found her even more lovely than her luck. He and she loved each other from first sight, and when the young man asked her father for her hand, permission was granted. They were wed and lived happily together, his bad luck more than balanced by the extreme good luck of his wife.[18]

The Wheel of Fortune

It was said of the sage known as Maimonides and the Rabbi Abraham Ibn-Ezra that though they were both born on the same day, the first was born when the Wheel of Fortune was at the top and Rabbi Abraham when it turned down. If Rabbi Abraham bought goods at such and such a price, that price was sure to fall the following day—his luck was always upside down. One day Maimonides, pitying his friend yet knowing the rabbi would never accept direct help, placed a purse full of money at a spot he knew Rabbi Abraham would pass on his way to the synagogue.

Meanwhile Rabbi Abraham was trying to cheer himself up by saying, "I must not bewail my fate. It could be worse; it is better to be poor but clear of eye than rich but blind."

And to teach himself humility, he walked to the synagogue with his eyes closed as though he were blind. Alas, his upside down luck held true! He taught himself humility—but since his eyes were shut, he walked right past the purse and never noticed it![19]

"My Luck Is Locked Up"

There was once a tailor who worked day and night. As he sat and sewed and sewed, never growing richer for all his work, he moaned over and over:

"I am helpless. My luck is locked up, my luck is locked up."

Now it happened that the sultan's vizier overheard the poor tailor and decided to play a pleasant trick on him. The vizier had a chicken roasted, secretly stuffed the chicken with coins, then gave the tailor the chicken on a tray. But to his annoyance, the tailor only thanked him absently and returned to his moaning:

"My luck is locked up, my luck is locked up."

The tailor's neighbor smelled the chicken and asked the tailor why he wasn't eating the nicely roasted bird.

"I am not hungry," said the tailor. "You take it." And he returned to his moan of:

"My luck is locked up, my luck is locked up."

The neighbor ate the chicken—and found the coins. He said nothing to the tailor, returning only the tray.

On the next day, the vizier returned for his tray and to see the tailor's gratitude. To his surprise, the tailor said only, "I did not eat the chicken as I was not hungry. Ah, my luck is locked up, my luck is locked up."

The vizier tried again with a nicely roasted turkey, stuffed with coins. Again, the tailor let his neighbor have it, continuing his moan:

"My luck is locked up, my luck is locked up."

On the next day, the vizier returned. And again was disappointed when the tailor said, "I did not eat the turkey. Ah, my luck is locked up, my luck is locked up."

"Indeed it is!" muttered the vizier. But he tried one more time, with a savory goose, stuffed with coins. Once again the tailor was so busy moaning his poor luck that he gave the goose away to his neighbor. But when the vizier returned in the morning, the tailor said to him, "I think I am hungry now. Today I am ready for a nice roasted chicken."

The vizier was furious. "You had your luck in your own hands!" he roared. "There were gold coins inside the chicken, and the turkey, and the goose! But did you look? No! It was far easier to sit and feel sorry for yourself! It is useless to help you, useless!"

And he stormed away. The tailor only sighed and returned to his moaning:

"My luck is locked up, my luck is locked up."[20]

THE KING HAS HORNS: TWO VARIATIONS ON A THEME

The Horned Sultan

Once, there lived a sultan with a shameful secret: two horns grew on his head. For a long time he would let no one cut his hair, lest his secret be revealed, but as time passed, the sultan's hair grew so long and wild that he called the royal barber to him and swore him to secrecy.

The barber cut the sultan's hair and saw the sultan's horns. Two neat little horns they were, and the weight of telling no one about them began to burden the barber till at last he went into a cave and whispered:

"Cave, cave, the sultan has horns!"

Feeling much better, he returned to the palace.

Reeds grew by the cave. A goatherd cut some of them and made himself a flute. But all the flute would play was:

"The sultan has horns! The sultan has horns!"

The astonished goatherd played his flute here and there. Even the sultan heard it and had the trembling barber brought before him. "I swore you to secrecy!" the sultan roared. "You were to tell no one about my horns!"

"I *didn't* tell anyone!" the barber wailed. "But my heart ached from holding in that secret! So I went to a cave and told the secret to it, only to it!"

The sultan sighed. "I believe you," he said. "And I forgive you. I should have known secrets will out, no matter how we try to hide them."[21]

Alexander of the Horns

King Alexander, Alexander the Great, had a secret shame: the two horns that grew on his head. He kept his secret by each month inviting a different barber to cut his hair, then having the barber slain before he could reveal the truth about the king. So things went till at last there was only one barber left in all the city. Alexander realized that if he killed this man too, there would be no one left to cut his hair. And so he made the barber swear not to tell another living human soul his secret, under pain of death.

The barber bore his secret and bore his secret till it wore at his health. He dared tell no one the truth, yet if he did not tell *someone,* he was sure his heart would burst. So each month, after he had tended the king, the barber raced down to the cellar of his house, to the spring of clear water that bubbled there and shouted into the water:

"Alexander has horns! Alexander is a Father of Horns!"

And his heart was light.

But some reeds sprang up around the spring. The barber cut them down and threw them away. A shepherd passing by picked them up and made a flute from one. And every time that flute was played, it whispered, "Alexander has horns! Alexander is a Father of Horns!"

The news reached Alexander's ears. He called the barber to him, and the trembling barber confessed what he had done. What could the King do but let the man go free? Since the barber had, indeed, told no living human soul the truth, he had kept his vow. A secret will out, no matter how it's hidden.[22]

CHAPTER SIX
TALES OF GHOSTS AND DYBBUKS

◇ ◇ ◇

Like every other people, the Jews have their share of supernatural, "scary" tales. Some of these tales involve such traditional otherworldly creatures as demons or the restless undead, others are about the perils of possession by wandering spirits, and still others concern such strange beings as the golem, the man of earth created by magic and the Holy Word.

GHOSTLY VISITORS

The Grateful Ghost

Once, a young Jewish man who was traveling in Turkey came across a coffin suspended by chains from a scaffold.

"Who is this who has been denied burial?" he asked a guard.

"That coffin holds the body of one of the sultan's advisors, a Jew." The guard added in a whisper, "That Jew had enemies who convinced the sultan the man was a thief and traitor. Therefore, the sultan denies him burial unless someone is willing to ransom the body."

The young man was moved to pity. "I shall," he said and paid for the body to be buried in sacred ground. His business in Turkey completed, the young man set out for the Holy Land, but a terrible storm overwhelmed the ship on which he sailed and sank it. Struggling in the waves, the young man was about to drown when an enormous eagle came soaring down out of the clouds, caught him in its talons, and carried him safely to land. As the young man stared, the eagle turned into the shrouded figure of a man.

"I am the ghost of he who was hung in chains," he told the young man. "I am he who your charity granted an honorable burial. I have returned only to repay your kindness."

With those words, the ghost vanished into air and was seen no more.[1]

The Restless Spirit

One day in Cracow, a sickly young man approached a cemetery caretaker and asked to buy a cemetery plot next to that of the great Rabbi Moses ben Israel Isserles. Alas, the caretaker was a crooked soul! He took the young man's money, planning to deny ever having sold that valuable plot. When the sickly young man died the very next day, the caretaker buried him in a pauper's grave.

But each night after that, the ghost of the young man returned to that caretaker in his dreams, insisting the ghost be given the plot he had bought. At last the exhausted caretaker fled to his rabbi and confessed all. The rabbi sternly told him a promise is a promise.

"When the ghost next appears to you, tell him that he may move to the plot he bought."

So the caretaker did. Most mysteriously, a new grave appeared on that spot the next morning. And the young man's ghost was seen no more.[2]

There's No Such Thing as Privacy!

Once, a man quarrelled with his wife over a gold coin he had given in charity during a famine; he wound up with no place to spend the night but in the cemetery. As he settled down as best he could to sleep, he heard two voices talking, and realized with a shock that they belonged not to living human beings, but to two girl-ghosts.

Said one, "Come, let us fly out and listen to what living folk say. And let us find out what ills await them!"

But the second ghost said, "No. I have only a straw shroud, and would be ashamed if I were seen in something so plain. You go, and tell me what you've seen."

Off flew the first ghost. When she returned, she told the second ghost, "Oh, what mischief! There will be a hail storm soon that will destroy the crops of any who sow their fields too early."

The man, hearing this, stole home. When it was time for sowing crops, he held back until all his neighbors had finished their sowing. Only then did he begin. And when the predicted hail storm came, his were the only crops still safe beneath the ground.

A year passed to the day, and the man went to sleep in the cemetery again. Once more he heard the two ghost-girls talking.

Said the first, as she had the year before, "Come, let us fly out and hear what living folk say. Let us see what misfortunes will overtake them!"

Again, the second ghost replied, "You go. I am ashamed to be seen in a plain straw shroud."

So off the first ghost flew. When she returned, she told the second ghost, "Oh, what mischief! The summer will be hot. Those who plant their crops too late will have them burned by the sun."

Home went the man and planted his crops in the springtime, before anyone else. And so his were the only crops ready to be harvested before the sun grew burning hot.

Now, by this time, the man's wife was consumed with curiosity. Where was her man getting his sudden wisdom? She questioned him till at last, just before his yearly trip to the cemetery, he pointed out the ghosts' graves to her and told her everything. She returned home, and he settled down for the night as before. And, as before, he heard the ghosts talking yet again.

"Come," said the first one, "let us fly and hear what living folk are saying!"

But the second ghost snapped, "Let us stay here and keep our mouths shut! Even as we speak, someone is eavesdropping on us! There is no such thing as privacy any more!"[3]

The Ghostly Congregation

Once, a laborer who had been working hard all day attended service in his synagogue, only to fall asleep during that service. When he awoke, it was fully night, but by the light of the moon, he could see that the congregation still seemed to be gathered.

But how strangely dressed they were! All of them were clad alike in flowing white robes!

Then, to his horror, the laborer realized he was not seeing robes. Those were burial shrouds. This was no living congregation, but a gathering of ghosts! He spied several members of the town who had died years back—but, to his bewilderment, among them were two fellows who he knew were still living.

It was far too much for the laborer to endure. With a shout of horror, he ran from the synagogue, ran till he was among living folk once more. He gasped out his story, omitting only that he had seen two living men among the ghosts.

But those two men died in an accident the very next day, and the laborer realized he had been granted a prophetic vision. To his great relief, he never had another—perhaps because he never dared fall asleep in the synagogue again![4]

Another Ghostly Congregation

It was a cold winter's night, and to entertain themselves, some men of the village were sitting in the synagogue, exchanging stories. One man, sitting a little apart from the others, fell asleep. Because he was sitting in shadow, his friends never missed him when they left, and the synagogue caretaker, locking up for the night, never noticed him.

About midnight, the sound of music woke the man. He found himself staring at a congregation of white-clad folk dancing to unearthly melodies—and knew these were never living people. Terrified, he dashed for the door, but a cold, cold hand tried to pull him back. The man wrenched free and ran to the window, yelling for help until the whole village was awakened. The rabbi and a *minyen* (the ritual number of men needed for prayer) entered the synagogue and carried him safely out, back to the world of the living.

And that adventure, it is said, is the reason why no man lingers too long in even the Great Jassy Synagogue of Rumania and why care is taken that prayers are completed long before the midnight hour.[5]

The Penitent

Once, Rabbi Akiba chanced to be crossing a cemetery when he saw a man burned black as charcoal running along as best he could, bearing on his back a load that would stagger a horse. The horrified rabbi stopped him, asking:

"My son, who are you? Why are you given such harsh labor? If you are a slave, I promise I will buy you and set you free. If you are a poor man, come with me and I will help you."

"Let this one pass, kind sir," the figure whispered. "I may not stop."

Rabbi Akiba suspected now he spoke to no living man. "Are you of humankind," he asked warily, "or are you a demon?"

"He to whom you speak," came the whisper, "is dead. He is sent every day to fetch the wood with which he is burned."

"My son," asked the rabbi, "what sins could you possibly have committed in the living world to be so punished?"

"In the living world, this one was a tax collector. He abused his position foully, loving the rich and slaying the poor. He took no notice of the Holy Laws and debauched a maiden, a bride-to-be, on the Day of Atonement itself."

Those were grave charges indeed, but Rabbi Akiba heard in the whispered voice a wish not merely to escape further punishment but also for genuine repentance. The rabbi was moved to ask:

"Is there no way for you to escape this dreadful fate?"

The dead man shivered, begging, "Do not keep this one any longer! Those who are his masters are masters of torment as well!" Then the dead man hesitated, whispering, "This one has heard that had he a son who could stand before the congregation and recite the holy prayers, then this one would be freed from torment. But that cannot be!" It was a wail of anguish. "This one never had a son! Even if this one's pregnant wife had borne a son, he would never have been taught the Torah, for this one left not one friend behind to guide him!"

"What was your name and city in the days of your life?" the rabbi asked. The dead man told him in a hasty whisper and hurried off. Rabbi Akiba went on to that city and asked if the tax collector had indeed left a wife and child behind.

At first, all the rabbi heard from the city folk were curses at the name of the dead man, but at last, he found the wife the tax collector had abandoned—and the son she had borne after his death.

The boy had been raised roughly. He knew nothing of his faith. But Rabbi Akiba took him and taught him till at last, with God's aid, the boy understood the Torah and came to believe in the One God.

At last, the day came when the tax collector's son stood up before the congregation and recited the proper prayers for the dead.

And that night, Rabbi Akiba had a dream. In it, the dead man, a burned slave no longer, came to him and thanked him for his mercy.

"May your mind forever be at ease as you have set my mind at ease," the spirit whispered and was gone.[6]

GILGLS AND DYBBUKS

A whole subgrouping of Jewish supernatural tales involve strictly Jewish creations, such as the *gilgul* (Hebrew) or *gilgl* (Yiddish), literally the "rolling" or "turning" of a wheel, which is a transmigrating soul temporarily possessing a living body in order to complete some unfinished task. The gilgl is a fairly late creation of Jewish mystics, becoming a major concept only in the thirteenth century. A very closely related—but not identical—Jewish supernatural figure is the *dybbuk,* which can be either an evil or amoral spirit or, like the gilgl, a human soul reluctant for one reason or another to leave the world of the living. The dybbuk also will possess a living body and must be exorcised.[7]

Undead Love

It happened in a Turkish seaport that a feebleminded young man suddenly sprang to his feet, his eyes blazing with an eerie new intelligence, and started into town. Ignoring everyone who tried to stop him, he burst into the house of the local rabbi, who saw the eeriness of the young man's eyes and asked, already suspecting the truth, "Who are you?"

"I am no one!" came the anguished reply. "I am nothing!"

By these words, the rabbi knew the truth. "Spirit, we will pray for you. But you have sinned by possessing this innocent's body."

"Aie, aie, what choice had I? I was drowned, drowned! My body is food for the fish! Who else was there? A cow? A donkey? Who else could hold me?"

"But why are you not at rest?"

"How can I rest, when a great sin has been committed? I was a man, I had a wife, a child. I went to sea and drowned, and she, my dear, sweet wife, had no family to help her! No one could prove my death, no one could legally name her widow. And so she could not remarry—and so, hopeless, moneyless, needing food for herself and our child, she has become a harlot!"

The rabbi sighed in pity. "What would you have us do? What will make you leave the body of this boy?"

The possessed young man shook with eagerness. "I am dead. She is a widow now, you can have no doubt of it! She and a neighbor boy loved each other as children. He is unwed now. Let him take her as wife!"

The man was called to the rabbi's home. When he heard the sad state of his childhood sweetheart, he cried out in horror. "Of course I will wed her!" he exclaimed.

One thing more the ghost requested, and that was that the prayers for the dead be read for him.

"It shall be done," the rabbi promised. "And we will mourn for you. Now, do no harm to the boy. Leave."

"I am gone."

It was the faintest, most joyous, whisper of sound.[8]

The Possessed Child

A little girl who had gone into the woods with her friends to gather mushrooms opened her mouth to cough and—flash!—just like that, a gilgl flew in and took possession of her. Her family, who of course knew nothing of what had happened, wondered why the child's nature had chanced from sweet to loud and demanding. At last the gilgl demanded to see the rabbi. The girl's grandfather pretended to be that rabbi, and insisted the gilgl leave his granddaughter alone.

"Call yourself a rabbi!" the gilgl taunted. "You're the one who ordered my tree cut down!"

"Who are you? Who were you?"

"I was a man. I died, and my spirit entered a dog. Rough boys killed the dog, so I entered a horse. The horse died, so I entered a tree. But then you had the tree cut down. There was nowhere else for me to go but into the girl!"

The frightened family called for the real rabbi. The gilgl agreed to leave if proper services for the dead were given. The rabbi agreed. With a wild shout and a tremendous "bang!," the satisfied gilgl vanished.[9]

The Gilgl Bride

There was much mourning when a beautiful young bride seemed to die on the very day before her wedding. Fortunately, the wise Baal Shem Tov had had a prophetic dream of such a happening and arrived just as the people were beginning to mourn.

"Don't weep," he told them. "Carry the girl to the cemetery. But take her bridal dress with you. Puzzled, the family and friends obeyed. At the Baal Shem Tov's commands, a grave was dug, and the girl placed face up in it. He ordered two strong men to stand on either side of her and do nothing but watch.

"If you see her eyes open, take her out of the grave at once."

Meanwhile, the burial ceremony continued. As soon as it was completed, save for the filling in of the grave, the Baal Shem Tov commanded:

"I order you to leave this girl."

The bride's eyelids fluttered open. She took a breath. Hastily, the two men lifted her out of the grave.

Smiling, the Baal Shem Tov explained what had happened. The bride had been temporarily possessed by a gilgl, a lost soul whose own body had never received proper burial and who had made it seem as though the bride too were dead. Now that the gilgl had finally received the burial ceremony for which it had hungered, it had gone. And the bride and groom were free to wed and be happy.[10]

A Pony's Debt

One day, the Baal Shem Tov went to see a villager's fine horses. The villager was willing to trade or sell every one of them save one: a stocky pony.

"This pony does more work than any horse I've ever owned," the villager claimed, "more work than a whole team of horses, and willingly, too!"

The Baal Shem Tov said nothing, only stared at the pony as though it was speaking silently to him. Then the Baal Shem Tov asked the villager about debts owed him. Surprised, the villager admitted that many people owed him money. Asking to see their debt accounts, the Baal Shem Tov studied one, then asked if he might keep it.

"If you wish it, take it," the villager said. "But it's worthless! That debt belonged to Chayim the coachman, a good fellow who always swore he'd pay whatever he owed, come what may." The villager shook his head. "Poor Chayim died several years ago, leaving not a coin behind to pay his debt."

"I would like it anyway," said the Baal Shem Tov. He took the paper, tore it to shreds and proclaimed, "This debt is cancelled. Now come, let us see your pony again."

The pony lay dead.

"You see," the Baal Shem Tov explained, "Chayim had sworn to pay all his debts. When he died, with his debt to you still unfulfilled, his spirit went into the body of a pony so he could work off that debt. He spoke to me as a pony and begged to be let go. I agreed that his debt to you had been fulfilled. And, now, he is free."[11]

THE GOLEM

Humanity has always had a fascination for the idea of artificial life, whether that life takes the form of a scientifically created robot or a clay, stone, or earth figure formed by magic. The golem, the artificial man made of earth—the literal translation of the word is "lifeless"—is the Jewish answer to this fascination and can be found in various forms in writings as early as the Talmud and as late as the twentieth century.[12]

A GOLEM

Rava was a great sage of Talmudic times. One day, he began musing about life and its creation. Surely, Rava reasoned, if the Just, the righteous men, wished to create a world, they would be able to do so. And so he set about creating a man from earth to prove his theory and sent it to Rabbi Zera.

65238

Alas, for Rava's theories: Rabbi Zera knew this was no living being. "You are a creation of magic," he said to the golem. "Return to your dust."

And the golem sank peacefully back into the earth and was no more.[13]

The Maid-Servant

It was said of Solomon ibn Gabirol of Valencia that the poet was dabbling in more than innocent philosophy. People murmured behind his back about the strange, blank-faced maid-servant who did her work willingly enough yet seemed to have no soul at all in her empty eyes. They began to murmur as well that Gabirol might be dealing with dark forces indeed. Word at last reached the king, who had the poet brought before him, threatening to put him to death for practicing foul arts. But Gabirol showed no sign of fear. The maid-servant that so worried the king, he said, was neither demon nor possessed woman. Indeed, it was no living thing at all, merely a golem created from earth. And to earth he sent it, reducing it once more to harmless dust before the king's eyes. So Gabirol was released, having suffered no worse than the loss of a useful servant.[14]

The Rabbi and the Living Idols

In a certain pagan land, its cruel rulers decreed that the Jews living there would be permitted to survive only if each year they picked one of their people to be sacrificed. One year Rabbi Abraham Ibn-Ezra was led by God to stop in that land, just at the time when the fatal lot must be drawn. It happened that the man chosen by chance was a young bridegroom about to be wed. When the rabbi heard the lamentations and learned the story behind them, he said:

"Don't be afraid. God will help you. Hand me over to the rulers instead of the young bridegroom, and go forward with the wedding."

"But we can't be so cruel to a stranger and a guest!" they argued.

"Don't be afraid," the rabbi replied quietly. "I am acting under Heaven's guidance."

So they brought him to the rulers, who had him taken into their pagan temple, which was lined with huge idols of wood and stone. As was the custom, the pagans asked the rabbi for his last wish.

"Bring me a bowl and jug for washing my feet," he said.

They brought him an empty bowl and jug. Rabbi Ibn-Ezra turned to an idol and commanded, "Go fill the jug with water and bring it to me!"

With that command, he murmured several secret words as well. And to the horror of the pagan folk, the idol creakingly dismounted its pedestal and stalked off, returning with a full jug. The rabbi proceeded to command other idols to warm the water and remove his shoes. He then turned to the chief idol, a huge creature of solid stone standing in the center of the temple, and commanded it:

"Come down here and wash my feet, and when you are done, drink the water!"

The chief idol began to groan and rumble into life, and that was too much for the terrified pagans.

"Stop!" they called to the rabbi. "We beg you, leave our idols in peace!"

"Only after you write it clearly into your laws that no Jew shall be put to death for those idols' sake."

So it was decreed. Rabbi Ibn-Ezra gestured, and the idols were lifeless wood and stone once more. And the Jews of that land were saved from a cruel death.[15]

The Golem of Chelm

In the middle of the sixteenth century, in the midst of intense persecution against the Jews in Poland, Rabbi Elijah, a scholar and student of the cabbala, decided to provide the Jews of his own town, Chelm, with a tireless protector. So he built up a man-shaped figure of earth and mud and brought it to life with the *Shem-Hamforesh,* God's Ineffable Name, which he wrote on a scrap of parchment and stuck against the figure's head. Instantly the figure became an animated golem, tall, powerful, and monstrous of aspect.

Alas, though the golem did, indeed, guard the Jews well, it grew more powerful and more monstrous with every passing day, till even the rabbi began to worry about what he had created. At last, the golem's power broke free into a mindless frenzy of destruction, killing men and animals alike, tearing down whole houses. No longer could it be allowed to exist.

And so Rabbi Elijah called the golem to him and withdrew the parchment with the *Shem-Hamforesh.* Instantly, the golem ceased to be, crumbling once more into lifeless earth.[16]

The Golem of Prague

King Rupert, sixteenth century ruler of Bohemia met with Rabbi Yehuda Loew, known as the pious Maharal, to put to rest rumors that the Jews were murdering Christian children. But even though the king had sworn this foulness was a lie, he never issued a formal proclamation. And so there was such unrest in the streets of Prague and such a swelling of anti-Jewish emotion that the Maharal knew it was just a matter of time before that growing hatred turned into open violence. His people needed a protector if they were not to be utterly destroyed.

So, together with his son-in-law and his chief disciple, the Maharal set about a rigorous program of prayer and fasting, as he prepared to work potent magic.

Early one morning, the three men went down to the riverbank and formed the figure of a gigantic man out of clay. First one man circled the figure seven times from left to right, chanting cabbalistic incantations.

The clay figure began to glow.

Then, the other man circled it seven times from right to left, and the glow faded, leaving the figure with hair and nails like a living man.

Next, the Maharal circled the figure seven times, and then, all three men called out the words from Genesis 11:7, "And he breathed into his nostrils the breath of life; and man became a living soul."

At that, the clay figure, the golem, opened his eyes. At the Maharal's command, he stood, and the three men dressed him and brought him back with them to Prague.

As they went, the Maharal told the golem, "You are to be called Joseph, and you will serve me even if I should tell you to jump into fire. Your purpose is to defend the defenseless Jews from harm."

The golem could not speak—the power of speech was God's alone to give—but he could hear and obey. Being a thing created from clay and magic, he could not, of course, reason, and folk soon thought him no more than a large but mentally innocent fool.

Even the Maharal's wife believed her husband's new helper was an idiot. She set Joseph to filling the house's water barrels, but she forgot to tell him to stop. And the Golem, mindlessly obediant creation that he was, tirelessly brought bucket after bucket till the Maharal's house was flooded, only stopping at the Maharal's hasty command.

But when evil men threatened the Jews, then the Golem proved his worth. No longer a figure of fun, he patrolled the streets, saving the

Jews again and again from any who meant to do them harm. And one night he surprised evildoers in the midst of a terrible plot. They had dug up the body of a Christian child in the cemetery and were planning to hide it in the Maharal's house, then to call in the guards of the city with "proof" that the Jews were murdering Christian children. But the Golem caught them before they could act, bound them fast, and dumped them and the child's body in the courtyard of the watchman's house.

Word of the plot reached King Rudolf's ears. This time, shocked and angered at what had almost happened in his own city, he issued a solemn decree forbidding any in his realm from raising charges of blood libel against the Jews again, nor were the courts to hear such charges.

The Maharal, after a peaceful year had passed, knew the golem was no longer needed. Together with his son-in-law and his disciple, they circled the golem seven times, chanting cabbalistic incantations. After the seventh encirclement, the golem lay as lifeless clay once more. They hid the clay under a pile of old parchments and prayer books.

Who knows? Perhaps the golem still sleeps there, waiting for the time when he shall be needed once more.[17]

CHAPTER SEVEN
CLEVER FOLK AND SURVIVORS

◇ ◇ ◇

Down through the ages, a persecuted people have always had to be quick-witted if they are to survive; the Jews most certainly have been both persecuted and survivors. Jewish folklore, understandably, has its share of wise and clever souls who overcome seemingly hopeless obstacles through the sharpness of their wits.

The Slave-Detective

In the days when the Greco-Syrians still ruled over the land of Israel, an Athenian came to Jerusalem to learn wisdom. Three years he spent and learned nothing, but at the end of that time, he purchased a Jewish slave. Only after the sale was complete did he realize the slave was blind in one eye.

"But this slave can see more with one eye than most men can see with two," the slave dealer assured him.

What could the Athenian do? The sale was already complete. So he set out for home with the one-eyed Jewish slave. Traveling alone was a dangerous thing to do, since that would make them easy prey for robbers, and so the slave cried, "Hurry, so that we may join the caravan up ahead!"

The Athenian stared into the distance but saw not the slightest sign of a caravan. "I see nothing. Where is this caravan?"

"Some four leagues ahead of us," answered the slave, studying the ground before them. "The lead camel is female and bearing twins. She is also carrying skin-bottles, one of which holds wine, the other vinegar. Ah, and she is blind in one eye."

"Now, how could you, with your one eye, know the camel was one-eyed too?" shouted the Athenian.

The slave shrugged. "I can see well enough to see that only one side of the road has been grazed."

"And how can you know she holds twins in her womb?"

"See, there, where she lay down to rest? There is a double depression in the earth."

"And how do you know the bottles hold wine in one and vinegar in the other?"

"Oh, that's simple. The drippings told me, there and there. Wine soaks right into the ground, but vinegar leaves bubbles."

"And how could you possibly know the caravan is four leagues ahead of us?"

"Free me, and I will tell you."

"You are free, you are free! Now, how did you know?"

"I can still just make out the mark of the camel's feet. A camel's footprints become unreadable right after four leagues."

The Athenian and the exslave went on their way. And the exslave was smiling.[1]

Jewish Wisdom

Two Jews were taken prisoners by a Persian, who warily had them walk before him. As they walked, one Jew commented to the other:

"A camel passed along this road before us. He was blind in one eye."

"Indeed," said the other. "He was also loaded with two kegs, one filled with wine, the other oil."

"And he was being driven by two men," added the first. "One was a Jew, the other a Persian."

That was too much for their captor. "How can you possibly know all that?"

"Simply thus," began the first Jew. "A camel, as you must know, usually grazes equally on both sides of the road. You can plainly see the grass here has been browsed on only one side. Therefore, the camel is surely blind in one eye."

"As for the kegs," added the second Jew, "all you need do to tell their contents is examine the dregs left behind."

"And as for the nationalities of the drivers," concluded the first Jew, "look at the crumbs of the bread they were eating. A Jew throws the crumbs aside, but a Persian tosses them right in the middle of the road."

Curious to find out if his captives were telling the truth, the Persian hurried them along till they had overtaken the camel and the two drivers. And all was exactly as the two Jews had told him. So overwhelmed with their wisdom was he that the Persian freed them on the spot, saying:

"Praise be the God of the Jews who has endowed His people with a share of His wisdom!"[2]

Do Unto Others

It was a cold, wet night, and a merchant from Jerusalem, traveling in Athens, was glad to find a tavern in which he could take shelter. But in that tavern were three Athenians. They were not pleased to have to share their tavern with a mere Jew. So they told him:

"We have agreed to let no man stay here unless he can jump three times."

The Jewish merchant knew these cold-hearted men would never let him share the inn with them, no matter how well he jumped. So he bowed his head meekly and said, "I do not know how to jump. Please show me how."

Laughing at this foolish Jew, one man jumped and reached the center of the inn. The second man jumped more powerfully and reached the doorway. The third man jumped a mighty jump, indeed, and landed in the courtyard outside. When the first two Athenians rushed outside to see how far their comrade had gone, the Jewish merchant calmly bolted the door behind them. The three Athenians shouted curses at him, but he answered calmly:

"I have only done that which you meant to do to me!"[3]

The Three Tests

A Jewish merchant had settled in a foreign town and there done very well. But illness overtook him, and just before he died, he told the innkeeper in whose home he lodged that all his wealth should go to his son.

"How can I recognize a man I've never seen?" the innkeeper protested.

The dying man assured him, "You will know my son by his wisdom. Test his wits three times, and if he succeeds, my money is his."

News of the Jewish merchant's death soon reached Jerusalem, where his son dwelt. After his mourning was completed, the young man set out for the foreign land. There he found that, according to his late father's wishes, no one would tell him the innkeeper's name or address. So the young man stopped a woodcutter, bought a load of wood from him, and ordered him to take the wood to the innkeeper. Of course the woodcutter went straight to the inn, and of course the young man followed, presenting himself to the innkeeper.

Since it was dinnertime, the innkeeper, pleased by the young man's cleverness, invited him to dine with his family. At the table were the innkeeper and his wife, their two sons, their two daughters, and the young man from Jerusalem. A dish of five squabs was placed before the young man, and he was told to serve the portions.

And so he did. One squab was divided between the innkeeper and his wife. Another went to the two sons, and a third to the two daughters. The remaining two squabs he took for himself. The innkeeper and his family were bewildered by this division, but kept silent, waiting.

At the next meal, a chicken was the main course, and the innkeeper again asked the young Jerusalemite to serve the portions. And so he did. The head he gave to the innkeeper, the stuffing to his wife, the legs to the two sons, and a wing to each daughter. The remainder he took for himself.

This was too much for the innkeeper. "Why have you divided the meals in this manner?"

The young Jerusalemite smiled. "At our first meal there were seven people and only five squabs. Since the meal could hardly be divided with perfect mathematical evenness, I decided to divide it numerically instead. You, your wife, and one squab equalled three. Your two sons and another squab equalled another three. Your two daughters and another squab equalled yet another three. And of course I and the remaining two squabs equalled the final three!"

The innkeeper laughed. "Very clever! But now, what of the chicken?"

"Why, since you are the head of the house, you deserved the head of the chicken. Since your wife has been blessed with fruitfulness, I gave her the inner portion, symbolic of that fruitfulness. Since your sons will, God willing, someday be the supporters of your house, I gave them the legs, supporters of the chicken! The wings went to your daughters to symbolize that someday they will fly away with their husbands. And the body of the fowl, with its keel-shaped breastbone, symbolic of a ship's hull, I kept for myself. For as soon as you give me my father's legacy, I will sail away for home. Have I, indeed, earned it?"

"You have, indeed, most clever young man!" said the innkeeper.

And with that, the innkeeper gave the young Jerusalemite his father's legacy and sent him on his way in peace.[4]

The Plucked Rooster

Once, in Poland, there lived a landowner who was a friendly, easy-going fellow who liked nothing so much as a clever exchange of words. Unfortunately, his steward was a mean, small-minded man who abused both his position and the tenants who farmed the land—particularly those tenants who happened to be Jewish. On those, the steward let loose the full measure of his nastiness.

Now, one wintery day the landowner went for a carriage ride across his lands with his steward, and saw one of his Jewish tenants breaking rocks industriously, keeping himself warm through his labor. Being the friendly fellow he was, the landowner climbed down to chat, while the disapproving steward remained in the carriage. Both landowner and Jew quickly realized the other liked a good turn of wits.

"Which is more," asked the landowner suddenly, "seven or five?"

"Thirty-two is more," the Jew replied.

"Agreed," said the landowner with a grin. "But what of your fortunes? Has your house burned down?"

"Oh, twice! And I expect it shall burn down yet a third time!"

"Indeed! It's a shame to see such a clever fellow in such sorry circumstances." The landowner glanced back towards his steward and frowned to see the cold hatred in the man's eyes as he stared at the Jew. "So . . . is *that* the way things are?" the landowner mused. He turned back to the Jew. "Tell me, my friend, how many handfuls would it take to pluck the rooster?"

The Jew laughed aloud. "For me, only two handfuls!"

Laughing with him, the landowner returned to his carriage and drove away. "Do you know what that was all about?" he asked the steward. "No? Take some time to think it over. But have the meaning of my first question and the meaning of the Jew's answer ready for me by Sunday."

The steward pondered and fumed, and at last went to the Jew and demanded to know the meaning of that first question. The Jew only smiled.

"That was between the landowner and myself. I will not tell you."

But the steward, afraid of his master's anger if he couldn't find the answer by Sunday, begged and pleaded and at last offered money. The Jew ignored him. At last, frantic, the steward offered fully half his wealth. Then the Jew told him:

"When the landowner asked which is more, seven or five, he was referring to the seven warm months and the five cold, asking if I shouldn't save my hard outdoor labor for warmer weather. When I replied that thirty-two was still more, I was referring to one's teeth. To give my teeth, and the teeth of my family, enough to eat, I have to work hard year-round."

The steward hurried back to the landowner and proudly told him the meaning of the first question. The landowner only smiled. "Now tell me the meaning of my *second* question!"

Once more the frustrated steward was forced to return to the Jew. This time it took the second half of his wealth before the Jew would tell him:

"The landowner asked if I was in such sorry straits because my house had burned down. You see, he knows and I know the proverb that says giving a daughter in marriage is as costly as having your house burn down. Well, I have already married off two daughters, so my house has burned down twice. And my third daughter will be married soon enough, which means my house will burn down one more time."

Back the steward went to the landowner with that answer. Again, the landowner only smiled. "Now tell me the meaning of my *third* question!"

Yet again, the steward was forced to return to the Jew. This time he had no wealth left with which to bargain, nothing but his position. "And I can't give you that!"

"You won't have to," said the Jew. "Another, I think, may do it for you. Listen. What the landowner asked me was in how many handfuls could one pluck the rooster. You, my hard-hearted friend, are the rooster. And I have, indeed, plucked you bare in but two handfuls!"

"But . . . my family . . . what will become of them?"

"You never worried about *our* families when you abused us!" But then the Jew smiled slightly. "Don't be afraid. I shall not be as cruel to you as you have been to my people. I give you back your wealth and tell you to go in peace. But leave your position behind."

Now, that was quite agreeable to the landowner. And he enjoyed many a witty chat after that with his new, Jewish, steward.[5]

Gold and Honey

Once, in the days when Saul was king in Israel, a wealthy widow was suddenly called away from home. How could she safely hide her gold coins in so short a time? She hastily emptied out several jars of honey, dropped the coins into the jars, topped the jars off again with some of the honey, and went on her way, leaving the honey jars in the safe-keeping of a neighbor.

Ah, but that neighbor chanced to need some honey and broached one of the widow's jars. Within, he found not honey alone, but a wealth of gold coins. Greed overcame honesty, and he hastily emptied all the jars, filling them once more with honey.

When the widow returned home and found how she had been robbed, she took her case to both civil and religious courts. In both cases, she was sent away, the judges arguing that there was no evidence save her word that the jars had ever held anything but honey.

Dejected, the widow happened to pass a young shepherd boy playing with the other children—this boy was David, who would one day be king. Seeing how sad she looked, he asked her story. When she had finished her tale, David smiled. "If King Saul will give me permission," he said, "I think I can help you."

The widow hurried to King Saul who, curious, gave the young shepherd boy his chance to solve the case. David had all the honey jars brought before the widow and her neighbor. Both agreed that those were, indeed, the jars in dispute. David proceeded to break them, one after another, until at last he found what he sought: honey is sticky, and two gold coins had stuck, unnoticed, to the inside of one jar. The widow's word was proven good, her coins were returned to her, and king and court were left in awe of the wisdom of a simple shepherd boy.[6]

The Wise Thief

A hungry man was caught stealing bread and was brought before the king, who ordered him to be hung. But before he could be sent to the gallows, the thief said that he knew a marvelous secret. With the help of this secret, a pomegranate seed planted in the ground would grow into a fruit-bearing tree overnight. The king and his court were amazed and wished to see this wonder for themselves. So the thief was taken into the royal garden, and a pomegranate seed given to him. The thief dug a small hole, then straightened.

"If the marvel is to work—and work safely—the seed can only be planted by someone who has never taken anything that did not belong to him. I, of course, as a thief, cannot do it."

He tried to hand the seed to the king's vizier, but the vizier shamefacedly confessed he had, indeed, taken a slave that did not belong to him. The treasurer admitted he might have entered a sum or two that might not have been quite honest. Even the king was forced to admit that as a prince he had taken a necklace from his father. The thief shook his head.

"You are all powerful men who want for nothing—and yet you cannot plant the seed. While I, who stole some bread only because I was starving, am to be hanged."

The king, pleased with the lesson the thief had taught, pardoned him.[7]

The Fox and the Angel of Death

In the beginning days, when the Angel of Death first walked the Earth and saw all the living creatures, the angel asked the Holy One, blessed be He, for permission to act. And the Angel of Death was given permission to cast one of each species into the sea and, by doing so, to gain authority over the rest.

The angel began casting one of each species into the sea, until he came to the fox. Before the angel could touch him, the fox began weeping and wailing.

The Angel of Death drew back in surprise. "Why are you weeping?"

"Oh, you took my dear, dear companion-fox and threw him into the sea!"

"I cast no fox into the sea!"

"You did, you did! Come, look!"

The fox stepped to the edge of the sea. The Angel of Death looked, saw the fox's reflection, and believed he had, indeed, already thrown a fox into the sea.

"Begone!" he told the fox angrily.

And the fox ran away, grinning.[8]

The Cunning of the Sons of Israel

A Jewish merchant had sold all his goods save a few spools of thread. He was returning happily homeward through the forest when he was suddenly stopped by an armed robber who shouted:

"Give me all you have!"

"Why, I have nothing with me but my donkey!" said the merchant with a laugh.

"I don't need a donkey! Give me . . . give me a cigarette, then, and go!"

"I fear I don't smoke. If I did, I would be happy to give you a cigarette."

The frustrated robber shouted, "I don't want anything from you! Just tell me: What is the meaning of 'The Cunning of the Sons of Israel'?"

Now for the first time the merchant was afraid. How could he possibly explain a verse from the Torah to this unlettered robber? "I'm afraid I don't know how—"

"Either explain it or die!"

The merchant realized the robber meant to kill him now, no matter what he said. He pulled out a spool of thread from his coat and handed the end of the thread to the robber.

"If you really must know the secret, hold fast to this thread and wait here till you feel a sharp pull. Then follow the thread until you reach a certain place. You will know it when you see it. And there, there you will find out the secret. But you must tell no one its meaning!"

The robber held the end of the thread and waited. The merchant set off quickly, unwinding the spool as he went. When he had finished one spool, he pulled out another and tied the end of one thread to the beginning of another. When he had finished the second spool, he pulled out a third and tied the end of the second thread to the beginning of the third. When at last the third spool ran out, he tied the end of the thread firmly to a tree—then hurried home.

And so the robber learned the meaning of "The Cunning of the Sons of Israel." And of course, ashamed and embarrassed, he kept his word and told nobody about it![9]

One Too Many

A Jew was returning home after three month's away, with his three month's wages in his pocket. As he passed through a dark wood, a robber sprang out at him, pointing a gun at his heart.

"Hand over your money!" the robber ordered.

What could the Jew do? If he argued, the robber would shoot him. But as he handed over his wages, he said:

"My wife will never believe me when I tell her all my money was taken by a robber."

"What is that to me?"

"Well now, you could help me a little, make things look more convincing."

"What do you mean?"

"Come, put a bullet through my hat so I look like I've been in a struggle."

The robber laughed, tossed the hat into the air, and fired a bullet through it.

"That's the way!" said the Jew. "Now, put a bullet through the corner of my coat, here."

The robber did.

"One more time," the Jew coaxed. "Through this side of the coat now."

"I'm out of bullets," growled the robber.

"Are you?" laughed the Jew. "Then to the devil with you!"

He flattened the robber with one punch, recovered his money, and went on his way.[10]

The King's Questions

The Sultan of San'a decided one day that since the Jews in his city would not follow the ways of Islam, they should all be cast out. But, he told them, he was not totally without mercy. If any Jew could answer the three questions he would pose, then there would be no expulsion, and the Jews would be left in peace.

Who could it be? Who deemed himself wise enough to risk his people's safety? No one dared take up the challenge save for one young boy. He boldly went before the sultan, trusting in God to see him through, and said:

"I am here. Ask your questions, oh sultan."

At first the sultan was angry that the Jews had sent a mere boy to answer him. Then he was amused. And at last he was puzzled. To hide his confusion, he asked the first question:

"How many stars are there in the sky?"

The boy answered with a large number chosen at random.

"Can you be so sure that's the right answer?" asked the Sultan.

"Have you counted the stars more recently than I?" countered the boy.

The sultan had to cede him the first question. For the second question, he led the boy out into the royal gardens. Sitting by the side of a rippling stream, idly letting his hand trail in the water, he said:

"Tell me, boy, how much water is there in these gardens?"

"First, answer me how many drops of water there are on your hand."

"That is impossible to answer!"

"No more so than your question, oh sultan."

The sultan had to cede the boy the second question. For the third question, he showed the boy three apples set on a table and asked:

"How many apples are there?"

Was this a trick? The obvious answer could never be the correct one, so the boy said simply, "One."

"How can there be only one apple?"

"The word 'one' means the One God. If I added two or three, that would be suggesting there are more gods than the One. And that would be against both the Jewish and Moslem faiths."

What could the sultan say to that?

"You are a wise young man. And you have answered my three questions correctly. Your people were right to send you—and the Jews of San'a may continue to live in my city in peace."[11]

An Eye for Horses, Gems, and Men

Once, long ago, there lived a Jew who could judge the worth of horses, gems, and men. Now, it happened that the king of that land saw a diamond necklace he wished to buy for his wife and sent for the Jew to examine it. The Jew studied the necklace, then shook his head.

"These are false diamonds, not worth the price."

The king was pleased to have saved his money. But he rewarded the Jew with nothing more than one small coin.

After a few days had passed, the king decided he wished to buy a handsome horse for his stables. He sent for the Jew, who studied the horse, then shook his head.

"This horse is treacherously wild. Do not try to ride him."

One of the king's horseman laughed and mounted. The horse went along quietly at first, then rolled a wild eye and began to rear and buck till he had thrown the rider to the ground. Again the king was grateful to the Jew. Again he showed his gratitude with nothing more than one small coin.

A few more days passed, and the king was in a joking mood. He called the Jew before him and asked, "Who am I?"

"A peasant," answered the Jew. "Nothing more than a simple peasant."

"How dare you!" the king exploded. "Guards! Imprison this fool!"

The Jew was cast into prison, and the king rushed off to his mother, the dowager queen, and asked, "Who am I?"

"What do you mean? You are a king and the son and grandson of kings!"

"No!" the king shouted. "Tell me the truth! Who am I? Who was my father?"

The queen shrank back in fear. "He was a peasant," she admitted. "I gave birth to my son the day the king, my husband, died. Alas, the child died too. Fearing the kingdom would be left without an heir, I . . . I had a servant steal a peasant woman's son. I've been a faithful mother, you know I have. But . . . you are a peasant's son."

The king ordered the Jew released from prison and brought before him. "I am setting you free. But, tell me, why did you say I was a peasant?"

"Oh, it was simple to deduce. When I saved you the money for that false diamond necklace, you sent me away with only one small coin. When I saved you from the wild and dangerous horse, you again sent me away with only one small coin. I kept quiet both times, but in my heart I knew the truth. No king would act that way. Only a poor, simple peasant would ever be so small!"[12]

Bird and Birdcatcher

A birdcatcher once snared a bird like none he had ever seen. And the bird said to him, "Free me, and I will tell you three wisdoms."

"First tell them to me."

"Swear you will release me."

"I swear. Now, what are your three wisdoms?"

"Listen well. The first wisdom: Never regret the past. The second wisdom: Don't believe the incredible. And the third wisdom: Never try for the impossible. Now release me, as you promised."

The birdcatcher released her. She promptly flew to the top of a tall tree and called down to him, "Fool! You let me go when I bear a priceless pearl of magic within my body!"

Now the birdcatcher regretted having let her go. He hastily tried to climb the tree. Halfway up, the branches grew too thin to support his weight, and down he tumbled to lie groaning on the ground. The bird laughed in scorn.

"Why, already you've forgotten the wisdom I told you! The first wisdom was: Never regret the past. Here you are already regretting letting me go. The second wisdom was: Don't believe the incredible. Yet you were willing to believe that I, a bird, would have a pearl inside me, like an oyster! The third wisdom was: Never try for the impossible. And here you were, trying to climb a skinny tree and catch a bird with your bare hands!"[13]

The Language of Signs

Once, a cruel priest who hated Jews decided to challenge the Jews in his city to a contest in the language of signs. "You will have a month in which to prepare," he told the chief rabbi of the city. "If after that time no one dares debate me in this language, I shall order that all your people be killed."

The rabbi told his people the dark tidings. A week went by, two weeks, three weeks, yet no one knew what the priest had meant by "the language of signs." Then, just when the month was nearly up, a Jewish poultry dealer who had been out of town buying chickens, returned to find his friends all with fearful faces. When he heard what the problem was, he laughed aloud.

"Is *that* all? The language of signs, eh? Go to the rabbi and tell him I am ready to meet this priest!"

So the poultry dealer met the priest. The priest promptly pointed a finger at him. The Jew pointed two fingers in reply. The priest picked up a piece of cheese. The Jew showed him an egg. The priest scattered grain on the floor. The Jew set loose one of his hens, which quickly pecked up the grain.

"Well done!" exclaimed the amazed priest. "Truly well done! Now I have to admit the Jews are wise folk. For even one of the humblest among them could understand me!"

And he sent the poultry dealer home richly clad.

Now, the Jews clustered around the poultry dealer, wanting to know what the sign language had meant. The poultry dealer replied:

"The priest pointed with one finger, meaning to take out my eye. I pointed with two to warn him I would take out both his eyes. He took out a piece of cheese to show I was poor while he had food. I showed him an egg to prove I didn't need charity. Then he spilled some grain on the floor, which was a waste, so I let my hungry hen feed. And that was that!"

But at the same time, the priest was answering his own followers:

"I pointed one finger, meaning there is only one king. He answered with two fingers, meaning there is a king in heaven and a king on earth. I took out a piece of cheese, asking, 'Is this from a white or black goat?' He countered with an egg, meaning, 'Is this egg from a white or brown hen?' I scattered grain on the floor, telling him the Jews are scattered all over the world. He let his hen scoop up the grain, meaning that the Messiah will come to gather all the Jews together once more."[14]

A Silent Duel

A cold-hearted king who fancied himself a clever man challenged the Jews in his royal city to a silent duel. Any of them who dared accept the challenge and lost would receive a hundred lashes. And if no one accepted that challenge, then all the Jews would be put to death.

It was a terrible choice. But one poor cobbler came forward, thinking that at the worst he would die but his people would be spared. The king looked at his humble opponent with scorn, then began the silent duel by raising his forefinger.

The cobbler countered by pointing straight down.

The king's eyes widened in surprise, and he thrust out two fingers at the Jew.

The cobbler thrust out one finger at the king.

The king thrust out his whole hand at the Jew.

The cobbler in turn held up his fist before the king.

The king held up a bottle of red wine.

The cobbler took out a piece of white cheese.

"Enough!" cried the king. "You have done well, remarkably well!"

And he ordered that the cobbler be richly rewarded, nor did he bother the Jews in his city again. When the king's puzzled servants asked for the meaning behind the silent duel, he said:

"My first gesture, pointing upwards, meant that the Jews were numerous as the stars. His answer, pointing down, meant that they were as the grains of sand beneath my feet.

"My second gesture, two fingers pointing, meant that there were two gods, one of good, one of evil. His answer, by pointing only one finger, stated there is only one God.

"My third gesture, my hand outstretched, fingers apart, said that the Jews have been scattered all over the world. His answer, the fist, answered that the Jews were still united.

"My last gesture, holding up the wine, told him his sins were red as the wine. His answer, holding up the cheese, said that they were white as cheese."

Meanwhile, the cobbler was telling his fellow Jews a different story:

"Well, first, he pointed up to tell me he wanted to hang me. So I pointed down to tell him to go to hell!

"Then, he threatened with his two fingers to gouge out my eyes, so I pointed at him, warning him it would be an eye for an eye.

"Then he showed by his open hand that he meant to slap me. I warned him with my fist not to try it.

"That scared him. He offered me a drink of wine. What could I do but offer him some of my cheese in exchange?" The cobbler grinned. "You see? It was easy!"[15]

The Rabbi and the Inquisitor

A Christian child had been murdered in Seville, and the cry went up that the Jews had killed him. The rabbi of the Jewish community was brought before the Grand Inquisitor to stand trial for his congregation. The Grand Inquisitor hated the Jews and did his best to prove them guilty, but the rabbi outwitted him at every turn and disproved the charge. The Grand Inquisitor was not about to give up so easily.

"We shall leave the matter to Heaven," he claimed to the rabbi. "There shall be a drawing of lots. I shall place two pieces of paper within a box. On one shall be written 'Guilty,' and on the other, 'Innocent.' If you draw the 'Guilty' lot, you shall be burned at the stake. And if you draw the 'Innocent' lot, I shall accept the will of Heaven and let you go."

Now, the rabbi knew he could never trust the Grand Inquisitor. And so it was, because on both pieces of paper the inquisitor had written "Guilty." The rabbi suspected just such a trick. When the time came for him to choose a lot, he picked a piece of paper—and popped it into his mouth and ate it.

"What nonsense is this?" roared the Grand Inquisitor.

"No nonsense at all," said the rabbi with a smile. "You have but to look at the remaining lot."

Of course it read "Guilty."

The rabbi's smile broadened. "Then, by the rules you've set, the lot I ate could only have been the one marked 'Innocent.' I am free, and my people are too."

Fuming, the Grand Inquisitor had to obey.[16]

Moses

In one faraway land, there lived a royal counselor who had once been a Jew but who had forsworn his faith. As a convert away from Judaism, he hated the Jews and plotted in every way to discredit them in the eyes of the king. One day he told the king:

"The Jews have a wonderworker among them, Moses, the very sorcerer who took them safely out of the land of Egypt. But he works his wonders only for them. They will reveal his existence to no one."

"Not even to me?" cried the king in anger. He ordered the Jews to have Moses step forth.

What could the Jews do? It was long, long years since the time of Moses. But how could they argue with the King? If they couldn't produce Moses for him, he would surely have them put to death. So the Jews fasted and prayed for guidance—except for one cheerful fellow, who acted as though nothing at all was wrong.

"I shall pretend to be Moses," he told the other Jews. "If the king believes me, well and good. If he doesn't believe me, all he can do is kill me for being a charlatan, and the rest of you will be safe."

That cheerful fellow went before the king, dressed in the finest robes he owned and proclaimed, "I am Moses."

The king sent for his counselor to see if this was true. The counselor, of course, knew that the man could not possibly be Moses. "Your Majesty, test the man and we shall learn the truth."

"If you are Moses," the king commanded the Jew, "you will work a wonder for me."

"Oh, I shall!" replied the Jew. "First bring me a great cauldron of boiling pitch."

Puzzled, the king had it done.

"Now," said the smiling Jew, "throw your counselor into it, and I'll pull him out unharmed as a young man."

The counselor trembled. "That . . . that will not be necessary," he stammered. "This man is Moses, of course he is Moses."

The king sent the Jew home a rich man—and all was well.[17]

Both Naked and Clad, Both Riding and Walking, Both Laughing and Crying

The king's vizier was an apostate Jew and hated the Jews with fervor. One day he whispered to the king, "They think they are so clever. But you are cleverer by far. Only you would challenge them to have one come to your court both naked and clad, both riding and walking, both laughing and crying."

The king could think of no way such a puzzle could be solved, but his vizier flattered him till he issued the challenge:

"Let a Jew come before me both naked and clad, both riding and walking, both laughing and crying."

There was great despair in the Jewish community. How could such a ridiculous feat possibly be performed? But it must be performed or the king would surely punish them.

A stranger, a travelling merchant Jew who happened to be stopping in their town, overheard their worryings and asked what was wrong. When he heard the king's command, he laughed.

"My friends, forget your worry! I know how to solve this puzzle. And tomorrow I shall appear before the King both naked and clad, both riding and walking, both laughing and crying!"

On the next day, the king and all his courtiers were waiting to see what the Jews would do. And what did they see? Before them came the merchant Jew, wearing only a fishnet wrapped about him so he was both naked and clad. He was hopping astride a broomstick so he was both riding and walking. He was laughing at the thought of the ridiculous sight he made, but he was also sniffing an onion, making the tears stream down his face, so he was both laughing and crying.

The king laughed so hard at what he saw that he too began to cry. He praised the Jew for his wisdom and asked him to name his reward. The Jew asked only to be allowed to ask the vizier three questions:

"The first: Why do Africans have dark skin?

"The second: Why does the sun rise in the east?

"And the third: Why can't a mule mare have foals?"

The answer to all three, of course, was simply, "God's will."

But the apostate could not remember that—and he was tied to the tail of a wild horse and driven out of town.[18]

The Mathematician

One day, a Jewish farmer died and left behind a will and three sons. In that will, he specified the following:

His eldest son should inherit one half of the farmer's cows.

His middle son should inherit one third of the farmer's cows.

And his youngest son should inherit one ninth of the farmer's cows.

Well and good, but the farmer had left behind seventeen cows. Try though they would, the three young men could figure out no way to carry out their father's wishes. At last, hopelessly confused, they went to the town rabbi for help. The rabbi puzzled over the problem for some time, then went out to the farm with his own cow, and added her to the herd, making a total of eighteen cows.

"Now the division is simple!" he said.

He gave the eldest son nine cows, half of the herd.

He gave the middle son six cows, one third of the herd.

And he gave the youngest son two cows, one ninth of the herd.

The last cow, the eighteenth cow, was of course, his, and the rabbi took it home with him, satisfied.[19]

The Clever Daughter

Once a noble landowner sent for his three leaseholders. One leased his woods, one his mill, and the third, the poorest, his inn. The nobleman asked them three questions.

"First, what is the fastest thing in the world?

"Second, what is the fattest thing in the world?

"And third, what is the dearest thing in the world?

"He who answers my riddles correctly will have to pay me no rent for ten years. But he who answers wrongly will be driven from my lands."

The leaseholder of the woods and the leaseholder of the mill thought they knew the answers right away. Surely the fastest thing in the world was the nobleman's horse, the fattest thing in the world was his pig, and the dearest thing in the world must be the woman he would someday marry.

The innkeeper went home in despair, because he knew that surely the answers must be more complex than that, yet he had no idea what they might be. His daughter, who was as clever as she was beautiful, asked him what was wrong. But when she heard the riddles, she only laughed and told him:

"Thought is the fastest thing in the world, the earth is the fattest, and sleep is the dearest."

So the innkeeper returned to the nobleman. Sure enough, the leaseholder of the woods and the leaseholder of the mill had guessed the wrong answers to the riddles and were sent away. But when he heard the innkeeper's answers, he frowned.

"You are correct. But these solutions never came from your own mind. Tell me who told you what to say?"

The innkeeper confessed it had been his daughter.

"If you have such a clever daughter," the nobleman said, "I wish to see her. Let her come to my mansion neither walking nor riding, neither dressed nor naked. And let her bring me a gift that is not a gift."

The innkeeper returned home more worried than before. But his daughter only laughed. "Don't be afraid, Father. There's nothing to worry about. Only buy me a fisherman's net, a goat, two doves, and a good chunk of raw meat."

Puzzled, he obeyed. The girl took off her clothes and wrapped herself in the net, so she was neither dressed nor naked. She sat astride the goat, her feet dragging on the ground, and so went along neither walking nor riding. When she had reached the nobleman's mansion, the dogs were set upon her, but she threw them the meat and went safely on her way right into the mansion. Going up to the nobleman, she told him, "I have brought you a gift that is not a gift," and released the doves, which flew out an open window.

The nobleman was delighted. "I wish to marry you, clever one," he told her. "But you must first agree never to meddle in the decisions I make at my law court."

She agreed, and so they were married and lived quite happily for a time. Then one day the girl saw a weeping peasant under her window and asked him for his story. He told her:

"My neighbor and I own a stable. I have a mare, he has a wagon. Now, my mare gave birth to her foal under the wagon, and my neighbor claims the foal is his. And when we brought the case to the nobleman, he agreed with my neighbor. That is why I weep."

"No need for tears. Go get a fishing rod and line and pretend to fish in the sand right under the nobleman's window. When he asks how you can possibly catch a fish in dry sand, you must answer, 'If a wagon can give birth to a foal, I can catch fish in dry sand.'"

The peasant did just as she told him and won his case. But the nobleman realized his clever wife must be behind his answer and told her:

"You failed to keep our agreement. Take the finest and dearest thing you can find in my mansion and return to your father's home."

She never begged, she never cried. "All right," she said calmly. "But first we must have one last meal together."

He agreed. She made sure he ate and drank enough to put him soundly to sleep, then had servants place him in his carriage. Together, she awake, he asleep, they drove to her father's inn. There, the nobleman awoke and asked in astonishment, "How did I get here?"

"Why, you told me to take the finest and dearest thing I could find in your mansion and return to my father's home. I could take no finer, dearer thing to me than you."

"I see," said the nobleman, pleased and embarrassed. "In that case, let us make up and go back home."

And so they did and grew old together in peace and happiness.[20]

The Most Precious Thing

There were a husband and wife living in Sidon who had been childless for ten years. The man, longing for a son, decided to divorce his wife and went to consult with the rabbi. The rabbi, knowing that there was genuine love between the couple, did his best to dissuade the man but without success. At last, with a sigh, he told the man:

"You made a banquet when you married, and it is my advice that you should part from that banquet good friends."

So the man prepared a feast for himself and his wife. She, suspecting, caused him to drink too much wine.

"My dear," he said, "you must take the most precious things in the house with you when you leave."

With that, he fell asleep. And his wife ordered their servants to carry him in his bed to her father's house. There, the man awoke and asked in surprise:

"Where am I?"

"In my father's house," his wife replied.

"What have I to do in your father's house?" he asked in growing astonishment. "How did I come here?"

"I have acted on your instructions," his wife replied sweetly. "You told me to take with me the most precious things in the house. But there is nothing more precious to me in all the world than you."

The husband was greatly moved by this, and in the morning husband and wife went together to the rabbi. He prayed to God in their behalf, and soon they had a son.[21]

The Master Thief

Once, there was a boy whose dead father had been a thief. His mother, wishing her son to have an honorable profession, tried apprenticing him to a barber, but after the boy stole the barber's razor and was thrown out for his troubles, he went home and asked his mother:

"What was my father?"

"He was a thief," the woman admitted reluctantly.

"Then I wish to be apprenticed to a thief," said the boy, and was apprenticed to his father's brother, who was also a thief. The boy learned well, until the time came for his final test: The uncle climbed a tree and stole eggs right out from under a nesting bird, then told his nephew to return them. The boy did, without so much as disturbing a feather, and his uncle cheered.

"Now you are a true thief and can be my partner!"

So the two stole whatever they desired and grew rich. They never grew weary of their profession and at last decided to rob the royal palace itself.

All went well the first night and the second night. They broke into the royal storehouse easily enough and took away several armfuls of treasure.

Unfortunately the king became aware he was being robbed. Following the advise of a clever minister, he had a big barrel of boiling pitch placed on the floor of the storehouse, right under the thieves' entryhole. The uncle fell right into the barrel of pitch and died.

The boy swung to one side and landed safely on the floor. He took several armfuls of treasure in his uncle's honor. Then, lest the king's guards track his family, the boy cut off his uncle's head and took that with him as well. He gave the treasure to his uncle's widow, consoled her with the treasure, and helped her bury the head.

In the morning, the king found himself with more missing treasure and a headless body, which no one could identify. At his minister's advice, he had the body hung in the town square and watched to see who came to mourn. But at the boy's advice, his aunt dropped a priceless vase right under the gibbet, so her weeping was taken for grief at having broken such a valuable object.

Meanwhile, the boy-thief bought a flock of forty sheep and tied forty candles to them, then drove them through the square at night. The guards were so frightened by these ghostly figures approaching through the darkness that they ran off, and the boy-thief calmly cut the rope holding his uncle's body and carried the body away for burial.

"Now what?" the irate king asked his minister.

"Tie a bejewelled ostrich to a long rope," advised the minister, "and have a guard hold the end of the rope. Then, when the thief grabs the ostrich, the guard can grab him."

But the boy-thief neatly cut the rope without alerting the guard, and stole the ostrich. He and his aunt ate the ostrich and kept the fat for medicine.

"Never mind," said the minister. "Send a spy dressed as an old woman out asking for ostrich fat. Who else but the thief will have any?"

The aunt felt so sorry for the old woman who was begging her for ostrich fat that she gave her a jar. But the boy-thief put a knife into the old woman before she could betray them and buried her secretly. When the king found his spy missing, he was furious. Now, the minister advised:

"Scatter gold coins in the street, as though a strongbox had burst open, and set guards all around to catch whoever takes the coins."

But the boy-thief hired a caravan of camels. In their right-hand saddlebags was flour. In their left-hand saddlebags was salt. And their feet were smeared with sticky soap. The guards fell to arguing what the camels carried: salt or flour. The sticky soap, meanwhile, picked up every one of the coins.

"I give up," said the minister. "Your Majesty, I simply have no more advice to give you."

"Then why should we go on hunting the thief?" wondered the king. "Far better to have such a clever fellow on my side!"

So he issued a proclamation offering the boy-thief a pardon and offering him the hand of his daughter. The boy-thief agreed. And, surprisingly enough, everyone, from thief to princess, lived happily after that!

Ah, but in a neighboring kingdom, word of the marriage of princess and thief reached the king's ears. And he sent a mocking letter to the thief's father-in-law, taunting him about having given in to a thief. The king was furious, and his daughter was hurt, and the thief, who by this point had fallen madly in love with his wife, announced:

"I'll simply have to teach the man a lesson. When I'm through, I promise I'll have him barking like a dog, braying like a donkey, and crowing like a rooster!"

Off he went to the neighboring kingdom. It was no challenge at all for him to work his way into the palace, into the room next to the king's bedchamber, even though he was dragging a large wooden chest after him. The thief wore away the dividing wall between that room and the king's bedchamber with acid till it was paper-thin, then called to the king in a grim, mysterious voice:

"I have come for you."

The king awoke in panic. "Who are you?"

"I am the Angel of Death. I have come to take you to Paradise."

With that, the thief burst through the wall, all covered with white plaster dust and looking truly frightening. "Come, enter this chest," he commanded, "and you shall be carried to Paradise."

The king was hardly happy at the thought of leaving the world of the living. But he certainly wanted to be carried to Paradise! So he crawled inside the chest.

Quickly the thief locked it. He brushed the dust off himself and his plain clothes till he looked like just a servant. He had other servants help him carry the chest down to a ship that took thief and chest home to where his father-in-law and wife waited.

"Before you may enter Paradise," he told the king in the chest, "you must purify your soul by ridding it of animal elements. You must bark like a dog, bray like a donkey, and crow like a rooster."

By this time, the king was eager to get out of that cramped, hot chest. He barked with good will, brayed with might, and crowed more loudly than a trumpet. The thief laughed.

"Now, enter Paradise!" he cried, and cast open the chest.

The king tumbled out, amid much laughter. Once he realized what had happened to him, he took the jest in good spirit. Apologizing for his letter, he told his neighbor king, "I see why you wanted this young man as friend, not foe! Indeed, were he not already married, I would want him for *my* son-in-law!"

And there was peace after that between the two lands.[22]

CHAPTER EIGHT
ALLEGORIES AND MORAL TALES

◇ ◇ ◇

Living an ethical life is one of the basic tenets of Judaism, and the emphasis on ethics is a feature common to much of Jewish folklore. Many of the stories in this section were compiled in the Talmud, the massive compendium of Jewish law and lore, in about the sixth century C.E. but are also very much a part of oral tradition.

THE REWARDS OF CHARITY

The giving of charity is very much a part of Judaism, and a good many folktales revolve around the saving of a charitable Jew by the metaphysical power of his or her good deeds and generosity.

Charity Repaid

Rabbi Akiba had a daughter whom he loved dearly. To his horror, when the astrologers read her stars, they proclaimed that on her wedding day she would be bitten by a snake and die. What could he do? Could he keep his daughter unwed and lonely? That was hardly the right thing to do.

And so the day of his daughter's wedding came about. As the guests sat rejoicing at the wedding feast, a beggar came to the door. No one wanted to notice him. What, leave the joyous feast to help a ragged stranger?

But the rabbi's daughter saw the sad-faced beggar. She went down from her place with her own portion of the feast and gave it to him. As she did, the ornamental clasp in her hair came loose. The young woman took the clasp from her hair and impatiently stuck it into a crevice in the wall, meaning to retrieve it later. But in the excitement of her wedding day, she forgot all about it.

The following day, the rabbi's daughter remembered her hair clasp. Pulling it free from the crevice, she screamed in horror as a poisonous snake tumbled out with it. On her wedding day, when she had stuck the clasp into the crevice, she had, by chance, stabbed the snake that had been about to strike her and killed it.

When Rabbi Akiba saw what had happened, he sighed in relief. His daughter's act of pure kindness had overcome the strength of the prophesy and saved her from a sure and painful death.[1]

The Charitable Child

Once, a boy who worked with his father as a woodcutter went to the synagogue. Next to him happened to be a boy of his own age, pale and thin. When the woodcutter's boy heard that the other was a poor orphan who had had nothing to eat all that day, he gave his own bread to the orphan. He then went on his way with his father out into the countryside, where they gathered more wood for their own fireside.

Now, what the woodcutter's boy didn't know was that in the wood he carried on his head lurked a scorpion. But that scorpion had no power to harm him. Why? The act of selfless charity the boy had performed protected him that day from death.[2]

The Waves Listen

To the horror of those standing watching on shore, an incoming ship was struck by a sudden windstorm and sank. Aboard that ship had been a kindhearted, pious man, a man who had always given charity to the needy. Rabbi Akiba had been one of those witnesses and sadly went before the law court to testify that the man had drowned and that his grieving wife was now a widow.

But before the rabbi could speak, the pious man himself appeared, wet and worn, but very much alive.

"Why, this is wonderful!" Rabbi Akiba exclaimed. "But how is it you are still alive?"

The pious man shook his head in wonder. "As I was drowning, being drawn down and down into the depths, I heard the roar of the waves all about me. And after a moment, I realized the waves were saying, 'We cannot drown the charitable man.' And with a great rush of water, I was cast up, safe, upon shore!"[3]

The Good Man and the Dragon

Ben Sever was a man who tried to do kind deeds all his life. One day he heard of a poor orphan who wished to marry but had no gold or silver with which to support a wife. So Ben Sever went into town and saw that a sufficient amount of his own wealth was secretly given to the orphan. Smiling, Ben Sever then set out for home.

But the river he needed to cross was swollen with spring rain, and the bridge had been washed away. Worse, in that river lived a dragon waiting to eat whomever tried to cross.

Yet when Ben Sever reached the riverbank, the force of his good deeds overwhelmed the dragon. It surfaced and stretched itself out, tip of its nose on one side, tip of its tail on the other. Ben Sever crossed that dragon-bridge in perfect safety.[4]

LIVING A PROPER LIFE

The Rabbi's Silence

One day, Rabbi Safra decided to sell some household goods for which he had no use. He asked ten gold pieces for them. Local merchants came to examine the goods, but offered only five pieces of gold. The rabbi refused. The merchants left, but after they had thought matters over for a time, they returned to offer seven gold pieces. But by the time they reached Rabbi Safra, he was at prayer. Although they offered him the seven gold pieces, he would not insult the Holy One by interrupting prayer for commerce. The merchants misunderstood. Mistaking the rabbi's pious silence for stubborn refusal, they sighed and argued and finally offered the full ten gold pieces.

But once his prayers were finished, Rabbi Safra called the merchants back to him and explained that he could not accept their offer of ten gold pieces. He refused to cheat men who, after all, had had no idea they were bargaining with someone who, at the time they were making their deal, couldn't listen to them.[5]

Don't Throw Stones from Yours to Not Yours

Once there was a rich man who was never satisfied with his large, splendid estate but was always after his servants to add a building here, dig a garden there. As they worked on that garden, the servants dug up many stones, which the rich man commanded be tossed over his walls out onto the public road. One day, a wise old man saw what was being done and asked the rich man to stop, saying:

"Why do you throw stones from yours to not yours?"

The rich man refused to listen. Why should he care what happened out there to the people beyond the walls of his estate? But nothing in life is permanent, least of all wealth, and the day came when that rich man was beggared and thrown out of his lovely estate. As he wandered the roads, his feet were bruised again and again by the very stones he had so thoughtlessly had his men toss from "his to not his."[6]

Scholarship

A scholar found himself on a shipful of merchants. They showed him their goods and taunted him, asking, "Where is *your* merchandise?"

Rather than becoming angry, he merely replied, "My merchandise is greater than yours."

The merchants searched the ship from bow to stern but found no hidden treasure, and they continued to mock the scholar. But then pirates fell on the ship and looted all their goods. The merchants and the scholar were set ashore with no more than the clothes on their back. The merchants wailed and wept, but the scholar went straight to the House of Study and proved his scholarship in learned discussions. Slowly, word of his learning spread, and soon the people of the city gave him a proper income as a teacher of wisdom. When the impoverished merchants heard of this, they begged charity of him and he aided them. And then the scholar reminded them gently of how they had taunted him. "You refused to believe me when I told you my merchandise was greater than yours. Now yours is lost, but mine remains!"[7]

The Honest Neighbor

King Philip of France decided in 1311 to banish all the Jews of Paris from his city. Many of them had no opportunity to see to their businesses before they were forced to leave. One Jewish merchant of gems found himself with no way to carry his valuable stock with him. Yet he could hardly leave it behind! He and his nextdoor neighbor had always been friends, even though one was Jewish and one Christian, so it was with this Christian friend that the Jewish merchant left his gems.

Years passed. King Philip died and his son decided to recall the Jews. The gem merchant returned to Paris, hesitant as to what he would find. Was his friend trustworthy? Would any of his gems be left? When he reached the neighbor's home, the gem merchant found to his dismay that the neighbor's business had failed, and he was living in poverty.

"But why didn't you use my gems to help you?" the gem merchant asked.

"I swore a sacred trust," the neighbor replied. "Your gems are safe, my friend."

The Jewish merchant was quick to set up shop once more. He shared his wealth with his faithful neighbor, and the Jew and the Christian lived as brothers.[8]

The Fox in the Vineyard

Once, a fox came to a vineyard that was surrounded by a high fence. But as the fox circled the fence, he found one small hole in it. What did that fox do? He fasted three days, till he had become so thin he could slip right into the vineyard through the hole. There, he feasted on the ripe, luscious grapes till he was sleek and round and fat.

When he wanted to leave the vineyard, the fox found himself far too fat to fit through the hole. Once again he was forced to fast for three days, till he was once more as thin as before. Sadly, the fox slipped out of the vineyard, then called back to it, "Vineyard, oh vineyard, your fruit is so good! But what use are you? As one enters you, so one must leave!"

What is the moral? Simply: As with the vineyard, so with life.[9]

A Pretty Girl

The pious folk of the small Jewish community were shocked. Their rabbi had been seen talking with a pretty girl—and right in front of everyone, right in broad daylight!

Well! How could such a shocking thing be allowed of their rabbi, their spiritual guardian? The elders of the congregation got together to lecture him on propriety. The rabbi listened patiently, then exploded:

"How self-righteous you all are! Tell me, which is worse: to talk to a pretty girl and think of the Almighty—or to talk to the Almighty and think of a pretty girl?"[10]

The Rewards of Faith

Once, a rich man, who had lost his faith through idle living, went down into the marketplace with a bag of money, planning to give it to the first beggar who admitted he too no longer had any faith in God. But for all his searching, he could not find any who was willing to forswear his faith. Even the poorest of the poor, lying nearly naked on ashes told the rich man, "Till my last breath, I shall not give up believing in the help of God. He who has faith in God is always rewarded."

Frustrated, the rich man decided to give his money to the dead, thinking that they, at least, had surely lost all hope. He entered the cemetery, buried the money in a hole under one of the tombstones and went his bitter way.

Time and ill luck brought the rich man down. His wealth gone, he was reduced to begging for crusts until at last, nearly starving, he prayed for help for the first time in years. Suddenly, remembering the buried sack of coins, he rushed to the cemetery and began digging under the tombstone. But no sooner had he closed his hand about the sack than the cemetery guards caught him and dragged him before the king for judgement as a grave robber. The prisoner stammered out his tale, ending, "In the name of the Lord, merciful king, have pity on me."

"In the name of the Lord, I shall," the king replied, commanding the guards to release the prisoner and return his money to him. "Do you not recognize me? I am the poor man you found sleeping on the bed of ashes. I told you then I would never give up my belief in the help of God. And God's help can come in the twinkling of an eye! With the Almighty's aid, I was recognized as the lost heir to the throne, and see, I have ascended to that throne. He who has faith in God truly is always rewarded."[11]

The Beggars and the King

Two beggars chanced to pass the palace of the king every day in their search for alms. And every day the king would give them charity. One beggar always praised his goodness, but the other always thanked God instead for helping the king be generous to his subjects. This angered the king, who told the beggar:

"*I* am the one who is generous to you, yet you always thank someone else!"

"Were it not for God's bounty," the beggar answered quietly, "you would not be able to be generous."

This hardly satisfied the king. He had his baker prepare two identical loaves of bread. Into one of them was stuffed precious jewels. The king ordered that this loaf be given to the beggar who praised only him.

As the two beggars left the palace with their loaves of bread, the beggar who praised only the king noticed that his loaf seemed heavy and decided it must be badly baked. So he asked the other beggar to exchange loaves. The beggar who always thanked God, suspecting nothing, agreed. But when he went to eat the bread, he found the gems inside. And he was truly thankful to God that he no longer needed to beg for a living.

The king was very surprised to see the beggar who praised only him return beneath the palace window. "What did you do with the loaf I gave you the other day?" he asked.

"It was hard," the beggar answered, "and did not seem well-baked. So I exchanged it with the other beggar."

Now at last the king understood what the beggar who praised God had been trying to tell him: Riches do, indeed, come from God alone.[12]

The Merchant's Leg

There was a merchant who was to set sail one day on an important trading trip. Just before he was to board the ship, he fell and hurt his leg so badly he had to give up the idea of the journey. As he watched the ship depart without him, the merchant cursed the bad luck that was keeping him from making what had promised to be an excellent profit. But, a few days later, word reached the city that a sudden storm had struck the ship, sinking it and drowning everyone aboard. The stunned merchant realized that had he been aboard he too would have died, and he was grateful for the first time that he had hurt his leg. He offered up thanks to God for having spared him. For, the merchant stated, even though it might not seem so at the time, everything that happens happens with God's will and happens for the best.[13]

One Golden Ruble

One Sabbath, long ago, a poor man went to the synagogue to pray. On his way, he found a pile of gold lying in the synagogue courtyard, but because he had no desire to violate the Sabbath, he left it untouched. When the Sabbath was done, he found all the money gone save one golden ruble, which he gave to his wife.

In that same town lived a wealthy merchant about to leave on a long trading voyage. Just as he was boarding his ship, the poor man's wife shyly approached with her ruble in hand and asked the merchant to buy her something from the far-off lands. On his voyage, the merchant acquired many goods but completely forgot about the poor woman's ruble, till he was about to set sail for home. He hurried ashore once more, planning to buy her the first thing he saw.

What he saw was a beggar man carrying a sack full of three young cats, which he meant to drown. The merchant bought the cats for the one ruble and sailed away. But his ship was caught in a storm and swept into the harbor of a barbaric people. When they trapped a stranger, they would lock him up in one of their houses, which swarmed with mice, until the mice devoured him. But no sooner was the merchant alone in his prison than he let loose the three young cats, which soon put an end to all the mice.

In the morning, his captors were amazed to find the merchant alive and healthy, with three purring, healthy cats at his side, and the mice quite dead. Seeing an end to their plague of mice, the people offered the merchant first one, then two, then three full sacks of gold for the marvelous cats. He took the gold and was set free.

Safely home, the merchant went to the poor man and his wife, and asked the woman where she had gotten her gold ruble.

"From my husband," she said.

"And where did *you* get the ruble?" asked the merchant.

The poor man sighed and told how he had found a pile of gold lying in the synagogue courtyard but had not wished to violate the Sabbath by picking it up. The merchant smiled.

"Was the pile of gold this big?" he asked, emptying one of his sacks of gold onto the floor. "Or perhaps this big?" he added, emptying the second sack. "I know: It must have been this big!"

And he emptied the third sack of gold onto the floor. Smiling, the merchant went his way, leaving the amazed poor man and his wife poor no longer.[14]

Tipping the Scales

Once, there was a wealthy man who had lived all his life neither truly good nor totally bad, but in idle, luxurious fashion. One night he was riding home in his fine carriage when he heard a muffled shout for help. There in a ditch lay an overturned farm wagon and trapped beneath it, nearly smothered in mud, was the farmer. Hastily, the wealthy man ordered his coachmen to drag the farmer out from under the wagon and free his fallen horse as well. While they were doing so, he tied a rope from his coach to the wagon. Climbing up into the coachman's seat, he urged his own horses forward, till they had pulled the wagon out of the ditch. Helping his servants wipe the farmer clean of his smothering coat of mud, the wealthy man saw that he was too badly shaken to handle his wagon. So he had the farmer driven safely home. He left the farmer and his family some money as well.

The wealthy man then went on his way and soon had put what had happened out of his mind. In the years to come, he went back to his idle—not good, not bad—way of life.

Time passed. The day came when the wealthy man was gathered up by God to his forefathers. And when he came up for judgement before the Accusing Angel, the wealthy man's idle life slanted the Scales of

Justice slightly away from Heaven towards Gehenna (Hell). The Angel of Mercy saw this and cried out that the man's good deeds should be weighed against his sins.

So the poor farmer and his family were placed in the scales.

"Not enough!" cried the Accusing Angel.

"Place the farmer's wagon and horse in the scales as well," pleaded the Angel of Mercy.

It was done, and the scales tilted ever so slightly away from Gehenna.

"Still not enough!" cried the Accusing Angel.

"Add to the scales the mud that covered that poor farmer," pleaded the Angel of Mercy.

It was done. And at last, thanks to the one great good deed the wealthy man had done, the Scales of Justice tipped towards Heaven![15]

Holy Man or Horse?

One winter, a young rabbinical candidate was boasting of his saintliness before his rabbi.

"I always clothe myself in spotless white, Rabbi, to show my purity, just like the sages of old. I never drink anything stronger than water. I keep nails in my shoes and roll naked in the snow to mortify my flesh. Every day, I complete my penance with forty lashes from the *shammes* [sexton]."

Just then, a white horse was led out from the stables to drink at the trough. It drank, then, in the fashion of horses, rolled happily in the snow.

"Do you see?" asked the rabbi gently. "He too is clad in spotless white. He too drinks only water, wears nails in his shoes, and rolls naked in the snow. And, you can be sure, he too gets plenty of lashes from his master. Now, I ask you, which is he: holy man or horse?"[16]

The Test

Three souls approached the Gates of Heaven, where they were stopped by the Recording Angel.

The first of the souls was a rabbi.

"Night and day have I proved myself learned in the Law," he said. "Night and day have I studied the Holy Word. Therefore, I deserve a place in Heaven."

"Not so fast," said the Recording Angel. "First we must investigate the reason behind your study, whether for the sake of honor or wealth."

Next came a pious soul.

"I fasted frequently in my life. I observed every religious obligation every day of my life. I deserve a place in Heaven."

"Not so fast," said the Recording Angel. "First we must investigate the reason behind your piety, whether for the sake of holiness or self-pride."

The third soul had been nothing more than a humble innkeeper in life. All he could find to say to the Recording Angel was:

"My door was always open to those in need."

"Step through the Gates," said the Recording Angel. "We need no investigation here!"[17]

Justice

Rabbi Wolf of Zbaraz was known far and wide for his wise judgements and incorruptible sense of justice. One day, his wife came crying furiously to him that her maid, an orphan girl, had stolen a fine piece of jewelry. The poor girl tearfully denied any wrongdoing.

"Enough of this!" cried the rabbi's wife. "We shall let the Rabbinical Court settle the matter!"

To her astonishment, as she left for the court, Rabbi Wolf put on his Sabbath robes and went with her.

"Why are you doing this?" she asked. "I can plead my own case!"

"So you can," the rabbi answered gently. "But who will plead the case of your orphan maid?"[18]

The Trapper Trapped

Once, a dishonest clerk stole from a merchant, who decided to take revenge on him for the theft.

The merchant waited till the clerk's wife gave birth to a son, then sent a man to steal the baby, place it in a chest, and throw the chest under a bridge.

A fisherman's hut stood near the bridge. The fisherman saw the chest fall and, wondering, went to investigate. He found the baby within, unharmed, and took it home to his wife. Childless, they decided to raise the baby as their own.

The years passed. The baby grew to a child, the child grew to a handsome young man. The merchant happened to see him one day and, not recognizing him as the stolen baby, set him to work for him. So pleased was the merchant with the boy's progress that he decided to give his own daughter to him for a wife.

One day, the fisherman happened to confess to the merchant that the fine young man was not really his son at all. He told how he had seen a chest fall, found a baby inside, and raised the baby as his own.

The merchant was stunned to hear the true identity of his son-in-law. He wrote a letter to his wife instructing her to hire someone to kill the young man, sealed the letter, and gave it, smiling falsely, to the young man to deliver.

By the time the young man reached the merchant's home town, it was very late. Rather than disturb the merchant's wife, the young man decided to spend the night in the synagogue. As he slept, the letter fell out of his pocket and tore open. The rabbi picked it up and read it, then tore it to bits. He wrote a second letter asking the merchant's wife to welcome the young man properly.

Time passed. The merchant returned home and was furious to find the young man still alive, so furious he could think of nothing else but revenge, nothing else but seeing that young man dead.

That very night, the merchant dug a deep pit right outside the front door, so that when the young man came out in the morning, he would fall into the pit and be killed.

And so it would have been. But it happened that morning that the young man chanced to go out the side door instead. The merchant saw him leave. How could this be? Hadn't the pit been hidden well enough? How could the young man have suspected? Frantic, the merchant went rushing out the front door to check his trap. He slipped and fell into his own pit—and was killed.[19]

What Happens, Happens for the Best

Once, Rabbi Akiba went on a journey, riding a donkey, carrying along with him a rooster to wake him at dawn and a torch to light his way should darkness overtake him.

Sure enough, he found himself riding right through sundown into night. He came to a village, but when the rabbi tried to find a villager who would grant him hospitality for the night, he found that not one of them showed even the slightest degree of charity. Not one would so much as heed his knocking, let alone unbolt a single door. At last Rabbi Akiba shrugged and told himself:

"What God wills is for the best."

He made himself as comfortable as possible out in the fields, and there, he spent the night.

But while the rabbi slept, the wild beasts ate both his donkey and rooster; a sudden gust of wind extinguished his torch.

When Rabbi Akiba awoke in the morning, it was to find that during the night the village of hard-hearted people had been looted by bandits.

"Had I lodged with the villagers," the rabbi marveled, "the bandits would have caught me too. And if my torch had continued to burn, if my donkey had brayed or my rooster crowed, the bandits would have found me in the fields. Everything God wills really *does* work out for the best!"[20]

The Silver Veneer

Once, there lived a rich but selfish man, who thought only of his ornate, expensive clothes and life and into whose heart the town's rabbi had tried in vain to instill a sense of charity towards others.

Then one day, the rich man came to the rabbi for a blessing. Without a word, the rabbi took the rich man into his house and led him to a window that looked out onto the street.

"What do you see?" the rabbi asked.

"Why, I see the street," replied the rich man in confusion. "What else should I see? I see the street and all the people going about their daily lives."

"Now come, look into this mirror. What do you see?"

"Myself, of course. Only . . . myself."

"I think you begin to understand," said the rabbi. "Both the window and the mirror are made of the same glass. The only difference is that the mirror has a veneer of silver. When you look through plain glass, you see other people. But when you cover that plain glass with silver, why, you stop seeing others and see only yourself."[21]

A Piece of Pastry

A miser bought himself a nice piece of pastry, but before he could taste it, he accidentally dropped it into the street. When the miser picked it up, he found to his disgust that the pastry had become covered with dirt. Just then a poor man asked him for charity. The miser was hardly about to part with good coins; he never had. He handed the poor man the dirty pastry and thought no more about it.

But that night the miser dreamed. And in his dream, he sat in a large restaurant, a crowded restaurant with waiters running about, bringing the customers the most wonderful cakes the miser had ever seen. Yet not one waiter came his way. At last, furious, he shouted for service. But all he was given was one dirt-covered piece of pastry.

"What is this?" he roared. "How dare you bring me this dirty pastry! I did not ask for charity! I have money enough to buy the finest cake!"

"I'm sorry," said one waiter. "You cannot use money here. This is Eternity, and here you can only eat what you, yourself sent ahead from the Mortal World. You, alas, sent only this one dirty piece of pastry, and I'm afraid that's all you may receive."[22]

CHAPTER NINE
HUMOROUS TALES

◇ ◇ ◇

IT COULD ALWAYS BE WORSE

One mercy Jews all over the world have been granted is a sense of humor—and a sense of just how ironic life may become. And so Jewish humorous tales often have a wry little moral attached to them.

It Could Always Be Worse

Once, a poor man went to his rabbi to complain.

"My house has only one room. I must share that room with my wife, my children, and my mother. It's so crowded in there! And so noisy! Rabbi, you must help me! What can I do?"

"Bring your goat into the house with you."

The bewildered poor man obeyed. A few days later he returned to the rabbi.

"Now it's even worse! The goat *maas* all the time. And the smell . . ."

"Fine. Now bring your cow into the house. And your chickens too."

The poor man obeyed. A few days later, he returned yet again. "Rabbi, you *must* help me! I can't move, I can't breathe, I can't even hear myself thinking!"

"Fine. Remove the chickens."

The poor man did.

"Now, remove your cow," the rabbi ordered.

Again, the poor man obeyed.

"Now, remove your goat, then tell me how things go."

The poor man removed the goat from his house, then came back to the rabbi in delight. "Oh, Rabbi, it's wonderful! So much room! And it's so nice and quiet now too!"[1]

You're a Fish, You're a Fish

During the Spanish Inquisition, a Jew, to survive, pretended to convert to Christianity. But one Friday night, agents of the Inquisition burst into his home and caught him cooking meat.

The Jew never panicked. He simply compared his cooking to what happened to him, repeating what he was told by the priests:

"You were born a Jew, you're now a Christian, you're a Christian."

And now, the Jew told the guards, that miraulous change had been repeated yet again. Gesturing over the sizzling steak, he solemnly intoned:

"You were born a steer, you're now a fish, you're a fish."[2]

Fresh Fish

One day a fish dealer stood with his wares beneath his sign: Fresh Fish Sold Here. A passerby stopped, studied the sign, then shook his head.

"Remove that 'fresh,'" he ordered. "Who would sell stinking fish?"

So the fish dealer eliminated "fresh" from his sign.

The next passerby stopped, studied the sign, and ordered, "Remove that 'here.' Obviously you're selling them here!"

So the fish dealer eliminated "here" from his sign, just in time for a new passerby to snap at him:

"What's this 'sold?' Of course you're selling them; that's evident!"

So the fish dealer eliminated "sold" from his sign, just in time for yet another passerby to argue:

"Why 'fish?' Anyone with an eye in his head can see those are fish!"

So the fish dealer eliminated "fish," and was left with a blank sign. Also, since not one of those critics had bought anything from him, he was left with aging, smelly fish as well.[3]

Pleasing the World

A man and his son were travelling, wearily, through the desert with their donkey. A traveller passed them and said:

"Now here's a foolish thing! You trudge on foot when you have a donkey to carry you!"

The traveller's words sounded wise. So the father climbed onto the donkey and rode, while his son continued on foot. After a time they met a second traveller, who said:

"How cruel! Here you ride like a noble, while your poor son, with his young, tender feet, is forced to trudge after you. How can you let your own child suffer?"

Abashed, the father climbed down from the donkey and put his son in his place. On they went, the son riding, the father walking. Awhile later, they came across yet another traveller, who said:

"How shameful! The son rides while the father trudges behind—a child has no right to ride while his father toils!"

The father looked at the son. The son looked at the father. They both climbed onto the donkey and rode along. But then they came to a fourth traveller, who stared at them in horror.

"How terrible! Abusing a poor, helpless animal like that, making him carry a double burden. For shame! Have you no pity?"

Father and son quickly dismounted. They sighed.

"There's no help for it," said the father. "We're just going to have to carry the donkey ourselves. Though someone's probably going to say that's wrong too! No matter what we do, we can't please the whole world!"[4]

The Dying Merchant

As a Jewish merchant lay dying in the apartment over his store, he murmured, "Is our oldest son, Jacob, here?"

"Yes, Pappa," he was assured.

"Is my oldest daughter, Rachel, here?"

"Yes, Pappa," she murmured.

"Is my second son, Isaac, here?"

"Yes, Pappa."

"My youngest son, Hershel?"

"Yes, Pappa."

"My youngest daughter, Miriam?"

"Yes, Pappa."

"And my wife of all these years, is she here too?"

"I'm here," came the tearful reply.

The dying merchant hoisted himself up in bed. "Then, *who's minding the store?*"[5]

From Minsk to Pinsk

A Jew hired a teamster to take him from Minsk to Pinsk. Off they went in the teamster's wagon, pulled by his horse, till they came to a steep hill.

"Would you mind walking up the hill?" the teamster asked. "I don't think my horse has the strength to pull the wagon and two people."

The Jew agreed. Up they walked. Soon they were about to go down the far side of the hill. The teamster asked:

"Would you mind walking down the hill? I don't think my horse has the strength to control the weight of a wagon with two people."

Again the Jew agreed. And so it went, he and the teamster walking up one side of a hill and down the other side, till at last they reached Pinsk. The weary Jew shook his head.

"Let me ask you a question. *I* needed to go to Pinsk on business. *You* needed to go to Pinsk to earn money. But tell me, friend teamster: Why did the *horse* have to go?"[6]

Where's the Cat

A husband and wife had a cat in their house that was a terrible nuisance, always getting into things that were none of its business.

One day, the wife happened to leave a kilo of butter on the table, and quick as thought, the cat devoured the butter, down to the last little smear. The furious wife chased the cat around the house, shouting at it that if she caught it, she would kill it.

Her husband stopped her. "You didn't actually see the cat eat the butter, did you?"

"No, but the butter is gone! *Someone* must have eaten it, and there was no one here but that thieving cat!"

"Ah!" exclaimed the husband. "I have an idea. We'll weigh the cat, and then we'll know if it really did eat the butter."

So they weighed the cat. And, sure enough, it weighed exactly one kilo.

"It *did* eat the butter!" cried the wife.

"But if the butter is all here," wondered the husband, "where's the cat?"[7]

The Woodcutter and Death

One day a poor woodcutter was struggling along under a heavy load of wood. The day was hot, the woodcutter was sweating, and the wood seemed to be growing heavier and heavier by the moment. At last, exhausted, disgusted with his lot, he threw down his burden and cried out:

"Oh, Death, release me!"

No sooner had he uttered these fatal words than the huge, shrouded figure of the Angel of Death appeared beside him. "You called me?" The terrified woodcutter could only stammer, "Uh . . . uh, yes, your . . . your most dreadful majesty. Would you . . . would you mind helping me get this wood back on my shoulders?"[8]

Tact

A Jew died suddenly in the marketplace. The rabbi sent the *shammes* (sexton) to break the sad news to the dead man's wife.

"For Heaven's sake, be tactful!" the rabbi warned. "Break the news to her as carefully as possible!"

The *shammes* agreed, and off he went to the dead man's house. He knocked, and a woman came to the door.

"Does the widow Rachel live here?" the shammes asked.

"My name is Rachel, and I do live here," the woman replied. "But I'm not a widow!"

"Wanna bet?" asked the *shammes.*[9]

LOGIC AND ILLOGIC

There is often impeccable, if incredibly convoluted, logic to Jewish folk humor, so convoluted it can sometimes leave a non-Jew with a headache!

The Poor Mourner

A bystander happened to see the funeral of the richest man in town pass through the streets. There in the procession was perhaps the poorest man the bystander had ever seen, a man in such worn clothing they were nearly rags. And this poor man was wailing and weeping more loudly and fervently than anyone else in the entire procession, beating his breast, tearing his already ragged clothing.

Moved, the bystander asked him, "Was the deceased a relation of yours?"

"No, no, not at all," the poor man replied.

"Then why are you weeping?" the puzzled bystander asked.

"*That's* why!" the poor man replied.[10]

A Glass of Tea

Two Jews sat together over a glass of tea. After a time of silence, the first mused:

"Life is like a glass of tea with sugar."

"Life is like a glass of tea with sugar?" his friend replied. "*Why* is life like a glass of tea with sugar?"

"How should I know? Am I a philosopher?"[11]

Everyone's a Critic

A poor student approached his rabbi with shy pride and handed him his commentary on the Talmud.

The rabbi read it and frowned. "Better to give up your writing," he told the student. "You'll never get anywhere with it."

The poor student looked down at his shabby clothes and shrugged philosophically. "And if I *stopped* writing," he asked, "would it get me anywhere?"[12]

Stamps

A Jew brought a package to the Post Office to be mailed. The clerk weighed it and told him:

"It's too heavy. You have to put more stamps on it."

"And if I put more stamps on it," the Jew retorted, "that'll make it lighter?"[13]

Cold Weather

"Husband, please close the window. It's cold outside."

"And if I close the window, will it be warm outside?"[14]

A Biting Dog

A Jew was brought to court by a neighbor who claimed the Jew's dog had bitten him.

"Your Honor," the Jew told the judge, "in the first case, my dog never bit anyone.

"In the second case, my dog has no teeth.

"And in the third case, I don't *have* a dog."[15]

The Pot

"You know that pot you borrowed from me? It's damaged! You'll have to buy me a new one!"

"First of all, that pot was in perfect condition when I returned it.

"Second, it was broken when you lent it to me.

"Third, I never borrowed your pot!"[16]

Questions

A Jew was on the witness stand. The lawyer asked him:

"Are you acquainted with the accused?"

"How should I be acquainted with the accused?"

"Did the accused ever try to borrow money from you?"

"Why should he want to borrow money from me?"

This was too much for the judge. Totally out of patience, he asked the Jew, "Why do you answer every question with another question?"

"Why not?"[17]

Herring

A Jew once thought up a riddle to confuse his friends:

"What's purple, hangs on the wall, and whistles?"

"We give up. What's purple, hangs on the wall, and whistles?"

"A herring."

"But a herring isn't purple!"

"It is if you paint it," crowed the riddler.

"But a herring doesn't hang on the wall!"

"It does if you hang it there."

"But a herring doesn't whistle!"

The riddler shrugged. "All right, so it *doesn't* whistle."[18]

Old Acquaintance

A man was walking down the street, minding his own business, when he was accosted by another man, who greeted him with a joyous cry of:

"Rosen! Moshe Rosen!"

"But I'm not—"

"It's been so long since I've seen you! Look at you!"

"I'm not—"

"Never mind, never mind. I can't believe how much you've changed. You used to be such a big man, strong as an ox. Now, you're smaller than I am, and thin as a stick! Have you been ill, maybe?"

"No, I—"

"Never mind, never mind. What have you done to your hair? You used to have a thick head of hair; now, you're completely bald! And you've lost your mustache, too! You know, Rosen, I almost didn't recognize you. Tell me, what has become of you?"

"I've been trying to tell you!" the exasperated man exclaimed. "I'm not Moshe Rosen!"

"What's this? You've gone and changed your name too!"[19]

Storm Warning

It was a bitterly cold day in Russia, with the wind howling wildly. The Jewish farmer was just about to harness up his horse when he heard a voice say, "Don't bother with this. A big blizzard is coming. Hurry home!"

The startled farmer glanced this way and that but saw no one. "W-what did you say?" he asked.

"I said, a big blizzard is coming. Hurry home!"

This time there could be no doubt about it. The only one who could have spoken was his horse. With a yell of fright, the farmer raced for home, slamming the door shut behind him and calling for his wife with all his might.

"What's the matter?" she asked. "Why are you shaking like that?"

"The horse!" he gasped out. "The horse *talked!*"

And he told her everything the horse had said. The woman sighed.

"All right, all right, so he said a blizzard is coming. No need to get so excited. What does a horse know about forecasting the weather?"[20]

Possibilities

Two Yeshiva students were discussing the possibility of war. One said:

"If there *is* a war, I hope I'm not called up. I dread the thought of it."

The other student shrugged. "Why worry?" he said. "Come, let us analyze the situation:

"There are two possibilities: Either war will break out or it won't. If there is no war, you have nothing to worry about. But if there *is* a war, there are two possibilities:

"Either you're called up or you're not. If you're not called up, there's nothing to worry about. But if you are, there are two possibilities:

"Either you're given combat duty or noncombatant duty. If you're given noncombatant duty, there's nothing to worry about. But if you're given combat duty, there are two possibilities:

"Either you're wounded or you're not. If you're not wounded, there's nothing to worry about. But if you're wounded, there are two possibilities:

"Either you're wounded gravely or you're wounded only slightly. If you're wounded only slightly, there's nothing to worry about. But if you're wounded gravely, there are two possibilities:

"Either you die or you recover. If you recover, there's nothing to worry about. But if you die there are two possibilities:

"Either you're buried in a Jewish cemetery or you're not. If you're buried in a Jewish cemetery, there's nothing to worry about. But if you're not . . ."

The student shrugged. "Why worry? There may not be a war at all."[21]

Reasoning

The same two Yeshiva students were puzzling over this question: "What makes tea sweet?"

The first student reasoned, "If I say that it is because of the sugar, then I must ask what the teaspoon's purpose might be. The answer, of course, is to sweeten the tea. After all, when you put sugar into the tea, the tea does not turn sweet until you have stirred that sugar into the tea. But that raises a new issue: Why, then, do we need the sugar?"

"Ah, I know the answer to that question," replied the second student. "It is, indeed, true that the teaspoon sweetens the tea. But the sugar is necessary because by watching carefully, we can see it dissolve. And we know by that sign that we may stop stirring."[22]

ROGUES AND TRICKY FELLOWS

The Jews may lack a codified Trickster figure, such as the Southwest's Coyote or West Africa's Ananse, but that does not mean Jewish folklore doesn't have its scoundrels, its witty rogues full of *chutzpah*—that supreme essence of cockiness and gall for which there is no easy English equivalent. A man with *chutzpah* has sometimes been defined as one who murders his parents, then asks leniency of the court because he is an orphan!

The Clever Thief

Once a thief was caught by the outraged citizens of a small town, right by the town's encircling fence. Inside was the town, outside was the forest and the wide world. As the citizens debated his punishment, the thief fell to his knees, pleading, "Whatever else you do to me, please don't throw me over the fence!"

The townspeople thought, "There must be something terrible waiting out there. What a perfect punishment!" And so they shouted, "How dare you appeal to our mercy, you . . . you criminal!"

With that, they threw the thief over the fence and went back to their homes, pleased at a job well-done. Not one of them realized that the thief, safe on the other side of the fence, was now free to run away. Which, of course, he did![23]

More than Enough

Once, an Athenian traveller in Jerusalem needed supplies for his journey. But he hardly wished to haggle in the marketplace! That would be far beneath his dignity. So the Athenian called a boy to him and gave him some money, saying:

"Go buy me something to eat. And get enough so that I can eat my fill now yet have some left over for my journeying."

The boy scurried away but returned with nothing more than a small sack of salt worth only a few small coins. "This is hardly what I asked you to buy!" the Athenian shouted.

"You told me to bring you something to eat, enough so that you could eat your fill now yet have some left over for your journeying," the boy replied. "And that is exactly what I've done!"

Grinning, he raced off into the crowd.[24]

An Orphan

A miserly rich man was asked by the members of his synagogue to donate money to the poor. He grudgingly gave a petty sum.

"Your son, who is a poor man," said the congregation, hoping to shame him, "has given generously. Won't you do the same?"

"How can you compare me to my son?" the rich man exclaimed. "*He* has a father who is a rich man. I am an orphan. *I* have no father at all!"[25]

A True Antique

Once a collector of antiques went into an antique dealer's shop and asked to see very rare objects. The shopkeeper opened his safe and removed a small box. Within the box was a watch.

"This is a nice old watch," said the antiques collector, "but it's nothing special."

"Nothing special! Nothing special! My friend, here you have a watch that's one of the great marvels of creation. You must certainly have heard that the *Rambam,* the wise Maimonides, was a doctor."

"Of course I have."

"Well, my friend, this was his watch. This is the very watch with which he took his patients' pulses, the very watch he brought with him on his visit to America."

"What *are* you saying?" asked the collector. "How could the *Rambam* have ever visited America? He lived ages ago, long before anyone had even *heard* of America!"

"Exactly!" crowed the shopkeeper. "That's precisely what makes this watch so valuable!"[26]

Chutzpah and More Chutzpah

An ailing miser held out as long as he could. At last, he grew so ill he knew he needed to go to a doctor. But the cost of an initial visit seemed so high! How could be bear to pay it?

Then, the miser had an inspiration. He entered the doctor's office with a cheerful, "Well, here I am again!"

The doctor never flickered an eyelid. He examined the miser with great care, then said, "Now, as for treatment: Continue exactly as before!"[27]

SOME HERSHELE TALES

Hershele Ostropoler comes as close as any folkloric figure to a Jewish Trickster, full of nonmalicious jests and practical jokes. Hershele actually existed, living in Eastern Europe in the latter half of the eighteenth century, though most of what is known about him comes from the cycle of folktales and jests that have grown up about his name. From what little can actually be traced of the real man, he lost his job through his constant joking and wandered throughout the Ukraine, finally becoming a regular in the circle of friends surrounding Rabbi Boruch of Miedzibezh, the grandson of the Baal Shem Tov, founder of the Hasidic movement. Hershele has been the subject of many a tale and poem, a novel, and even a television play produced in the United States in the 1950s!

Hershele at the Inn

One time Hershele stopped at an inn for the night and asked the innkeeper's wife for something to eat. She took one look at this ragged, disreputable fellow and decided he surely had no coins with which to pay.

"I'm sorry," she told Hershele, "but we're all out of food."

Hershele drew himself up to his full height. "Then I'm going to have to do what my father did."

He looked so frightening that the woman stammered, "What . . . what did he do?"

"He did what he had to do."

Now the poor woman was even more frightened. What if this stranger was the son of a dangerous madman, a murderer even? "I think I remember where we might have some food," she said, and hurried off to the kitchen, returning with a whole feast for Hershele, who devoured it gladly. When he was done, and smiling peacefully, she dared ask him:

"Good sir, what . . . what was it your father did?"

"When there wasn't any food?" Hershele's smile broadened. "Why, he went to bed hungry, of course!"[28]

A Golden Lie

Hershele gained such a reputation as a teller of tales that one day a wealthy merchant stopped him and said:

"Hershele, if you can tell me a lie without even stopping to think, I'll give you a ruble."

"One ruble?" exclaimed Hershele. "You promised me two!"[29]

A Sorrowful Dinner

One day, Hershele took it into his head to dine in a fine restaurant, even though the prices were outrageous. But the portion of meat that arrived on his place was so tiny that Hershele burst into loud sobs.

The owner of the restaurant came running. "What's wrong, sir? Please, what's wrong?"

"Oy!" cried Hershele, and "Oy!" again. "To think that for such a tiny scrap of meat a whole big ox had to be slaughtered!"[30]

Hershele the Carriage Driver

One day Hershele ran totally out of money. But though he might have no coins, he still had his wits! He borrowed a whip from a carriage maker and went out into the street, cracking the whip loudly. "Hey, everyone! I'm taking anyone who wants to go to Letitshev for half fare, today only!"

That was quite a bargain, and soon Hershele had gathered a cluster of eager customers. Hershele collected their money gladly.

"But where are your horses?" one man asked.

"Follow me," Hershele replied. "Don't worry. I'll take you right to Letitshev."

They followed him. And they followed him. By now they had left their town behind—but there was still no sight of a team of horses!

"Don't worry," Hershele repeated. "I'll take you right to Letitshev."

And so he did—on foot.

"You thief!" his customers screamed. "Give us back our money!"

"I am no thief!" said Hershele. "Did I not promise to take you right to Letitshev?"

"Yes, but in a horse-and-carriage, not on foot!"

"Did I ever say anything about horses or a carriage?" asked Hershele.

And as they stood there, dumbfounded, Hershele hurried away.[31]

Hershele the Artist

Now, it must be understood that Hershele had no talent as an artist, none at all. But that didn't stop him from deciding to make some money from art! He found himself a large, totally blank canvas, set it up in a prominent place and waited. Sure enough, a passerby stopped to ask why a blank canvas should be on display.

"Blank!" Hershele exclaimed. "Blank! Hardly that! But the mystery of this great and famous painting can only be learned by those who pay me one silver crown."

Overcome by curiosity, the passerby handed over a silver crown.

"This painting, this great and famous painting," Hershele declared, "is the actual depiction of the crossing of the Red Sea by Moses and the Israelites."

The passerby peered at the blank canvas. "But there's nothing there! Where are the Israelites?"

"When this painting was made, they had already crossed over."
"Then where are the Egyptians?"
"They hadn't yet arrived."
"But . . . but the sea! The Red Sea! Where is the water?"
Hershele shook his head. "My poor friend, don't you remember our history? The waters had already parted when this painting was made!"[32]

THE WISE MEN OF CHELM

The people of Chelm are no fools, it's only that foolish things happen to them.[33]

Bread and Butter

One of the wise men of Chelm brought a problem to his rabbi:
"Why is it that bread always falls butter-side down?"
"Does it?" wondered the rabbi. "Let us see."
He buttered a slice of bread and dropped it—and it landed bread-side down. "You see?" said the rabbi.
But the Chelmite wasn't satisfied. "That's because you buttered the wrong side!" he cried.[34]

Higher Mathematics

Two Chelmites were sitting one day over their glasses of tea, puzzling over the marvels of modern travel.
"Let me see if I understand this properly," said one. "It takes a horse and carriage only four hours to go from here to Pinsk. Am I correct?"
"You are. But if you had a carriage with *two* horses, it would take only two hours."
"Indeed," said the first. "Then, if you had a carriage with *four* horses, you could get there in no time at all."
"It would seem so. But if that is the case, why bother to go to Pinsk at all? Why not simply harness up your four horses and stay right here?"[35]

Faster Travel

The same two Chelmites were puzzling over the wonders of the modern world.

"Did you know," said one, "that with the marvel that is the steam locomotive, you could leave Chelm at noon and be in Warsaw by midnight?"

The second Chelmite shook his head, unimpressed. "What in the world would I do in Warsaw in the middle of the night?"[36]

Golden Shoes

The wise men of Chelm decided one day that, to heighten their importance in the world, they would appoint the wisest of them the Chief Sage.

"But how will anyone *know* I'm the Chief Sage," their choice argued. "There must be something special about me to say, 'Here is an important man!' "

The wise men of Chelm agreed. And they bought him a pair of golden shoes.

Alas, the streets of Chelm were not paved. And the first time the golden shoes were worn, the Chief Sage stepped right into a mud puddle, which covered up every trace of gold. And without the golden shoes, no one could recognize the Chief Sage.

"This will never do!" he complained. "Now no one knows I am the Chief Sage! If no one knows who I am, I . . . I'll resign!"

"We must do something about this!" cried the wise men of Chelm. What they did was have the shoemaker make a fine pair of leather shoes for their Chief Sage to protect the golden ones.

Unfortunately, the fine leather shoes covered up every glint of gold. And without the golden shoes, no one recognized the Chief Sage.

"Everyone's ignoring me!" he cried. "The Chief Sage should not be ignored!"

"You're right," the wise men of Chelm agreed. "We shall do something drastic about this!"

So they had the shoemaker make a new pair of leather shoes for their Chief Sage. But this pair had holes cut carefully into the sides and tops so that the golden shoes gleamed through.

Unfortunately, the first time the leather shoes with the holes and the golden shoes underneath were worn, the Chief Sage stepped into another mud puddle. Mud seeped right in through the holes, and soon the gold was covered up once again. And since no one could see the golden shoes, no one recognized the Chief Sage.

"This is an outrage!" cried the Chief Sage. "This is an insult to my dignity!"

"Don't worry," said the wise men of Chelm. "We shall defend your dignity."

They stuffed straw into the holes in the leather shoes to protect the golden shoes underneath. It kept out the mud very well. But unfortunately, now it was the straw itself that hid the gold! No one could catch even the faintest glimmer of the golden shoes. Once again, no one recognized the Chief Sage.

"This is humiliating!" cried the Chief Sage. "Why, I'm ashamed to be seen on the streets!"

So the wise men of Chelm thought and pondered, pondered and thought. At last, they came up with a solution:

"You shall wear ordinary leather shoes on your feet. But in order that everyone shall know you are the Chief Sage of Chelm, you shall also wear the golden shoes—on your hands!"

So he did. From then on, everyone in Chelm could recognize their Chief Sage. And everyone was happy.[37]

His Father's Beard

Soon after the Chief Sage became well known in Chelm, a worried young man went to him. "Chief Sage, oh wisest of the wise, you must help me. Can you tell me why I have no beard on my chin? I have no reason not to trust my mother—and yet my father, as you know, has a fine, thick beard!"

The Chief Sage pondered awhile, stroking his own beard. Then, his face brightened. "Perhaps," he suggested, "you take after your mother?"

"Of course!" cried the young man. "My mother has no beard at all! What a wonderful Chief Sage you are!"[38]

Umbrella

Two Chelmites were strolling along when all of a sudden it began to rain.

"Quick!" said one. "Open your umbrella!"

"It won't do any good," said the other. "My umbrella is all full of holes."

"Then why did you bring it with you?"

"I didn't think it would rain."[39]

The Rock

A high hill overlooked Chelm, and on that high hill stood a large rock. Looking at that rock, the Chelmites began to worry that it would someday come loose from the hill and fall down upon the town. They decided to bring the rock down by themselves.

But how should they move it? That was a problem worthy of much consideration. At last, all of Chelm, men and women, boys and girls, climbed up that high hill and began to drag the rock down. When they, groaning and struggling, had managed to wearily pull it almost halfway down, a stranger saw what they were doing and started to laugh.

"Why bother dragging the stone?" he asked. "Just give it a good push, and it will roll down all by itself!"

That sounded like good advice to the Chelmites. They dragged the rock all the way back up the hill, gave it a push, and sure enough, it rolled all the way down the hill by itself.[40]

The Worrier

The people of Chelm spent a lot of time worrying—so much, in fact, that they began to worry they wouldn't have any time left to do anything else. So all the wise men of Chelm met to decide what to do about this problem.

They wrestled with it by day and night for a week. At the end of that week, they announced their solution: They would appoint Chelm's chimney sweep, Yossel, the official Worrier of Chelm. In exchange for a salary of one ruble a week, he would do all the worrying for the town.

Everyone agreed this was a fine solution. But just before they were about to vote the post of official Worrier of Chelm into existence, one small voice called out:

"If Yossel gets a nice salary of one ruble a week, what has he got to worry about?"[41]

Sun and Moon

The people of Chelm took it into their heads to wonder which was more important: the sun or the moon. They began to argue about it, some yelling, "The sun!" others yelling, "The moon!" At last, afraid that they were going to come to blows, they took the whole matter to the Rabbi of Chelm, asking him:

"Which is more important, the sun or the moon?"

The rabbi pondered the question for a time, then decided, "The moon. It shines in the night, when it would otherwise be dark. The sun, however, isn't so useful. After all, it shines when the day's already light!"[42]

The Cat

At one time, there were no cats at all in the entire town of Chelm. What there were instead were mice! Oy, were there mice! People used to kick mice out of their way in the streets and knock them off the tables at home.

Then one day, a merchant came to town and mentioned a mystical creature to the Chelmites, a being called a "cat" that caught and ate mice. When the Chelmites heard of this, they were delighted and paid the merchant a huge sum to find them this "cat." Sure enough, the merchant returned with a nice tabby, and the Chelmites quickly put it into a house. To their delight, they saw it chase out the mice in no time at all.

Unfortunately, no one in Chelm knew that cats can run away. One day, someone left a window open, and out the cat went, leaping up onto the roof. So the people of Chelm called a meeting. How were they going to catch the cat? They thought of this and that and finally decided the only thing to do was to set the house on fire so that the cat would jump down. They burned the house down—but the perverse cat only jumped to the roof of the next house. They burned that one down too—but the cat jumped to the roof of a third house. They burned that one down too. And by the time the cat finally deigned to jump down, the Chelmites had burned down half the town.[43]

Counting Months

There was a young man of Chelm who was totally ignorant of many facts of life. One day, he went running frantically to the rabbi, crying:

"Rabbi, can you explain this extraordinary thing? My wife and I have been married only three months, and everyone knows it takes nine months for a baby to be born—yet she's just given birth! How can this be?"

The rabbi sighed. "I see, my son, you don't understand the simplest arithmetic. I ask you: Have you lived with your wife for three months?"

"Yes."

"Has she lived with you three months?"

"Yes."

"Together you have lived three months?"

"Yes."

"And how much is three plus three plus three?"

"Why, nine, of course, Rabbi!"

"Then why bother me with silly questions?"[44]

Catching the Moon

The people of Chelm were very worried about the dark nights when the moon didn't shine. Maybe someone would fall and hurt himself, maybe even, God forbid, break an arm or leg!

So the wise men of Chelm held a meeting. What could they do about the darkness?

"We will catch the moon," they decided.

They set up a great barrel of water in the center of town and waited for the moon to rise and move across the sky. Soon it would be in just the right place, and then . . .

"We have it!" the Chelmites cried.

Sure enough, there was the moon, right in the middle of the water, in the middle of the barrel!

Quickly, the Chelmites covered the mouth of the barrel with planks, nailing them firmly in place. Then, satisfied, they all went home.

The next night was cloudy and dark, and the Chelmites decided it was a perfect time to let the moon shine a little. So they all went down to the town square, where the barrel stood. Carefully, they pried back one of the planks . . .

Nothing happened.

They pried back another plank . . .

Still nothing happened.

They pried off all the planks and stared into the barrel.

"The moon is gone!" they cried.

Just then, the clouds parted. The moon shone overhead.

"Someone must have let it out," the people of Chelm decided.[45]

The Sundial

How proud the people of Chelm were of their new sundial! They stared at it and polished it. Then, a storm came along. Rain poured down on the sundial. That would never do! So the Chelmites built a roof over their sundial to protect it.[46]

A Thief in Chelm

To everyone's horror, a thief broke into the Chelm synagogue one night and made off with the poorbox. The wise men of Chelm promptly gathered together to make sure such a scandal could never happen again.

"We shall install a new poorbox," they decided, "but we shall hang it from the ceiling, right up near the beams, so no thief can reach it."

"Wait, wait," called out a voice from the back of the room. "If you do that, how will the charitable folk be able to reach it?"

Now there was a question worth pondering. And ponder it, the wise men did, till at last the gathered wisdom of Chelm saved the day. It was decreed that a ladder would be built so that the charitable could easily reach the new poorbox.[47]

Fire!

One dark, moonless night, long after the Chelmites had given up on capturing the moon, a fire broke out in Chelm, and everyone came running to the fiercely burning building to help put out the blaze. Once it was safely out, they sat down to bewail their misfortune. But the rabbi cried out:

"My friends, this wasn't a misfortune! It was a miracle sent from Heaven!"

How could such a thing be? The rabbi hurried to explain.

"If the fire hadn't been burning so brightly on such a dark night, how would we ever have been able to see how to put it out?"[48]

The Pit

The Chelmites decided one day that their synagogue was just too small and too old to serve their needs. They would have to build a new synagogue. Well and good, but all of them knew a building, even a holy one, first needed a foundation. So they all picked up their shovels and set to work digging one.

Suddenly, one man stopped. "Wait a minute," he said. "What are we going to do with all the earth we've dug up?"

That was a problem no one had considered. What *were* they to do with it?

"I know!" said a second Chelmite. "We'll dig a new pit, and into that we'll dump all the earth from this one!"

"Then what will we do with the earth from *that* pit?" asked the first Chelmite.

"I have it!" cried a third man. "We'll dig *another* pit. Only we'll make it twice as big and twice as deep as the first, and into it we'll shovel all the earth from the first two pits!"

"Of course!" everyone cried. And, satisfied, they all went back to digging.[49]

DEFIANT HUMOR AND BITTER JESTS

Anti-Semitism has, sadly, been a fact of Jewish life for millennia. Faced with all the many forms of cruelty and fear, Jews have fought back with whatever weapons came to hand. Even when, all too often for a people outnumbered and surrounded, there was no hope of victory or escape, there was still the last defiant weapon of humor.

Courtesy

The eighteenth century philosopher, Moses Mendelssohn, was walking down a busy Berlin street when he accidentally bumped into a Prussian officer.

"Swine!" the officer bellowed.

"Mendelssohn," the philosopher replied with a gracious bow.[50]

A Hat

A Jew walking past a Czarist officer forgot to doff his hat as Jews were required to do. Instantly the officer shouted:

"What do you mean by such insolence! Where are you from?"

"From Minsk," the Jew said with proper humility.

"And what about your hat?" thundered the officer.

"Also from Minsk."[51]

Quick Thinking

A Jewish man fell into the river and was drowning. He shouted frantically for help. Two Czarist officers heard him, and came running.

But when they realized he was a Jew, they drew back from the edge in contempt.

"Bah. Let the Jew drown."

When the drowning man heard them and realized he wasn't going to be rescued, he gathered the last of his strength together and managed to pull himself above the surface long enough to shout with all his might, "Down with the Czar!"

Hearing these treasonous words, the officers hurriedly dragged the Jew out of the river and arrested him.[52]

Politics

A Jew, travelling by train in Czarist Russia, found himself sitting across from a Russian lieutenant and his dog. The Russian made a big point of loudly addressing the dog by the name "Yankele."

"What a shame," said the Jew quietly, "that your dog has a Jewish name."

Instantly the officer came alert. "Why is that?"

"Otherwise," the Jew replied, "he could have become a lieutenant."[53]

Quiet Logic

A group of Nazis surrounded an elderly Jewish man and demanded of him:

"Tell us, Jew, who caused the war?"

The elderly Jew answered quickly, "The Jews—and the bicycle riders."

"Why the bicycle riders?"

"Why the Jews?" he replied.[54]

The Rescuer

Hitler went horseback riding one day, only to have his horse bolt. Before Hitler could be thrown, a man came running to grab the bridle and bring the horse to a stop.

"You have saved your Fuehrer!" gasped Hitler. "Who are you?"

The man paled. "I am Isadore Cohen," he said.

Hitler was stunned to hear that his rescuer was a despised Jew, but he said, "You have saved my life, and I wish to reward you. Just name the favor you wish granted."

"The biggest favor you can do for me," murmured the sorrowful Jew, "is not to breathe a word about this to anyone!"[55]

Wrestling the Tiger

During the height of Nazi power, a circus in Germany offered a job to any man who would put on a lionskin and wrestle their tiger. To the manager's dismay, no one took up the challenge, except for one man who wore the yellow armband marking him as a Jew.

"Who else but a Jew would accept such a job?" the man said bitterly. "I have a family to support, and no one else will hire me."

"But the tiger may kill you!"

The Jew shrugged in resignation. "I repeat, I have a family to support."

So he was hired. The time came for the main event: lion-man against tiger. Trying not to show his fear, the Jew put on the lionskin and entered the tiger's cage. Roaring as much like a real lion as he could, he rushed forward on all fours—and found himself face to face with the furious tiger. Sure he was about to die, the Jew began a resigned prayer:

"Hear O Israel—"

But to his astonishment, the tiger concluded, "The Lord our God, the Lord is One."

"You scared me half to death!" the Jew whispered. "I thought you were a real tiger!"

"Listen, my friend," the false tiger whispered back, "do you think you're the only Jew in Germany trying to make a living?"[56]

Meat

On a cold day in Moscow in the time of Stalin, a long line had formed outside a meat market, drawn by the rumor that a big shipment of meat was due to arrive. After two hours of waiting in the bitter chill, the manager of the market came outside to announce:

"Comrades, I have been advised that the shipment is on its way. But there isn't enough meat arriving for all the people waiting here. We're going to have to shorten the line. So I must ask all the Jews to go home."

They did. After another hour or two in the freezing cold, the remaining people on line saw the manager appear again.

"Comrades, I have been advised that the shipment is still on its way. Unfortunately, there are still too many people on line. Will all those who aren't party members please leave?"

The line shortened again. Again there was an hour's wait in the freezing cold before the manager appeared again.

"Comrades, I have bad news for you. The truck broke down. There will be no delivery of meat today."

As they trudged away, one party member muttered to the other, "Damn Jews have all the privileges!"[57]

Mail Delivery

In Moscow, Goldberg was awakened at 3 a.m. by pounding on his door.

"Who's there?" he asked.

"The mailman," came the reply.

Warily, Goldberg opened the door. Two KGB agents stormed in. "Are you Goldberg?" they asked.

"I am."

"And you made an application to go to Israel?"

"I did."

"Don't you have enough food to eat here?"

"I do."

"Don't your children get a good state education?"

"They do."

"Then why do you want to leave Russia?"

Goldberg smiled faintly. "Because," he said, "I don't like living in a country where they deliver the mail at three in the morning."[58]

NEW WORLD JESTS

As Jewish immigrants to the United States grew used to their new country, old forms of humor evolved in different ways. In the New World, the immigrants found that they no longer had to fear that practicing their religion would mean their death. They learned that though the ugliness of anti-Semitism still existed, it was illegal in this new country; it could be fought with law. And though no Jew will ever forget the horrors of the past—as, indeed, no human being should ever forget—Jewish-Americans are able to jest openly both about anti-

Semites and about their own sometimes exaggerated sensitivity to even the slightest hint of an ethnic slur.

Assimilation

An Americanized Jew, a former Talmudic scholar, returned years later to the Old Country for a visit. His old mother took one look at him and cried:

"Moishe! Where's your beard?"

"Ah, Mama, in America no one wears a beard."

"I see, I see. But you do still keep the Sabbath?"

"Mama, you know, business won't wait. In America, many people work on the Sabbath."

"I see, I see. But at least you do still eat kosher food?"

"Mama, I'm afraid it's very difficult to keep kosher in America."

"I see, I see." Mama hesitated a moment, then whispered in her son's ear, "Moishe, tell me this one thing: Are you still circumcised?"[59]

A Southern Belle

During World War II, a Southern lady of the old school of southern breeding decided she would do something for the boys in uniform for Thanksgiving. She telephoned the local army base and told the lieutenant to whom she was referred:

"Send me three nice, lonely boys, and I will be happy to treat them to Thanksgiving dinner. Oh, but lieutenant, one little thing: I don't care if they are Northerners or Southerners. Just do *not* send me any Jews. No Jews, please!"

The lieutenant told her he understood her perfectly.

Sure enough, when Thanksgiving Day came around, the lady heard a knock on her door. She opened it to see three young men in army uniform—three black young men.

"Oh . . . oh my!" she gasped in shock. "There . . . there must be some mistake!"

"Oh no, ma'am," said one of the soldiers, smiling broadly. "Lieutenant Goldberg *never* makes mistakes!"[60]

The Restaurant

An elderly Jew from the Lower East Side went into a posh uptown New York restaurant, only to be told by a haughty waiter:

"I'm sorry, sir. We don't serve Jews here."

"Don't let that worry you," the elderly Jew replied tranquilly. "I don't eat Jews either."[61]

Discrimination

Two American Jews met in the street. Said one to the other, "How goes it?"

"N-n-not so good," the other replied. "I j-j-just was t-turned down for a j-j-job."

"That's too bad. Where was it?"

"At a r-r-r-adio s-s-station. L-l-lousy anti-Semites!"[62]

Borrowing

A Jewish traveling salesman, whose suitcase had been lost in transit, stopped in a men's room in the train station to wash up. He asked the man next to him:

"Excuse me, could I borrow your soap?"

"Sure," said the man. "Go ahead."

A few moments later, the salesman asked, "Now, do you mind if I borrowed your razor and a bit of shaving cream?"

The man looked at him a little strangely but passed them over. A few minutes later, the salesman asked, "Could I borrow your towel, too?"

The man sighed. "Sure. Why not?"

A few moments later, the salesman asked, "One more thing: Can I borrow your toothbrush?"

This was too much for the man. "No! Of course not! Go buy one in the corner drugstore!"

"Anti-Semite," muttered the salesman.[63]

A Baseball Question

A little Jewish boy who had been to Yankee Stadium came running home, laughing with excitement, to tell his grandfather all about the game.

"You should have seen it, Grandpa! Babe Ruth hit three home runs today!"

The old man carefully considered what his grandson had told him.

"Tell me," he said at last. "What this Babe Ruth did: Was it good for the Jews?"[64]

The Elephant

A professor of zoology once had a graduate class full of international students. He set them all the assignment of writing papers regarding the elephant.

The English student wrote, "Elephant Hunting."

The French student wrote, "The Love-Life of the Elephant."

The German student wrote, "An Introduction to the Bibliography for the Study of the Elephant."

The American student wrote, "Breeding Bigger and Better Elephants."

And the Israeli student wrote, "The Elephant and the Jewish Problem."[65]

Thirst

A man had just settled down for the night in his bunk aboard a train. All was silent. Then, a heartrending sigh shattered the still air:

"Oy, am I thirsty!"

The man settled down once more. But again he heard:

"Oy, am I thirsty!"

It was coming from behind the curtains of the bunk opposite his own.

"Oy, am I thirsty!"

After several repetitions of this cry, the man could stand it no longer. He wrapped his robe about himself, climbed down from his bunk, and padded along the dark, swaying length of the train till he had reached the water fountain. He filled a cup to the brim, then padded back along the length of the train, struggling not to spill any water, till he had reached the bunk from which had come the heartrending sighs.

"Here," he said, thrusting the cup past the curtains. "Enjoy."

The man climbed back into his own bunk, threw off his robe, and settled down once more. All was still, blessedly still, and he was just drifting off to sleep—when the night was shattered by a new heartrending sigh.

"Oy, was I thirsty!"[66]

Telephone Call

A Jewish housewife in the Bronx answered the phone one day and was astounded to hear a very, very proper British voice say:

"This is Mrs. Vanderbilt's secretary speaking. I am calling to confirm her luncheon engagement with Mrs. Astor at the club today. Am I correct?"

The housewife could only gasp out, "Oy, have *you* got a wrong number!"[67]

Dinner Party

Sophie Goldberg was social climbing and had gone so far as to change her last name to Mont d'Or. At a society dinner party, she asked, in her best false-British accent:

"I beg your pardon. Would you please pass the butter?"

But as the butter was passed, it fell right into her lap. "Oy veh!" she yelled. Then, hastily composing herself, she added, "Whatever *that* means!"[68]

An Emergency

One way for a synagogue to earn needed revenue is to sell tickets for seating during the High Holy Days. Since an observant Jew is forbidden to work during those days, a non-Jewish gatekeeper is usually hired to collect those tickets.

One Yom Kippur, a frantic man came running up to the door of a New York synagogue and tried to get in without a ticket. The gatekeeper stopped him.

"No ticket, no admission."

"But I've got to get in!"

"No ticket, no admission," the gatekeeper repeated.

"You don't understand! My business partner is in there, and I've got to speak to him!"

"I'm telling you, no ticket, no admission!"

"But I just need to speak to him for a few moments!" the man insisted. "It's a matter of life and death!"

"Well . . . all right," the gatekeeper said. "I'll let you in for a few moments. But don't let me catch you praying!"[69]

OY AND AHA!

It's quite possible for Jews, particularly Yiddish-speaking Jews, to gather information, carry on a conversation, or make a point conveying a maximum amount of meaning through a minimal number of words. Sometimes, indeed, one word alone can speak volumes![70]

Chicken Soup

A Jew dining in a kosher restaurant said, "Waiter! Taste this chicken soup."

"What do you mean, taste the chicken soup? There's nothing wrong with that soup!"

"Just taste the soup."

Grumbling, the waiter went to taste the soup. "How can I taste the soup?" he asked. "Where's the spoon?"

"AHA!" the Jew exclaimed.[71]

Politics

Three Jews were sitting in the synagogue. After a few moments of silence, one of them sighed and said:

"Oy."

After a few more moments of silence, the second Jew sighed and said:

"Oy veh."

The third Jew stood up, put on his coat and said, "If you can't talk about something other than politics, I'm leaving!"

Children

Three Jewish mothers were sitting around the kitchen table. One woman shook her head and said:

"Oy."

The second woman sighed. "Oy veh."

The third woman glanced at the other two. "I thought we weren't going to talk about the children!"[72]

Conversation

Two Jews, old friends, ran into each other on the street. Asked one:

"How's by you?"

"Eh-eh."
"And how's business?"
"Hah!"
"And your wife, is she in good health?"
"Mmm-mmm!"
"So! It's been a treat to have a heart-to-heart talk with an old friend!"[73]

THE JEWISH-AMERICAN MOTHER

The Jewish-American Mother as stereotype is a fairly recent folkloric creation, dating from the middle of this century. She is portrayed as a woman overly protective of her young—her battle cry being, "Eat, eat!"—overly, and loudly, self-sacrificing, with a strong martyrdom complex that instills a guilt complex in those young. Impossible to please, she is obsessed with seeing her daughters married well and her sons successful in honorable, money-making professions; "My son, the doctor" is one of her goals. In short, the Jewish-American Mother is the personification of caring raised to the point of the ridiculous.

The Gift

A Jewish-American mother gave her son two neckties for his birthday, one blue, one green. After much deliberation, he wore the blue necktie when he took her out to dinner. His mother took one look at what he was wearing and said:
"What's the matter, you don't like the green tie?"[74]

El Al, Airline of Israel

There are said to be two signs on El Al airplanes. One reads, "Fasten Your Seat Belts." The other reads, "Eat, eat!"[75]

The Israeli Navy

The Israeli Navy is said to have a new ship, the S.S. Mein Kind (Eat, Eat, My Child).[76]

The Magic Lamp

A Jewish-American mother was walking on the beach when she stumbled upon a brass lamp. Rubbing it, she found herself staring at an enormous genie, who bowed before her and promised the woman her heart's desire.

"What is your wish?" he asked.

"Nothing."

"Nothing!"

"You heard me. Go away, genie. I don't want to wish." The Jewish-American mother smiled with satisfaction. "I have everything I want: a daughter married to a doctor, and a son who calls me regularly."[77]

THE JEWISH-AMERICAN PRINCESS

Where the Jewish-American Mother is seen in folklore as overbearingly protective but basically loving, her daughter is often portrayed as a dainty, perpetually calorie-counting, spoiled creature, a princess who lives for shopping and loathes the very thought of cooking, sex, or other "onorous" chores.

The folklore surrounding the Jewish-American Princess—usually abbreviated in folk jokes to the J.A.P.—is of even more recent vintage than that referring to Jewish-American Mothers. The earliest examples of J.A.P. folklore date only to about the 1970s, and new variants are constantly being created; some have even come out of the 1991 Desert Storm campaign.

The J.A.P. folk joke usually takes the form of tongue-in-cheek riddles rather than actual stories—and is usually vicious, frequently bordering on, or crossing over into, the obscene. While there is still an undertone of love in even the nastiest of the Jewish-American Mother folktales, there is little love lost for the Jewish-American Princess stereotype.

A Sampling of Jewish-American Princess Riddles

[Q.] What does a J.A.P. make for dinner?
[A.] Reservations.

[Q.] What is a J.A.P.'s favorite wine?
[A.] I wanna go to *Hawaii!*

[Q.] What is a J.A.P.'s idea of perfect sex?
[A.] Simultaneous headaches.

[Q.] Why does a J.A.P. close her eyes during sex?
[A.] So she can pretend she's shopping.

[Q.] How many J.A.P.s does it take to change a light bulb?
[A.] 1. None: "What, and ruin my nail polish?"
2. Two: one to pour the Diet Pepsi, and one to call Daddy.[78]

[Q.] What is the difference between a Libyan terrorist and a J.A.P.?
[A.] A terrorist makes fewer demands.

[Q.] What would a J.A.P. in the Army Reserve do during a nuclear holocaust?
[A.] Run for her sun reflector.

[Q.] What do you call an Israeli Army doll for girls?
[A.] GI J.A.P.[79]

CHAPTER TEN
A SAMPLING OF PROVERBS AND RIDDLES

◇ ◇ ◇

HEBREW PROVERBS

Few are they who see their own faults.[1]
The rose grows among thorns.[2]

No man is impatient with his creditors.[3]

When wine enters the head, the secret flies out.[4]

What the child says outdoors, he has learned indoors.[5]

Without law, civilization perishes.[6]

Say little and do much.[7]

A small coin in a large jar makes a great noise.[8]

Too many captains sink the ship.[9]

Men should be careful lest they cause women to weep, for God counts their tears.[10]

Silence is the fence round wisdom.[11]

The poor is hated even by his own neighbor; but the rich hath many friends.[12]

A wise son maketh a glad father; but a foolish son is the grief of his mother.[13]

A soft answer turneth away wrath; but a grievous word stirreth up wrath.[14]

Give every man the benefit of the doubt.[15]

When in a city, follow its customs.[16]

One good deed leads to another.[17]

All's well that ends well.[18]

YIDDISH PROVERBS

If they give, take; if they take, yell![19]

The wheel turns round.[20]

Talk less, do more.[21]

When you grease palms, you ride.[22]

A liar should have a good memory.[23]

When you have no linen you save the laundry bill.[24]

Petty thieves are hanged, major ones go free.[25]

Time is the best healer.[26]

Too smart outsmarts itself.[27]

No one is deaf to praise.[28]

None so deaf as those who will not hear.[29]

If one man calls you a donkey, ignore him. If two men call you a donkey, think about it. If three men call you a donkey, buy a saddle.[30]

What one has, one doesn't want; what one wants, one doesn't have.[31]

Don't spit in the well; you might drink from it later.[32]

You can't chew with someone else's teeth.[33]

When a rogue kisses you, count your teeth.[34]

When it falls, it falls butter-side down.[35]

Your friend has a friend, and your friend's friend has a friend; be discreet.[36]

An insincere peace is better than a sincere war.[37]

If grandma had wheels, she'd be a wagon.[38]

The highest wisdom is kindness.[39]

One fool makes many fools.[40]

The sun will set without your help.[41]

What is cheap, is dear.[42]

Death is the only certainty.[43]

The whole world is one town.[44]

RIDDLES AND PUZZLES

[Q.] Everyone loves me, yet no one can look into my face. What am I?
[A.] The sun.[45]

[Q.] Who had thousands of grandchildren yet no parents?
[A.] Adam and Eve.[46]

[Q.] When did one-fourth of the world's population die in one struggle?
[A.] When Cain killed Abel.[47]

[Q.] It's not a shirt, yet it's sewed. It's not a tree, yet it's full of leaves. It's not a person, yet it talks. What is it?
[A.] A book.[48]

[Q.] A man dreams he was on a ship with his father and mother. The ship begins to sink. He can save himself and one other only. What should he do?
[A.] He should wake up.[49]

[Q.] Who can speak in all languages?
[A.] Echo.[50]

[Q.] How many sides has a bagel?
[A.] Two: an inside and an outside.[51]

[Q.] What does a pious Jew do before he drinks tea?
[A.] He opens his mouth.[52]

[Q.] What causes neither pain nor grief yet makes everyone weep?
[A.] An onion.[53]

[Q.] What were the only living creatures not included in Noah's ark?
[A.] Fish.[54]

[Q.] What kind of water can be carried in a sieve?
[A.] Frozen water.[55]

[Q.] Three merchants and three thieves needed to cross a lake. Unfortunately, they had but one boat, and that boat could hold only two people at a time. Since no one merchant could be left alone with two thieves, how did they all safely cross?
[A.] First two thieves crossed. One then brought the boat back for the third thief. He returned once more and stayed on the near shore. Then two merchants rowed across the lake. One merchant and one thief returned with the boat. The thief got out of the boat, and two merchants rowed across, making a total of three on the far side. Then one thief returned to pick up the last thief.[56]

NOTES

◇ ◇ ◇

Motif types and numbers refer to Stith Thompson's exhaustive *Motif-Index of Folk-Literature* (6 vol. Bloomington: Indiana University Press, 1932–36), which is a classification of the elements in folktales, legends, fables, and other folkloric narratives. Tale types and numbers refer to Antii Aarne and Stith Thomson's *The Types of the Folk-Tale* (FF Communications No. 74, Helskini, 1928).

INTRODUCTION

1. William Wells Newell, "On the Field and Work of a Journal of American Folk-Lore," *Journal of American Folklore,* 1 (1883): 3.
2. Between 1883 and 1911 Krauss edited a series of yearbooks titled *Kryptadia* that has been called "the pioneer work in the study of erotic folklore" (Frank Hoffmann, *Analytical Survey of Anglo-American Traditional Erotica*, Bowling Green, Ohio:Bowling Green University Popular Press, 1973, p. 26) and from 1904–1929 he edited a more broad ranging set of yearbooks dealing with the same subject titled *Anthropophyteia.*
3. Friederich S. Krauss, "Jewish Folk-Life in America," *Journal of American Folklore,* 7 (1894): 73.
4. Raphael Patai, *On Jewish Folklore* (Detroit: Wayne State University Press, 1983), p. 36. Although published in 1983 this article titled "Jewish Folklore and Jewish Tradition" was originally published in a 1960 volume titled *Studies in Biblical and Jewish Folklore.*
5. Leah C. Yoffie, "Yiddish Folk Stories and Songs in St. Louis," *Washington University Record,* 5 (1920): 20–22.
6. Leah Yoffie, "Present-Day Survivals of Ancient Jewish Customs," *Journal of American Folklore,* 29 (1916): 412–17.
7. This article appeared in the 1946 issue of the *Journal of American Folklore* and is reprinted in Patai, *On Jewish Folklore,* pp. 17–34.
8. Jacob Richman, *Laughs From Jewish Lore* (New York: Hebrew Publishing Company, 1954; reissue of a book originally published in 1926), xxiv.
9. Ibid., xii.
10. Ibid., xxiv. See, for example, the stories given of pp. 72 and 88.
11. *Ibid.* See, for example, the stories given on pp. 72 and 88.
12. Richard M. Dorson, "Jewish-American Dialect Stories on Tape" in Raphael Patai, Francis Lee Utley, and Dov Noy, eds., *Studies in Biblical and Jewish Folklore* (Bloomington: Indiana University Press, 1960), pp. 111–74.
13. Nathan Ausubel certainly deliberately excluded such materials from his *A Treasury of Jewish Folklore* (New York: Crown Publishers, 1948) because he says, p. 265, "A large body of so-called 'Jewish dialect stories' are not Jewish at all, but the confections of anti-Semites who delight in ridiculing and slandering the Jews."
14. Richard M. Dorson, "More Jewish Dialect Stories," *Midwest Folklore,* 10 (1960): 133–46.
15. Naomi and Eli Katz, "Tradition and Adaptation in American Jewish Humor," *Journal of American Folklore,* 84 (1971): 215–20.
16. Ibid., 219.
17. Ed Cray, "The Rabbi Trickster," *Journal of American Folklore,* 77 (1964): 331–45.
18. Ibid., 343.

19. Alan Dundes, "The J.A.P. and the J.A.M. in American Jokelore," *Journal of American Folklore,* 98 (1985): 456–75.
20. *Ibid.,* 456.
21. Heda Jason, "The Jewish Joke: The Problem of Definition," *Southern Folklore Quarterly,* 31 (1967): 48–54.
22. Dan Ben-Amos, "The 'Myth' of Jewish Humor," *Western Folklore,* 32 (1973): 112–31.
23. Elliott Oring, "The People of the Joke: On the Conceptualization of a Jewish Humor," *Western Folklore,* 42 (1983): 261–71.
24. Ibid., 268.
25. Joseph Boskin, "Beyond *Kvetching* and Jiving: The Thrust of Jewish and Black Folkhumor" in Sarah Blacher Cohen, *Jewish Wry: Essays on Jewish Humor* (Bloomington: Indiana University Press, 1987), pp. 59–60.
26. Ibid., 71.
27. Henry Eilbirt, *What Is a Jewish Joke?: An Excursion into Jewish Humor* (Northvale, N.J.: Jason Aronson, Inc., 1991), p. 127.

PART ONE: LIFE CYCLES

Chapter One: Life and Celebrations

1. Psalms, 66:1.
2. An interesting but almost certainly coincidental parallel can be found in pagan Celtic holidays, which also ran from sundown to sundown.
3. For more about Rosh Hashanah, see Philip Goodman, ed., *Rosh Hashanah Anthology* (Philadelphia: Jewish Publications Society, 1970).
4. For more about Yom Kippur, see Philip Goodman, ed., *Yom Kippur Anthology* (Philadelphia: Jewish Publications Society, 1971).
5. The idea of petitioning heaven with objects symbolic of the petitioner's desire is very old indeed and common throughout the world. The concept of "like calls to like" idea is also the motivating force behind what anthropologists know as "sympathetic magic," in which the rites of a would-be rainmaker might include the sprinkling of a few drops of water on the ground.
6. B.C.E. (before the common era) and C.E. (common era) are often used by Jews in place of B.C. (before Christ) and A.D. (anno Domini).
7. An electric menorah, its bulbs lit one by one, sundown by sundown, often takes the place of candles in Jewish-American homes; although it may offend purists, an electric menorah is considered just as holy.
8. For more about Hannukah, see Theodor H. Gaster, *Purim and Hanukkah in Custom and Tradition* (Boston: Beacon Press, 1950). See also

Philip Goodman, ed., *Hanukkah Anthology* (Philadelphia: Jewish Publications Society, 1976).

9. For more about Purim, see Gaster, *Purim and Hanukkah.* See also Philip Goodman, ed., *Purim Anthology* (Philadelphia: Jewish Publications Society, 1949).
10. The seder's use of red wine has, alas, been the basis for anti-Semitic horror stories claiming the wine is really the blood of murdered Christian children. These stories were particularly virulent during the Middle Ages; in 1256, for example, the Jews of Lincoln, England, were believed to have ritually murdered a little boy, and examples of anti-Semitic ballads from that era are sadly not uncommon. See, for instance, "The Jew's Daughter," in Thomas Percy's *Reliques of Ancient English Poetry* (London: George Routledge and Sons, n.d.)
11. See Theodor H. Gaster, *Passover: Its History and Traditions* (Boston: Beacon Press, 1962). Cumulative, or counting, songs are common throughout the world. Other songs of this sort, familiar to most English speakers, are "I'll Sing You One—Oh" and "Old MacDonald Had a Farm."
12. For more about Shavuoth, see Philip Goodman, ed., *Shavuot Anthology* (Philadelphia: Jewish Publication Society, 1975).
13. Other peoples include a holy day of rest in their weekly rounds as well. In some West African tribes, such as the Ga and the Ibo, the first day of each new week is taken as a day of rest. The same is true of the Lolo people of China. See Theodor H. Gaster, *Festivals of the Jewish Year* (New York: William Morrow, 1952.)
14. Exodus 16:23.
15. Ezekiel 20:12.
16. Abraham Joshua Heschel, *The Sabbath: Its Meaning for Modern Man* (New York: Farrar, Straus & Giroux, 1951), p. 10.
17. Almost every culture marks these dualities in some way, a familiar example being the oriental yang and yin.
18. Note the English saying, "Bread is the staff of life."
19. For more about Sabbath observation and its meaning, see Heschel, *The Sabbath.*
20. Deuteronomy 6:4, 6:4–9.
21. Alfred J. Kolatch, *The Jewish Book of Why* (Middle Village, NY: Jonathan David Publishers, 1981), pp. 113–19.
22. For more about modern customs surrounding mezuzot, see Anita Dimant and Howard Cooper, *Living a Jewish Life* (New York: HarperPerennial, 1991), pp. 28–32. For details about a modern hanukkat habiyat, or housewarming, party, see Mae Shafter Rockland, *The Jewish Party Book* (New York: Schocken Books, 1978), pp.69–79.
23. For an introduction to the writings of Maimonides, see Isador Twersky, ed., *A Maimonides Reader* (New York: Berhman House, 1972).

24. The Jewish cleanliness in food and home was, ironically, nearly the Jews' downfall during such Medieval plagues as the Black Death. To a large extent, the Jews remained healthy during plagues, in part, because rats were not tolerated in Jewish homes. But hysterical Christian neighbors decided that the plague was the result of Jewish sorcery, and did their best to eliminate the "sorcerers." The sudden influx of Jews into fourteenth century Russia was the result of Bohemian Jews fleeing for their lives, not from plague but from angry, witchhunting Christians.
25. Calf or kid seethed in its mother's milk was a dish with religious and ethnic significance for the Canaanites; the earliest reference to the ritual surrounding it can be found on line 14 of the "Poem of the Gracious Gods," a first millennium B.C.E. clay tablet text discovered at Ras Shamra in Syria. Because the Canaanites were both pagan and the enemies of the early Israelites, this custom may have been the cause first for the ban on Jews serving such a dish and then for mixing meat and dairy products at all. See Theodor H. Gaster, *Thespis* (Boston: Beacon Press, 1950) for a translation and discussion of the Ras Shamra tablet. For a discussion on the political, social, and possible magical implications for the Canaanites, see Menahem Haran, "Seething a Kid in Its Mother's Milk," *Journal of Jewish Studies* 30, No. 1 (Spring, 1979): 23–35.
26. Leviticus 7:26.
27. For details about the *kashering* process, see Ben M. Edidin, *Jewish Customs and Ceremonies* (New York: Hebrew Publishing Company, 1941), chapter 3.
28. For more about keeping a kosher house, see Diamant and Cooper, *Living a Jewish Life.* See also Shonie B. Levi and Sylvia R. Kaplan, *Guide for the Jewish Homemaker* (New York: Schocken Books, 1964).

Chapter Two: Love and Marriage

1. Song of Songs 6:7.
2. Genesis 2:18.
3. For more about the use and status of the *shadhan,* see Kolatch, *Jewish Book of Why,* pp. 28–29. See also Lilly S. Routtenberg and Ruth R. Seldin, *The Jewish Wedding Book* (New York: Schocken Books, 1968), p. 4.
4. Leviticus 18:6ff.
5. Routtenberg and Seldin, *Jewish Wedding Book,* pp. 4–5.
6. The idea of a groom paying compensation to a bride's family is one that has been common throughout the world. Among the Plains tribes of Native Americans, for example, it was customary for a prospective groom to offer as many horses—valuable currency—for his bride as he could afford. See Josepha Sherman, *Indian Tribes of North America* (New York: Portland House, 1990), pp. 55–56.

The reverse idea, that of a bride adding to her worth by bringing a dowry to her wedding, is also one that has been known worldwide; many a medieval European marriage hinged not on the bride herself but on the value of the lands she might inherit as her dowry. Ideas on who actually owned a bride's dowry varied from culture to culture: a Christian medieval woman's dowry belonged legally to her husband, but a pagan Celtic woman's dowry belonged only to her, even after marriage. See Patrick C. Power, *Sex and Marriage in Ancient Ireland* (Dublin: Mercier Press Limited, 1976), chapter 2.

7. For a description of a modern-day Jewish engagement celebration, see Anita Diamant, *The New Jewish Wedding* (New York: Summit Books, 1985), pp. 137–43.
8. For more on favorable and forbidden times for Jewish weddings, see Edidin, *Jewish Customs and Ceremonies*, pp. 66–67.
9. Diamant, *New Jewish Wedding,* p. 53.
10. For a more detailed look at the time before a modern Jewish-American wedding, see Diamant, *New Jewish Wedding,* "Before the Wedding."
11. Most Americans are familiar with the superstition that it is unlucky for the groom to see the bride right before the wedding, particularly for him to see her in her wedding gown before the wedding.
12. Routtenberg and Seldin, *Jewish Wedding Book,* pp. 81–82. See also Levi and Kaplan, *Guide for the Jewish Homemaker,* p. 50.
13. For those interested in the *ketubah* as a work of art, there are elegant examples in the collections of The Jewish Museum in New York City and the Museum of the Hebrew Union College, Jewish Institute of Cincinnati.
14. For a look at Jewish-American wedding ceremonies in more detail, see Routtenberg and Seldin, *Jewish Wedding Book,* chapter 5.

Chapter Three: Birth and Childhood

1. Oral tradition. See Leo Rosten, *Leo Rosten's Treasury of Jewish Quotations* (New York: McGraw-Hill, 1972).
2. However, a couple unable for physical or emotional reasons to have children are placed under no religious or moral handicap. See *Gates of Mitzvah: A Guide to the Jewish Life Cycle* (New York: Central Conference of American Rabbis, 1979).
3. See *Midrash Rabbah* (London: The Soncino Press, 1961).
4. For a more complete description of the *mikvah,* see Kolatch, *Jewish Book of Why,* pp. 123, 144–45.
5. For a detailed analysis of the many superstitions surrounding pregnancy among Near Eastern Jews, see Raphael Patai, *On Jewish Folklore* (Detroit: Wayne State University Press, 1983), chapter 21.
6. Exodus 15:16.

7. Again, for a study of Jewish birth superstitions, see Patai, *On Jewish Folklore,* chapter 21.
8. The author has seen most of these superstitions and admits to having knocked on wood a few times herself! Not one of the women questioned knew why they had tied a red ribbon to their baby carriages, other than commenting, "It's what my mother always did," adding the quintessentially Jewish, "It couldn't hurt." This tradition reaches partially around the Mediterranean: A non-Jewish Italian-American acquaintance remembered seeing her mother tying a red ribbon onto her baby carriage. Red ribbons can also be seen warding off the evil eye in such twentieth century communities as Bensonhurst, Queens, where cars may sport those protective ribbons on their dashboards; it may or may not be coincidence that members of Mothers Against Drunk Driving hang red ribbons in their cars!

   Red is a color frequently associated with the chasing away of evil. For example, an old English charm for keeping away witches consists of a rowan twig bound round with red thread. For more on the subject of Jewish birth superstitions, see Anita Diamant, *The Jewish Baby Book* (New York: Summit Books, 1988), pp. 209–10.
9. Ibid., p. 188.
10. Ibid., part 4.
11. For more on the *Shalom Zachar* and *Shalom Nekavah,* see ibid., pp. 205–7.
12. See Kolatch, *Jewish Book of Why,* pp. 22–23.
13. Genesis 17:12.

    The Jews are not the only people to practice circumcision. Many Native Americans, Africans, and Australians included circumcision in their puberty rites, and Islamic boys are circumcised upon coming of age at thirteen. In addition, some non-Jewish American babies have been circumcised for health reasons. For more on the subject of circumcision as part of a rite of passage, see Arnold Van Gennep, *The Rites of Passage* (Chicago: The University of Chicago Press, 1960).

    Although the high infant mortality rate in antiquity imposed a waiting period to see if the new baby would survive, and is probably the reason for the seven-day wait before the *brit milah,* folk belief blamed the delay on Lilith, the first wife of Adam, who was cast out for refusing to submit to her husband's will and who became a life-hating demon. She might kill any baby who had been brought to her attention by having been named before the sacred seven days were completed. Lilith (who has become something of a folk heroine for Jewish feminists for her refusal to submit to male domination) was also a succubus, stealing both the sexual vigor and sometimes the life from young men, and almost certainly has her origin in the Babylonian demon, Lilitu, usually portrayed as a winged, taloned woman.

14. Kolatch, *Jewish Book of Why,* p. 17. The belief that sharp implements, specifically those made of iron, chase away evil spirits or witches has been shared by many cultures; it was particularly common in pre-nineteenth century Great Britain, where a knife might be placed under a baby's cradle to scare off baby-stealing fairies. See, for example, the various protective charms listed in Walter Yeeling Evans-Wentz, *The Fairy Faith in Celtic Countries* (reprint edition, University Books, 1966).
15. Diamant and Cooper, *Living a Jewish Life,* pp. 246–47.
16. Ibid., pp. 247–50.
17. The inviting of fairies to christening ceremonies is a not-uncommon European folk motif, best known, perhaps, in the very wide-spread tale of "Sleeping Beauty."
18. For more about Lilith, see note 10. For more about pre-brit superstitions, see Diamant, *Jewish Baby Book,* pp. 206–7. Almost every culture has some variation on the magic circle, the symbol of the whole, with neither beginning nor end, which is drawn either to hold in some evil force or to keep evil out.
19. For a crosscultural examination of rites of passage, see Van Gennap, *Rites of Passage.*
20. For a concise look at the prehistory and history of the Bar Mitzvah, see Jane Lewit and Ellen Robinson Epstein, *The Bar/Bat Mitzvah Planbook* (Briarcliff Manor, NY: Stein and Day, 1982), chapter 1.
21. Edidin, *Jewish Customs and Ceremonies,* pp. 57–58.
22. For a look into the elaborate preparations behind a modern Bar Mitzvah ceremony, see Hattie Eisenberg, *Bar Mitzvah with Ease* (Garden City, NY: Doubleday and Company, 1966). See also Lewit and Epstein, *Bar/Bat Mitzvah Planbook.*
23. For more on the origin of the Bat Mitzvah, see Lewit and Epstein, *Bar/Bat Mitzvah Planbook,* p. 7.
24. Diamant and Cooper, *Living a Jewish Life,* pp. 254–55.

Chapter Four: Death and Mourning

1. Isaiah 40:1.
2. The autopsy is still a subject of much controversy in Israel. For more on the subject of Jewish autopsies, see Kolatch, *Jewish Book of Why.*
3. See Maurice Lamm, *The Jewish Way in Death and Mourning* (New York: Jonathan David Publisher, 1969), pp. 26–27.
4. For example, an American bride, of course, traditionally dresses in virginal white.
5. The practice of covering mirrors or turning them face to the wall in the house of the deceased is an ancient one, widespread throughout the

world—wherever mirrors are known—and very common. Superstition has it that the soul is reflected in a mirror. Therefore, the soul of the deceased could conceivably be trapped on leaving the body if reflective surfaces were not covered. For some examples of this and other beliefs about the magical powers of mirrors, see James George Frazier, *The Golden Bough* (one volume abridged edition, New York: Macmillan Company, 1960), chapter 18.

6. Deuteronomy 21:23.
7. See the story of Joseph in Genesis; Genesis 50:26 in particular.
8. Genesis 3:19.
9. There was once a very practical—if distasteful to our "nice" modern sensibilities—reason for those floral arrangements: in cultures where it was common to keep a corpse on view for a time, in the days before refrigeration, flowers and spices were used to sweeten the air! Jewish burials, taking place almost immediately, did not need those masking scents.
10. In some cultures, there are similar pauses to give the deceased a chance to say farewell to life. The author once saw a funeral procession drive through the streets of Tblisi, Georgia, with the deceased riding in the place of honor in an open car, in an open coffin, so he could say goodby to his old neighborhood—and not try to return.
11. For more on the subject of pausing to and from the cemetery, see Kolatch, *Jewish Book of Why,* pp. 61–62.
12. Mutilation of clothing or bodies is a way of expressing grief common to folk the world over. Some Central Australian people used to gash themselves over the gravesite; among some Native American peoples, such as the Lakota Sioux, it was customary for members of the immediate family to either gash themselves or sacrifice a finger joint. The ancient Egyptians settled for a rending of clothing similar to that of the Jews. The practical Egyptians often hired professional mourners to take the strain off the family; there was even a mourner's guild, and apprentice mourners can be seen in some wall reliefs. For more on sacrificial rites of mourning and rebirth, see James George Frazier, *The New Golden Bough,* edited by Theodor H. Gaster (New York: Criterion Press, 1959), parts 3 and 4.
13. The egg and the never-ending circle have been signs of eternal life for many cultures, from pagan Roman and Saxon to modern Christian Easter symbolism.
14. For more about sitting *shivah,* see Lamm, *Death and Mourning.*
15. For details on modern Jewish memorial observances, see Levi and Kaplan, *Guide for the Jewish Homemaker,* chapter 4.
16. Edidin, *Jewish Customs and Ceremonies,* chapter 7.

PART TWO: FOLKLORE

Chapter Five: Wonder Tales

1. Known to the author, source unknown. See also Moses Gaster, *The Exempla of the Rabbis: Being a Collection of Exempla, Apologues and Tales Culled from Hebrew Manuscripts and Rare Hebrew Books* (London: Asia Publishing Society, 1924). This tale was also the inspiration behind the operetta "Shulamis," by Abraham Goldfaden, and versions of the story of an unfaithful lover turned faithful once more are to be found throughout the world. Compare, for example, Tale 186, "The True Bride," in *The Complete Fairy Tales of the Brothers Grimm,* translated by Jack Zipes (New York: Bantam Books, 1967), pp. 583–88, in which the forsaken young woman follows her lover to his home with the aid of a magical calf and successfully reminds him of their vows.

   Motifs include C920.1. "Death of children for breaking tabu"; D2003. "Forgotten fiancee"; H1385.5. "Quest for vanished lover" and the closely related H.1385.4 "Quest for vanished husband"; K2094. "Love falsely pledged"; Q252. "Punishment for breaking betrothal"; and R141. "Rescue from well." The tale type is 425, The Search for the Lost Husband.
2. Collected by Leo Wiener from an anonymous Rumanian informant in the late nineteenth century, no specific date or site included. See Beatrice Silverman Weinreich, *Yiddish Folktales,* (New York: Pantheon, 1988), pp. 73–76. This is a Yiddish version of a very old tale type, The Magician and His Pupil, the details of which remain surprisingly constant from culture to culture. A father apprentices his son to a magician, and may have his son back at the end of a specified time (in this story a ritual three years) if he can recognize him. The boy transforms himself into a saleable animal, frequently a horse, to help his father, with the caveat that the father retain the bridle lest the boy be an animal forever. Despite this warning, the father gives up the bridle, and the boy is the sorcerer's prisoner till he succeeds in freeing himself from the bridle, then conquers the magician in a shape-shifting contest, which usually involves the boy transforming himself into a ring and being temporarily rescued by a princess. He then turns himself into seeds or grain to trick the magician into becoming a vulnerable bird; the boy then becomes a predator, a fox or in this case, a polecat, to kill the bird. The oldest forms of this tale come from India and date to at least the first millennium B.C.E., though it is known throughout Europe and Asia—over thirty-six variants appear in Turkey alone—and has travelled with Jewish, French, Spanish, African, and other ethnic groups into the New World as well.

   One element that helps give this particular version its essential "Jewishness" is the appearance of the helpful old man in the father's dream; this archetypical "Wise Old Man" figure is almost certainly the Prophet

Elijah, who is one of the most popular Jewish folk heroes and who often gives folktale characters aid through the medium of dreams. For more about Elijah, see Louis Ginzberg, *The Legends of the Jews* (Philadelphia: Jewish Publications Society, 1909–46), vol. 7, pp. 133–35.

For a more detailed discussion of the tale and its migration, see Stith Thompson, *The Folktale* (Berkeley and Los Angeles: University of California Press, 1977), pp. 69–70.

Motifs include C837. "Tabu: losing bridle"; D610. "Repeated transformation"; D612. "Protean sale"; D615. "Transformation contest between magicians"; D630. "Transformation at will"; D671. "Transfomation flight"; D1711.01. "Magician's apprentice"; H161. "Recognition of transformed person among identical companions"; and L142.2 "Pupil surpasses magician." The tale type is 395, The Magician and His Pupil.

3. Recorded in Israel by M. Ohel from Menahem Mevorakh, originally of Tripoli, Libya, date unknown. See Dov Noy, *Folktales of Israel* (Chicago: University of Chicago Press, 1963), pp. 150–52. Compare with note 2. This Sephardic tale is not as "perfect" an example of The Magician and His Pupil as the above version—it lacks the formal contract between sorcerer and parent, the recognition by the parent of the transformed son, and eliminates the capture of the boy by the sorcerer completely—but it adds intriguing elements as well. The human sorcerer here is replaced by a devil (an amoral creature not to be confused with the Christian Devil), and the story includes the "forbidden chamber" theme used in such European folktales as the German "Bluebeard."

   Motifs include C611. "Forbidden chamber"; D610. "Repeated transformation"; D615. "Transformation contest between magicians"; D630. "Transformation at will"; D671. "Transformation flight"; D1711.01. "Magician's apprentice"; and L142.2 "Pupil surpasses magician." The tale type is 395, The Magician and His Pupil.

4. Known to the author, source unknown. This Yiddish folktale is of a remarkably widespread story type, with variations collected from throughout Europe and Asia, though in many non-Jewish versions the demons are replaced by various types of fairy folk. See, for example, the Irish "Legend of Knockgrafton" in Joseph Jacob, *More Celtic Tales* (New York: Dover Publications, 1968), pp. 156–63, which even includes the tune the fairies were singing! See also the Japanese "How the Old Man Lost His Wen" in *Japanese Fairy Tales,* compiled by Yei Theodora Ozaki (New York: A.L. Burt Company, n.d.), pp. 282–92.

   Demons are not necessarily out-and-out creatures of evil in Jewish folklore. Though some are definitely creatures of darkness, others are described variously as mischievous, amoral spirits—possibly related to pagan nature spirits—living souls without bodies, or even as members of a totally different species that had inhabited the earth prior to the creation of humanity.

Motifs include F261. "Fairies dance"; F344.1. "Fairies remove hunchback's hump"; F953.1. "Hunchback cured by fairies"; K611.4. "Man in devils' power makes them believe he will return and is permitted to leave"; and N471. "Foolish attempt of second man to overhear secrets." The tale type is 503, The Gifts of the Little People.

5. Collected from an anonymous informant from Lodz, Poland, date and name of collector unknown. See Weinreich, *Yiddish Folktales,* pp. 359–60. For a discussion of Hoshana Rabba, the willow twigs, and Succoth in general, see chapter 1 of the present volume; see also chapter 1, note 6.

   This story falls into the category of "Changeling Tale," a familiar folkloric type more often found in Western Europe. See Katherine Briggs, *A Dictionary of British Folk-Tales* (Bloomington: Indiana University Press, 1971), vol. 1, part B, for a comparative collection of these tales. The substitution of a magicked bunch of straw or block of wood for a living baby to trick its parents is a standard element in such tales, just as the touch of holiness repels evil creatures. In this Jewish tale, though, the baby-stealing fairies of standard Celtic lore, who have no place in Jewish folklore, have been replaced by a demon.

   Motifs include F321.1 "Changeling"; F321.1.4. "Disposing of a changeling"; and R10.3. "Children abducted."

6. Collected from an anonymous informant from Lodz, Poland, date and collector unknown. See Weinreich, *Yiddish Folktales,* p. 348. The mischievous little demon in this Yiddish tale makes up in playfulness what it lacks in malice, and as a prankster, has its parallels in such equally mischievous, amoral nature spirits as the British Hedley Kow and Puck, who often took the form of animals to trick human farmers or travellers. See Briggs, *Dictionary of British Folk-Tales,* vol. 1, part B, for examples of both.

   An applicable motif is 6303.3.3.1. "Devil in form of domestic beast."

7. First heard by the author, source, unfortunately, unrecalled, in New York in the 1970s. See Noy, *Folktales of Israel,* pp. 31–32, for a version collected in Israel in the 1950s by Uri Baranu from Avigdor Hadjadj, a Libyan Jew, and for a brief discussion of the tale's worldwide dissemination. This folktale type is extremely popular with Jews and non-Jews alike. One hundred and sixteen related versions have been collected in Ireland alone, and even more have been found in Eastern Europe and Central Asia. Two versions collected in Michigan in 1954 from non-Jews (names of collector and informants unrecorded) replace the horse with a picture of a horse, which falls on the man trying to cheat death. In a medieval Russian tale, a prince who has been warned that his favorite horse will kill him has the horse slain—only to be fatally bitten, years later, by a snake living in the horse's skull.

   The horse, whether alive or reduced to only a skull, is a focal point of great and incredibly varied power in world folklore, representing everything from life or death to the justification of a king or regime's rule. See

M. Oldfield Howey, *The Horse in Magic and Myth* (New York: Castle Books, 1958).

Motifs include M341.2.5. "Prophesy: death by horse's head"; M370. "Vain attempts to escape fulfillment of prophesy"; and M370.1. "Prophesy of death fulfilled." The tale types are 934, The Prince and the Storm, and 934A, Predestined Death.

8. Collected by Elisheva Schoenfeld in Affula, Israel, in 1955, from Obadia Pervi, a Yemenite Jew. See Noy, *Folktales of Israel,* pp. 22–24. One of the cruelest anti-Semitic slurs has always been the blood libel, the rumor that the Jews murder gentile children (see chapter 1, note 10). This Sephardic tale is one version of a widespread legend in which Jews are miraculously defended from false accusations of murder. As in "The Sorcerer's Apprentice" (see this chapter, note 2), the Prophet Elijah appears in a dream as a protector and savior. In a similar Yiddish tale from Eastern Europe, the story is set in Jerusalem, the murdered boy is the son of the governor, and his corpse is temporarily returned to life by Rabbi Kalonymos, who places on the boy's forehead a paper on which is written the secret Name of God. See Angelo Rappoport, *The Folklore of the Jews* (London: Soncino Press, 1937), pp. 136–38. The idea of the dead being raised to catch murderers runs through Old World folklore, though usually the life of only one man, the falsely accused, is at stake. In an Italian folktale known to the author, for instance, an innkeeper is accused of murdering one of his guests and is about to be hung when St. Oniria appears and commands the corpse to name his murderer. The corpse announces that his traveling companion was the killer, and the innkeeper is freed.

   Motifs include D1817.0.3. "Magic detection of murder"; E234.3. "Return from dead to avenge death (murder)"; K2116. "Innocent person accused of murder"; K2110. "Slanders"; Q211.4. "Murder of child punished"; and V229.1. "Saint commands return from dead with supernatural information."

9. Known to the author, informant unknown. The motif of a man accidentally marrying a demon, in particular a man who finds he has wed a demon on whose finger he unwittingly placed a ring, is a fairly common one in late medieval Sephardic and Ashkenazi Jewish folklore traditions, turning up in both Yiddish and Palestinian tales of the sixteenth century, although there are older variants in European folklore that may have been transmitted to the Holy Land by the Jews. One variant even turns up in the biography of the cabbalist Rabbi Isaac Luria (1534–72). See Micha Joseph Bin Gorion, *Mimekor Yisrael* (Bloomington and Indianapolis: Indiana University Press, 1990), pp. 194–95. See also Pinhas Sadeh, *Jewish Folktales* (New York: Anchor Books, 1989), pp. 241–42. Another Yiddish version of this story, taken from a sixteenth century manuscript in Trinity College, Cambridge, tells of a boy climbing a tree who sees what looks like a finger-shaped branch. He puts his ring on it, pretending to recite

the wedding vows, and only when he has grown up does he learn he actually did marry a demon. She kills each human woman he marries, until his last wife strikes a bargain with the demon: they will share their husband. See Howard Schwartz, "Jewish Tales of the Supernatural," *Judaism,* 36, No. 3 (Summer, 1987): 339–51.

An applicable motif is F402.2.3. "Child of demon king marries mortal." The tale type is 421*, The Youth Wed to a She-Devil.

10. Original informant and date unknown; this folktale has been circulating in anonymously printed handbills and penny booklets throughout Europe since the last century. Novelist Meyer Levin came across some of these booklets in Paris in 1929 and later included them in his *Classic Hassidic Tales* (New York: Dorset Press, 1985), pp. 93–100. See also Nathan Ausubel, *A Treasury of Jewish Folklore* (New York: Crown Publishers, 1949), pp. 182–86. Rabbi Israel Baal Shem (1700–1760) is the legendary founder of the Hassidic movement of Judaism, and as the Baal Shem Tov, has become the focal point for a cycle of much older folktales that involve him in adventures against werewolves, sorcerers, and other fantastic beings.

This Yiddish wonder tale has definite links to similar European types in which a father, to escape a perilous otherworldly being, often a water-spirit, promises to give the spirit the first thing he meets—which, of course, turns out to be his child. In the European versions, all the attempts to protect that child turn out to be in vain, with the emphasis of the story then switching to the child's adventures with and escaping from the otherworldly captor. How this tale differs from the non-Jewish versions is in its emphasis on ethics—if the rabbi had been pure-hearted and not morally polluted the lake, there never would have been a problem—and its matter-of-fact logic in merely keeping the boy safely locked up till the dire thirteenth birthday is done. That it should be the thirteenth birthday can hardly be an accident, since that is the day on which a Jewish boy legally becomes a man.

Motifs include A1003. "Calamity as punishment for sin"; M341.2. "Prophesy: death before a certain age"; and M391.1. "Fulfillment of prophesy successfully avoided." The tale type is 934D, Outwitting Fate.

11. Collected by Khaim Lunyevski from Tsvi Moyshe (no surname recorded), originally of Podlbrodz, Poland, no date recorded. See Weinreich, *Yiddish Folktales,* pp. 79–83. This is a true fairy tale, of a type that should be familiar to practically everyone, with more parallels to world folklore than can be enumerated here. Certain necessary folkloric elements are missing from this tale, though: the beautiful girl, unlike her counterparts in similar world tales, does nothing to earn the water-spirits' gifts, and neither the wicked stepmother nor the sorceress are punished.

The magical reward of the "good" daughter and punishment of the "evil" one runs through European folklore. It should be noted that unlike the dark spirit of the previous tale (see note 10) these are potentially friendly water-spirits, akin to the three magical beings in the British tale, "The Three Heads at the Well." For the complete story, which parallels the Yiddish tale relatively closely up to the marriage of prince and princess, see Joseph Jacobs, *English Fairy Tales* (New York: Dover Publications, 1967; reprinted from G.P. Putnam's Sons and David Nutt, 1898), pp. 222–27. See also Jacobs' notes regarding the tale type's distribution, p. 261.

A common theme in folktales is the false accusation of the heroine—often a commoner raised to royalty by marrying a prince—of the murder of her child, and of her restoration through magical aid. See, for example, *Tales of the Brothers Grimm,* trans. Zipes, "The Maiden Without Hands," pp. 118–23, in which supernatural forces in the form of a devil and an angel vie for the souls of the heroine and her prince.

Motifs include D 1500.1.18. "Magical healing water"; D1860. "Magic beautification"; D1870. "Magic hideousness"; D2161.3.1. "Blindness magically cured"; E323. "Dead mother's friendly return"; E323.6 "Mother returns to encourage daughter in great difficulties"; K2116. "Innocent person accused of murder"; L55. "Stepdaughter heroine"; L162. "Lowly heroine marries prince (king)"; Q2. "Kind and unkind"; S31. "Cruel stepmother"; and S165. "Mutilation: putting out eyes." The tale types are 480, The Spinning-Women by the Spring, the Kind and Unkind Girls, and 706, The Maiden Without Hands.

12. Collected from an anonymous Tunisian Jew, date known. See Sadeh, *Jewish Folktales,* pp. 98–101. There are parallels to be found to this Sephardic tale throughout North Africa—in particular, the heroine, like Morgiana in "Ali Baba and the Forty Thieves," kills forty men—although this is not a particularly widespread folktale. Guardian lions do, however, turn up in European folklore, even in countries in which lions are hardly native, from Britain to Russia, showing how widely a specific folk theme can travel.

    Motifs include K1810. "Deception by disguise"; K1916. "Robber bridegroom"; P14.22. "Lions as king's pets"; and S62. "Cruel husband." The tale type is 956B, The Clever Maiden Alone at Home Kills the Robbers.

13. Collected by folklorist Yehude-Leyb Cahan, date unknown, from Khave Rubin from Smargon, Poland. See Weinreich, *Yiddish Folktales,* pp. 85–88. See also her notes, p. 384, in which she notes that this tale and its other Yiddish versions were traditionally told by women. This is, very obviously, a variation on the Cinderella theme, one of the most popular types of folktales in the world; over nine hundred versions of Cinderella have been collected throughout every corner of the world, with the earliest variants—so far—dating from first millennium B.C.E. China and Egypt. For further reading on the story and its distribution, see Alan Dundes, *Cinderella: A Casebook* (Madison: University of Wisconsin Press, 1982).

    The theme of "Love Like Salt," in which a daughter is cast out of her father's house for what seems at the time a trivial answer, is also a very common one, occurring in Cinderella variants such as the British Cap O'Rushes (see Jacobs, *English Fairy Tales,* pp.51–56 and notes, pp. 237–38) and even in Shakespeare's folklore-inspired *King Lear*.

For all the similarities in this Yiddish tale to the usual Cinderella type, there are details that are specifically Jewish. The most noticeable, of course, is the replacement of a fairy godmother by the Prophet Elijah. The prince or nobleman whom the heroine marries here becomes a rabbi's son, and prophetic dreams help his parents accept the marriage to which they would otherwise object.

Motifs include D1050.1. "Clothes produced by magic"; D1254. "Magic stick"; D1718.1. "Magic powers in stick"; H36.1. "Slipper test"; H151.6. "Heroine in menial disguise discovered in her beautiful clothes; recognition follows"; H.592.1. "Love like salt"; J1146.1 "Detection by pitch-trap"; N711.6. "Prince sees heroine at ball and is enamored"; and V238. "Guardian angel." The tale type is 510, Cinderella and Cap O'Rushes.

14. This Yiddish folktale, first collected by folklorist Yehude-Leyb Cahan from an anonymous Eastern European Jew in 1931, has almost exact parallels in Sephardic Jewish folklore as well. For a Yiddish variant, see Pininnah Schram, *Jewish Stories One Generation Tells Another* (Northvale, NJ: Jason Aronson, 1989), pp. 162–68. The old man in this story is, of course, the Prophet Elijah, who in some versions oversees the snake boy's religious education. *Rosh Hodesh* is the Jewish celebration of the new month; for more about this and other celebrations of Judaism, see chapter 1.

Several elements in this story are common to folktales the world over. The breaking of a magical prohibition and its consequences is one of the most common, ranging from the refusal to allow a beggar the place of honor, as in this story, to the disobedient opening of a forbidden door, as in "Snow White" or "Bluebeard." Childless couples who will welcome even a child born in animal form abound in world folklore. See, for instance, "Hans My Hedgehog" in *Tales of the Brothers Grimm,* trans. Zipes, pp. 393–97, in which the father's foolish words—he wants a son, even if that son is born an animal—result in a hedgehog son who, as is the norm for this tale type, goes on to win human shape and a princess-wife. The "Beauty and the Beast" theme, in which the hero is trapped by a spell into a terrifying animal shape—often a giant snake or a bear, sometimes an outright monster—that can only be removed by a youngest daughter's love or determination, is equally common. See, for example, "The Story of Five Heads" in George McCall Theal, *Kaffir Folk-Lore* (Westport, CT: Negro Universities Press, 1970), pp. 48–55, in which the heroine must obey a long list of magical prohibitions before she can wed the monstrous five-headed snake and turn him back into his rightful human form.

Motifs include B646.1 "Marriage to person in snake form"; C758.1. "Monster form because of hasty (inconsiderate) wish of parents"; D191.

"Man transformed to snake"; S215.1. "Girl promises herself to animal suitor"; and T554.7. "Woman bears snake-child." Tale types are 425A, The Monster (Animal) as Bridegroom and 433, The Prince as Serpent.

15. Collected from a Moroccan Jew, names of collector and informant and date of collection unknown. See Schram, *Jewish Stories* pp. 352–57. Almost identical versions of this Sephardic folktale have been collected at various times ranging from the last century up to the 1950s from Jews from Iraq, Turkey, Palestine, and Central Asia. This tale is one of a type known as "The Fairy Midwife," and very similar variants, almost always substituting the fairy folk for demons, can be found throughout Great Britain and across Europe. See, for instance, "The Fairy Midwife" in *Folktales of England,* edited by Katherine M. Briggs and Ruth L. Tongue (Chicago: University of Chicago Press, 1959), pp. 38–39, for a version collected in Somerset. In most stories of this type, the human protagonist is warned against tasting the Otherworldly food or taking Otherworldly treasure, lest she (or, more rarely, he) be forced to remain in that Otherworld forever. For more on the changeling motif, see note 5.

    Motifs include C242. "Tabu: the eating of food of fairies or witch (demon)"; F321.1. "Changeling"; F33. "Fairy grateful to human midwife"; F340. "Gifts from fairies"; F342.1. "Fairy gold"; F372.1 "Fairies take human midwife to attend fairy woman"; and F379.2 "Objects brought home from fairyland." The tale type is 476*, In the Frog's House.

16. Collected by folklorist Yehude-Leyb Cahan from a Russian Jew, Yosl Cutler, date unknown. See Weinreich, *Yiddish Folktales,* pp. 10–11. This tale of a sleeping luck who needs to be awakened is, indeed, as much Slavic as it is Jewish. In fact, a more detailed but very similar version can be found in Aleksander Afanas'ev, *Russian Fairy Tales* (New York: Pantheon Books, 1973), pp. 501–4, in which the peasant does not just beg his luck to awaken but actually threatens him, then goes on to bury Luck's antithesis, Misery.

    A pertinent motif is N113. "Good luck personified."

17. Known to author, source unknown. A Byelorussian Jewish version of this sad little story can be found in Sadeh, *Jewish Folktales,* p. 302, and non-Jewish parallels can be found throughout Europe and Asia. See, for instance, the similar Lincolnshire folktale of "Yallery Brown," a rather demonic luck who attaches himself permanently to the farmer who has the misfortune to uncover him, in Joseph Jacob, *More English Fairy Tales* (New York: Dover Publications, 1967), pp. 26–33.

    Motifs include N112. "Bad luck personified" and N250.2. "Persecution by bad luck." The tale types are 947A, Bad Luck Cannot be Arrested, and 947A*, Bad Luck Refuses to Desert a Man.

18. Collected from a Moroccan Jew, names of collector and informant and date of collection unknown. See Sadeh, *Jewish Folktales,* pp. 285–87. Similar versions have been collected throughout the Near East.

Motifs include C242. "Tabu: the eating of food of fairies or witch (demon)" and N134. "Persons effect change of luck."

19. Collected from S. Gabai, an Iraqi-born Jew, date, place, and name of collector missing. See Noy, *Folktales of Israel,* pp. 20–22. Both Maimonides and Abraham Ibn-Ezra, a poet and scholar, were historical personages and contemporaries, but there is no evidence that they ever met, let alone became friends. And though the rabbi certainly did lead an impoverished life, this tale, with its parallels throughout Eastern Europe and the Near East, can hardly be called anything but apocryphal! See note 10.

    The tale type is 947A, Bad Luck Cannot be Arrested.
20. Collected in Israel in the 1950s by Elisheva Schoenfeld from Mordechai "Marko" Litsi, a Sephardic Jew from Turkey. See Noy, *Folktales of Israel,* pp. 183–84. Though strictly speaking this Sephardic tale of self-pity is not a wonder tale, it does have the final word on the subject of luck.
21. Collected from a Moroccan Jew, names, date and location unknown. See Patai, *Gates to the Old City,* pp. 663–64, who cites a similar version collected in Jerusalem. See also Sadeh, *Jewish Folktales,* pp. 323–24, for a very similar version collected in Afghanistan.

    The theme of the ruler with some shameful, inhuman attribute that must be hidden is a very common one in folklore, with parallel tales to be found throughout the world. The most blatantly obvious parallels are probably the Greek story of King Midas and his donkey's ears and the British tale of King Mark of Cornwall (the King Mark of the "Tristan and Iseult" legend) and his horse's ears. In all cases, it is talking reeds that finally give the ruler's secret away.

    The tale type is 782, Midas and the Ass's Ears.
22. Collected from an Iraqi Jew, names, date, and location unknown. See Patai, *Gates to the Old City,* pp. 664–65. Compare this to the previous tale. One folkloric phenomenon is the attaching of a motif to an historical personage; in this case the very real Alexander the Great, who certainly did not bear horns on his head! Other historical folk, such as King Mark, mentioned in note 21, and Tzar Peter the Great, have also had totally irrelevant folktales attached to their names.

    The tradition of a horned Alexander is also known in Arabic lore; he is called Alexander of the Horns in the Koran.

    The tale type is 782, Midas and the Ass's Ears.

Chapter Six: Ghosts and Dybbuks

1. Collected in Eastern Europe, date, collector, and informant unknown. See Rappoport, *Folklore of the Jews,* pp. 132–36. See also Howard Schwartz,

Miriam's Tambourine: Jewish Folktales from Around the World (Oxford: Oxford University Press, 1986), pp. 264–66, for a retelling of a similar version from Poland. The theme of "The Grateful Dead" who return to aid a rescuer is a common one throughout European folklore. It should also be pointed out that the redeeming of prisoners, even deceased ones, is considered a great act of charity in Judaism.

Motifs include E341.1. "Dead grateful for having corpse ransomed"; Q271.1. "Debtor deprived of burial"; R163. "Rescue by grateful dead man"; and S142. "Person thrown into water and abandoned." The tale type is 506.1, The Grateful Dead Man.

2. Collected in Cracow, Poland, in the twentieth century, collector and informant unknown, this local legend dates to approximately the seventeenth century. See Weinreich, *Yiddish Folktales,* p. 338. Rabbi Moses ben Israel Isserles, who lived in the sixteenth century, was one of the great authorities of Jewish law.

   The world of folklore is full of tales of ghosts who return to haunt those who have broken a promise made while they were alive. The use of dreams that are more than dreams is a particularly Jewish motif. See chapter 5, notes 2 and 8.

   Motifs included are E235.2. "Ghost returns to demand proper burial"; E459.3. "Ghost laid when wishes are acceded to"; and E586. "Dead returns soon after burial."

3. This wry little folktale was first written down in the Talmud, although tales of humans overhearing—and benefiting by what they hear from—supernatural beings are to be found in every culture. The indignant ghosts bewailing the lack of privacy, however, is a specifically Jewish twist. See also Ausubel, *A Treasury of Jewish Folklore,* pp. 616–17.

   Motifs include E401. "Voices of dead heard from graveyard"; and N451.1. "Secrets of animals (demons) overheard from tree (bridge) hiding place."

4. This anonymous Yiddish folktale, which was first written down in about the twelfth or thirteenth century, is cited by Schwartz in "Jewish Tales of the Supernatural," pp. 339–51. The concept of those about to die or very newly dead being seen in visions or dreams as already dead is common to almost every culture's folklore, though usually the vision is seen by a relative or lover.

   Motifs include E283. "Ghosts haunt church"; and E492. "Mass of the dead."

5. Collected from a Jew from Yas (or Jas, or Jassy), Rumania, collector, informant, and date unknown. See Weinreich, *Yiddish Folktales,* p. 348. This Yiddish tale is obviously very similar to the previous medieval Jewish tale, although the element of the vision of the soon-to-die is missing here, and the story has been attached to a real site. A good story lasts!

Motifs include E283. "Ghosts haunt church"; and E493. "Dead men dance."

6. Original source unknown. See Gaster, *Exempla of the Rabbis,* pp. 84, 92–93. This folk legend has been attached to various semi-mythical rabbis in addition to the second century C.E. Rabbi Akiba. It was used during the Middle Ages as a teaching lesson on the value of saying the Kaddish, the mourner's prayer for the dead. It makes use of one of the most universal folk themes, that of the soul that cannot find rest until a ritual obligation is fulfilled.

   Motifs include E754.1.3. "Condemned soul saved by penance"; and F171.6. "Mysterious punishment in otherworld." The tale type is 326A, Soul Released from Torment.
7. S. Daniel Breslauer, "The Ethics of Gilgul," *Judaism,* 32, no. 2 (Spring, 1983). The dybbuk is a more familiar figure in Jewish-American lore, and has even turned up in plays such as S. Anski's Yiddish play, *The Dybbuk.*
8. Collected in America from a Turkish Jew, collector, informant, and date unknown. Other Sephardic versions have been found in Israel as well. Under traditional Jewish law, a woman cannot be declared a widow without proof of her husband's death. For a literary retelling of this folktale, see Judith Ish-Kishor, *Tales from the Wise Men of Israel* (Philadelphia and New York: Lippincott, 1962), pp. 103–11. The transmutation of souls is a feature common to folk culture worldwide.
9. For a "true" version of this Yiddish folktale, collected in Poland (details of collection unknown) and related as though it actually happened to the teller's family, see Weinreich, *Yiddish Folktales,* pp. 331–32. The gilgl tends to be much more reasonable than its demonic counterpart; once the gilgl's demands are met, it is usually willing to depart in peace. The series of the soul's transmutations listed here is reminiscent of those found in Celtic folklore, such as the many transmutations of Taliesin and Amairgen, the mystical Celtic bards. See John Rhys, *Celtic Folklore: Welsh and Manx* (London: Wildwood House, 1980; originally published by Oxford University Press, Oxford, 1901), vol. 2, pp. 614ff.
10. As with note 10, chapter 5, this is one of a series of anonymous folktales distributed through the medium of penny booklets. See Levin, *Classic Hassidic Tales,* pp. 45–57, for a much longer version of this story (described as a "true story"). For comparison, see Weinreich, *Yiddish Folktales,* pp. 342–43, for a version collected by Barbara Kirshen-blatt-gimblett from Ben Schneider of Ludz, Poland, who in turn remembered hearing it in Berlin after World War II.
11. Another anonymous folktale spread via the medium of penny booklets. See Levin, *Classic Hassidic Tales,* pp. 87–91, and Sadeh, *Jewish Folktales,* p. 354, for versions of this Yiddish Hassidic tale.
12. For a brief history of the golem and its many relations, see Ausubel, *Treasury of Jewish Folklore,* pp. 603–5.

13. This tale is, indeed, from the Talmud, *The Babylonian Talmud,* Sanhedrin, 65b. Many a story of wonder-working has been attached to various sages of the era; in fact, some of those sages have been labeled, rather contemptuously, as "magician-scribes" by their contemporaries. For more on this subject, see the introduction to Patai, *Gates to the Old City.*

    An obviously pertinant motif is D1635. "Golem."

14. Known to the author, original source unknown. Solomon ibn Gabirol was a poet and philosopher who did, indeed, live in Valencia in the eleventh century. As often happened with scholarly men of the period, he was suspected of practicing forbidden magics; the most fantastic tale is this one of his robotic maid-servant. See Ausubel, *Treasury of Jewish Folklore,* p. 604, for a summary of this tale and a comparison with other medieval golem tales.

    Motifs include D1620.1.6. "Magic statue of man labors for owner"; and D1635. "Golem."

15. Original source unknown. See Asher Barash, *A Golden Treasury of Jewish Tales* (New York: Dodd, Mead & Company, 1966), translated by Murray Roston, pp. 69–71. This is the same Rabbi Abraham Ibn-Ezra involved in "The Wheel of Fortune" tale in chapter 5 (see note 19, chapter 5). Though the rabbi was, as stated before, a perfectly real person, a cycle of wonder tales have built up about him.

    An applicable motif is D1635. "Golem."

16. Known to the author, original source unknown. See also Ausubel, *Treasury of Jewish Folklore,* p. 604. This version of the golem story, with its hint of power gone out of control, was frequently told in America after the Atomic Age began, as a parable of the potential for nuclear destruction. Interestingly enough, the town of Chelm is also the site for a completely different cycle of folktales, humorous stories totally unrelated to the golem tale (see chapter 9, note 33).

    Other cultures have their variants of the "power gone mad" theme. See, for instance, the Siberian folktale, "The Clayman and the Golden-Antlered Elk," in James Riordan, *The Sun Maiden and the Crescent Moon* (New York: Interlink Books, 1991; originally published by Cannongate Publishing, Edinburgh, 1989), pp. 164–65, in which a huge clay man made by a fisherman goes wild and eats up everyone and everything it meets till it is destroyed by the charging elk.

    Motifs include D1620.1.6.1. "Magic statue of man fights for master"; and D1635. "Golem."

17. Known to the author, original source unknown. For one version, see-Ausubel, *Treasury of Jewish Folklore,* pp. 605–12. For a variant, see Sadeh, *Jewish Folktales,* pp. 228–30. See also Beverly Brodsky McDermott, *The Golem: A Jewish Legend* (Philadelphia and New York: Lippincott, 1976). "The Golem of Prague" is perhaps the most well-known story of the golem, and has been the inspiration for everything from a silent

movie and Leivick's Yiddish play, *The Golem,* to such novels as Sulamith Ish-Kishor's *The Master of Miracle: A New Novel About the Golem* (New York: Harper & Row, 1971) in which the golem becomes a symbol of tragic alienation. It has even been suggested that Mary Shelley may have used the Golem of Prague as an inspiration for her *Frankenstein.*

Cabbala, or Kabbalah, literally means "to receive" in Hebrew, and is the term for the study of Jewish mystic texts.

An interesting subplot in the story of the Golem of Prague is the incident of the water barrels, which the golem, without a command to stop, continues mindlessly to fill. This is a variant on the "Sorcerer's Apprentice" theme of the boy who, toying with magic, sets a broom or, in some versions, a demon the task of filling the water barrels, only to realize he does not know how to stop his magical helper. It is a story known in different variations throughout the world and should be very familiar to anyone who has seen Walt Disney's film *Fantasia.*

Motifs include D1620.1.6. "Magic statue of man labors for owner"; D1620.1.6.1 "Magic statue of man fights for master"; and D1635. "Golem."

Chapter Seven: Clever Folk and Survivors

1. This "Sherlockian" story comes from the Midrash, Lamentations Rabbah, I:1, 12. See also Hyam Maccoby, *The Day God Laughted* (New York: St. Martin's Press, 1978), pp. 43–44.

   Tales of pre-Sherlock Holmes detectives who solve mysteries by the powers of deduction are not uncommon in the Near East. In a similar story collected in Uzbekistan, three observant brothers are brought before the king because they describe the camel a missing woman and child are riding so well, down to the fact that the camel is large and blind in one eye, that it is thought they kidnapped the woman. They defend themselves. They knew the camel was large because its prints were deep, and blind in one eye because only one side of the road was grazed. They knew the camel was carrying the missing woman and child since they dismounted at one point and left their footprints. The brothers further prove their powers of deduction when they are ordered to identify an object in a sealed chest. They declare it to be a green pomegranate. They knew the object was light because only one man carried the chest, and round because they heard it rolling. Also, they had noticed the man coming from the pomegranate garden, and because the season was too early for ripe fruit, the pomegranate had to be still green! See Irina Zheleznova, *Folk Tales from Russian Lands* (New York: Dover Publications, 1969), pp. 218–23.

   Motifs include H692. "Tasks performed by close observation"; J1661.1. "Deduction from observation"; and, more specifically, J1661.1.1. "Deduction: the one-eyed camel." The tale type is 655A, The Strayed Camel and the Clever Deductions.

2. This very similar detection story comes from *The Talmud.* See the previous note.
3. This tale is from the Midrash, though the use of pretended stupidity to outwit tormentors or predators is a theme found in folktales from around the world. One of the most familiar parallels can be found in the story "Hansel and Gretel," in which little Gretel saves herself and her brother from being baked by the evil witch by pretending she doesn't know how to look into an oven.

   An applicable motif is K17. "Jumping contest won by deception."
4. This story of a clever son posing curious riddles to his host was written down in the Midrash, but is probably much older; it has parallels (as do the riddles themselves) in tales from Asia and Eastern Europe. In a Russian folktale known to the author, for example, a clever peasant manages to outwit the tzar, telling him that of his income, twenty rubles go to his past, twenty to his future, and twenty go flying out the window. By this riddle he means that twenty rubles go to support his parents, who supported him when he was a child, twenty rubles go for his son's upkeep in the hope that the boy will someday return the favor, and twenty rubles go for his daughter's upkeep, although she will someday go flying off with her husband.

   Motifs include H507. "Tests of cleverness or ability: miscellaneous"; and H601. "Wise carving of the fowl." The tale type is 1533, Wise Carving of the Fowl.
5. Known to the author, who heard it in New York, possibly in the 1970s, from a Jew of Polish decent, name not noted. This tale has a good deal in common with the previous tale, with its cryptic riddles, and with Slavic folklore, in which a peasant often gets the better of the authorities through his cunning. What makes this tale a little unusual is the sympathetic treatment of the landowner; aristocrats in such tales are usually portrayed as cold-hearted villains. For a literary treatment of this story, see Ish-Kishor, *Wise Men of Israel,* pp. 160–70.

   Motifs include H540. "Propounding of riddles"; H561. "Solvers of riddles"; H561.6.1. "King and peasant: the plucked fowl"; and H580. "Enigmatic statements."
6. This folktale from the Midrash about the young King David is unusual in that it is about David, rather than his son, Solomon, about whom a whole cycle of folktales revolve. The use of simple logic (that is, the knowledge that honey is sticky enough to snag a coin or two) to solve a problem can be found in "puzzle" tales throughout the world. In most stories of this type, either a child or an apparently simple peasant proves wiser than king or court.

An applicable motif is J30. "Wisdom (knowledge) acquired from inference."

7. Known to the author, original source unknown. See also Moses Gaster, *The Exempla of the Rabbis* (London: Asia Publishing Company, 1924). This wryly wise little fable has been used as a parable by rabbis both in the Old and New Worlds. The "miraculous" pomegranate seed is, of course, only a trick, reminiscent of other trick taboos, such as the universal one—known in one form or another by a good many American children—that a fabulous treasure can only be uncovered by someone who can avoid thinking of the right eye of a camel, crocodile, or other animal (an impossibility, given the power of suggestion). The world of folklore is also full of some very real taboos, however. The Irish River Shannon, to take one example, is said to have come into being when a woman disobeyed the ban on uncovering a magical well.

   An applicable motif is J1370. "Cynical retorts concerning honesty."
8. Original source unknown. Although this particular tale has been found in manuscripts dating only from about the eleventh century C.E., it is of a very old type, indeed. There are parallels to be found in first millennium B.C.E. Sanskrit folklore, in which the trickster-hero, a hare or other "underdog," tricks a dangerous foe—a demon, lion, or elephant—through use of a reflection.

   An applicable motif is J1791. "Reflection in water thought to be the original of thing reflected."
9. Collected in Israel in 1952 by Mila Ohel from Meachem Kamus, originally from Libya. See Noy, *Folktales of Israel,* pp. 100–101. This Sephardic trickster tale has parallels in similar survival tales in Europe and the New World. Folk jokes about escaping would-be assailants through trickery abound in such modern American cities as New York.

   An applicable motif is K500. "Escape from death or danger by deception."
10. Known to the author, who first heard it in New York in the 1970s, informant unknown. See also Ausubel, *Treasury of Jewish Folklore,* pp. 370–71. While this tale, like the last, involves an escape from a robber through trickery, the hero here has a much more modern idea of self-defense. In fact, this Yiddish folktale could just as easily be set in New York or some other modern urban setting as in the forests of Eastern Europe.

    Motifs include K500. "Escape from death or danger by deception"; and K550. "Escape by false plea."
11. Collected in Israel between 1949 and 1950 from a Yeminite Jew, names of collector and informant unknown. This Sephardic tale, which was collected in the years when "Operation Magic Carpet" airlifted most of the Jewish population out of Yemen to Israel, is yet another "riddle" tale. See also notes 3 and 4.

    Motifs include H540.3. "King propounds riddles"; H541. "Riddles propounded with penalty for failure"; H561.4. "King and clever youth"; and H583. "Clever youth (maiden) answers king's inquiry in riddles."

12. Recorded by Nehama Zion from her Hungarian-born grandfather, name and date unknown. See Noy's *Folktales of Israel,* pp. 91–93. Similar deductive tales are more popular in the Sephardic tradition than the Ashkenazi, and can also be found throughout Central Asia and the Orient. See also notes 3, 4, and 6.

    Motifs include J1661.1. "Deduction from observation"; and J1661.1.2. "Deduction: king is a bastard."

13. Original source unknown. See Ausubel, *Treasury of Jewish Folklore,* p. 628. This is yet another ancient tale.

    Although this particular version is from Yiddish folklore, it has direct parallels both in the medieval collection known as the Gesta Romanorum, tale number 187, and in both Chinese and Sanskrit folklore, where the characters are sometimes a birdcatcher and a bird, or they are a hungry, foolish tiger and a clever cat, but in which the three wisdoms generally remain the same.

    An applicable motif is K604. "The three teachings of the bird (fox)."

14. Recorded by S. Gabai from Shlomo Haim, originally from Iraq, date unknown. Oral tradition. See Noy, *Folktales of Israel,* pp.94–97. The irony of this Sephardic "riddle test" tale, in which each contestant thinks that the other meant something else entirely, has made it popular in North and South America as well as in the Near East. A note about the third riddle: Jews believe that the Messiah has not yet arrived. See Gastner, *Exempla of the Rabbis,* pp. 177, 269, for a similar version dating at least from the twelfth century. See also Zheleznova, *Tales from Russian Lands,* pp. 148–52, for a non-Jewish Azerbaijani variant, in which a humble weaver successfully wards off the threats of an enemy ambassador through the language of signs. This tale includes the episode of the hen and the grain, though in this case there is no ambiguity of interpretation: the grain represents the enemy soldiers, and the hen represents the weaver's counterthreat that those soldiers would be easily destroyed.

    Applicable motifs are H607.1. "Discussion between priest and Jew carried on by symbols"; and K510. "Death order evaded." The tale type is 924A, Discussion between Priest and Jew Carried On by Symbols.

15. A Yiddish folktale known to the author, provenance unknown. See also Henry D. Spalding, *Encyclopedia of Jewish Humor* (New York: Jonathan David Publishers, 1989), pp. 13–14. The humor in this version is even broader than in the previous tale, but the point is the same (see note 14).

    An applicable version is H607. "Discussion by symbols."

16. Known to the author in both this specifically Jewish version and in a non-Jewish variant. See also Ausubel, *Treasury of Jewish Folklore,* p. 36. The idea of rigged lots, with a clever person overcoming the fact that both

papers have been marked "Guilty" (or, in the case of a nonliterate culture, both pebbles painted black) by swallowing one of the lots is a common folkloric "gimmick" throughout the world. Most of the time, the gambler is risking his own life, though, not the life of a whole community as well, and often the gambler is guilty, a rogue managing to escape justice.

Motifs include H233. "Ordeal: taking stone out of bucket"; J1130. "Cleverness in law court—general"; and K510. "Death order evaded."

17. Collected by an unknown collector from a Moroccan Jew, name unrecorded. See Sadeh, *Jewish Folktales,* pp. 298–99. Versions of this Sephardic tale have been collected from Jews from Tunisia and Yemen as well. Indeed, the basic theme of a trickster who bluffs his way out of trouble is found throughout the world. Many of the evil viziers or counselors in Sephardic tales are apostate Jews with a true convert's hatred for their former people.

    Motifs include K500. "Escape from death or danger by deception"; J951. "Lowly masks as great"; and K1700. "Deception through bluffing."

18. Same source as the previous tale. See ibid., pp. 297–98. Like the previous tale, this is a Sephardic story, and like the previous tale, it features a converted Jew as villain. The elements in the king's challenge are found throughout the Middle East and Europe. The answers vary in details—sometimes, for example, the solver of the puzzle rides a broomstick, sometimes, a goat so small the rider's feet drag on the ground—but follow the same general pattern. See notes 16 and 17. The vizier's fate has particularly strong parallels to European folklore, in which villains are frequently torn apart by or dragged to their death behind wild horses. The idea of the fishnet is a singularly old one; a second millennium B.C.E. Egyptian papyrus includes a scene in which the Pharaoh Snefru's boredom is relieved by the sight of his wives "both naked and clad," wrapped fetchingly in nets.

    Motifs include H541. "Riddle propounded with penalty"; H960. "Tasks performed through cleverness or intelligence; H1050. "Paradoxical tasks"; H1053.3. "Task: coming neither on horse nor on foot (comes with one leg on animal's back, one on ground)"; and H1054.1. "Task: coming neither naked nor clad (comes clothed in net or the like)."

19. Known to the author, source unknown. See also Spalding, *Encyclopedia of Jewish Humor,* p. 26. While this puzzle is Yiddish in origin, the author is also familiar with versions involving English or American wills in which odd numbers of items must be successfully divided among the heirs.

    An applicable motif is H960. "Tasks performed through cleverness or intelligence."

20. Known to the author, who probably heard it in childhood from her Russian Jewish grandmother. This story of a clever wife and her riddle-solving abilities is a very popular folktale type, found among Jews and

non-Jews alike, although the specific riddles vary from tale to tale. Most versions collected come from Eastern Europe and the Near East, though there are Scandinavian variants as well. For two Yiddish variants, see Weinreich, *Yiddish Folktales,* pp. 207–9, and Ausubel, *Treasury of Jewish Folklore,* pp. 95–97. For a very similar Russian version, see Afanas'ev, *Russian Fairy Tales*, pp. 252–55. For a Norwegian variant, see *Norwegian Folktales: Selected from the Collection of Peter Christen Asbjornsen and Jorgen Moe,* translated by Pat Shaw and Carl Norman (New York: Pantheon Books, 1960), pp. 137–38. For a Sephardic riddle tale involving some of the same riddles, see note 11.

Motifs include H632.1. "What is the swiftest? Thought"; H633.1. "What is the sweetest? Sleep"; H960. "Tasks performed through cleverness or intelligence"; H1050. "Paradoxical tasks"; H1053.3. "Task: coming neither on horse nor on foot (comes with one leg on animal's back, one on ground)"; H1054.1. "Task: coming neither naked nor clad (comes clothed in net or the like)"; J1111. "Clever girl"; J1191.1. *"Reductio ad absurdum:* the decision about the colt"; and J1545.4. "The exiled wife's dearest possession." The tale type is 875, The Clever Peasant Girl.

21. From the Midrash. This is a version of the previous tale type but with a little moral implied about relying on God's mercy. A Jewish man could legally divorce his wife for barrenness, as could a Moslem. This practice is still performed in some Islamic countries, King Hussein of Jordan, who divorced his much-loved first wife for her barrenness, being a case in point.

    An applicable motif is J1545.4. "The exiled wife's dearest possession."

22. Collected from a Tunisian Jew, date and names of collector and informant unknown. See Sadeh, *Jewish Folktales,* pp. 291–95. This is a beautifully complicated version of a very wide-spread folklore category: "Master Thief" tales turn up all over the world in one form or another. See, for example, "The Master Thief" in Joseph Jacobs, *European Folk and Fairy Tales* (New York: G.P. Putnam's Sons, 1916), pp. 121–28, 245–46, n. 16, which compares this tale to that of Rhampsinitus in Herodotus and to other Old World and Asian variations. For a somewhat similar Sephardic version collected in Israel from a Kurdistani Jew, see Noy, *Folktales of Israel,* pp. 80–83. In Noy's version, the thieves are brothers, not uncle and nephew, and the boy-thief cuts out the spy's tongue instead of killing her. She marks the houseposts with her blood, but the thief marks the houseposts of all the other houses with sheep's blood as well. The episode with the neighboring king is omitted.

    Several trickster tales in world folklore utilize the idea of an animal bearing different loads on each side or a coat having two colors, one on each side, usually to cause trouble between two observers or to win a "sucker" bet. The concept of stealing eggs out from under a nesting bird is a familiar theme in European folklore as well, usually being part of a competition between thieves rather than being a graduation test.

Motifs include H500. "test of cleverness or ability"; H961. "Tasks performed by cleverness or intelligence"; K301. "Master thief"; K301.2. "Family of thieves"; K305. "Contest in stealing"; and K714. "Deception into entering box (or prison)." The tale type is 1525, The Master Thief.

Chapter Eight: Allegories and Moral Tales

1. From the Talmud. The protective power of charity is a theme that runs throughout Jewish folklore.
   An applicable motif is V411. "Miraculous reward of charity."
2. As with the previous tale, a version of this fable was first written down in the Talmud. See the Babylonian Talmud.
   An applicable motif is V411. "Miraculous reward of charity."
3. This wonder tale of charity rewarded was first written down in a commentary on the Talmud dating to the second century.
   An applicable motif is V411. "Miraculous reward of charity."
4. Original source unknown. This fable combines elements of the "protection of charity" tale with the wonder tale, and is part of a longer, episodic story concerning the adventures and trial of Ben Sever. The complete story, with all its episodes, was transcribed by Moses Gaster in Hebrew in 1896, and translated into English by Patai in *Gates to the Old City,* pp. 588–90.
   Motifs include B549.2. "Dragon makes bridge across stream for holy man"; and V411. "Miraculous reward for charity."
5. A tale from the Midrash. Although it has elements of a trickster tale about it—there are a good many folktales of scoundrels, such as the Teutonic Til Eulenspiegel, tricking merchants into paying too much or giving away their goods for nothing—this story quickly shows its basic morality.
6. Although this fable has entered the world of oral tradition, and has been told both in America and in Israel, it is originally from the Talmud. See *The Babylonian Talmud* (London: Soncino Press, 1935–52), chapter 2. For an Israeli version, see Harold Courtlander, *Ride with the Sun: Folk Tales and Stories from All Countries of the United Nations* (New York: Whittlesey House, McGraw-Hill, 1955), pp. 99–100.
   Motifs include L400. "Pride brought low"; and Q331. "Pride punished."
7. Known to the author, original source unknown. This fable concentrates on one of the basic themes of Jewish life, the value of learning, and probably dates from about the ninth or tenth century.
8. Original source unknown. This refreshing Yiddish folktale, in which Jew and Christian can actually be friends, was first published in German. For an English version, see Ausubel, *Treasury of Jewish Folklore,* pp. 586–87.
9. From the Midrash, Ecclesiastes Rabbah, 5:14. Parallels to this story can be found throughout the Near East. A Berber tale from Morocco involves a hedgehog and a fox, both of whom slip through a hole in the fence into

a melon patch. The hedgehog is wise enough to eat only enough to let him still fit through the hole. The fox, on the other hand, gorges himself until he is too fat to fit. He is caught by the farmer, who chases him, beating the fox till he has sweated off all his stolen gains and can fit through the hole. See Rene Basset and Chauncy C. Starkweather, "Popular Tales of the Berbers," *Moorish Literature* (New York: Colonial Press, 1901), pp. 215–48.

10. Known to the author, source unknown. This Yiddish tale probably originated in the Soviet Union, since most versions place it in a Ukrainian village. See, for example, Ausubel, *Treasury of Jewish Folklore,* pp. 109–10.

11. Recorded by Hanina Mizrahi, originally from Iran, in Israel, no date. See Noy, *Folktales of Israel,* pp. 12–13. This is a fable with particularly widespread roots, both within and without Judaism. There are variants to be found in such dissimilar collections as Boccaccio's Decameron, tenth day, first tale, and the sixth century Indian collection of tales known as the Pantschatantra.

    Motifs include Q4. "Humble rewarded, haughty punished"; Q22. "Reward for faith": Q112.0.1.1. "Kingdom as reward for piety"; and Q221.6. "Lack of trust in God punished."

12. Collected by Zvulun Korb in Israel, date unknown, who heard it from the late Rabbi Joseph Gurgii, chief rabbi of the Afghanistan Jews in Jerusalem. See Noy, *Folktales of Israel,* pp. 83–85. This Sephardic tale is of a type found primarily in the Near East and Central Asia.

    An applicable motif is Q22. "Reward for faith." The tale type is 934D, Nothing Happens Without God.

13. Original source unknown. One version of this fable on accepting God's will was collected in Hebrew in the nineteenth century by Rabbi Joseph Shabtai Farhi. For a version translated into English, see Sadeh, *Jewish Folktales,* p. 285. Although there have been cases of people who really have, for one reason or another, missed what turned out to be a fatal flight, this theme has entered American urban folklore, often with a similar moral attached.

    The tale type is 934D, Nothing Happens Without God.

14. Collected by Toyvye Yafe from Yehoshua Yafe, no date. See Weinreich, *Yiddish Folktales,* pp. 161–62. In this Yiddish tale, both the poor man and the merchant show themselves as moral men; the first, because he will not break the prohibition against handling money on the Sabbath; the second, because he freely repays the poor man the gold that, indirectly, does belong to him. The motif of rescue and riches thanks to cats catching mice is a popular one throughout Europe and is perhaps best known in the story of Dick Whittington, who lived in the fourteenth century and who did go on to become Lord Mayor of London; he fits the theme of an historical personage to whose name a legend is attached. For the com-

plete tale of "Dick Whittington," see Jacobs, *English Fairy Tales,* pp.167–78; see also his notes, p. 255.

Motifs include F708.1. "Country without cats"; N411.1. "Whittington's cat"; and Q40. "Kindness rewarded."

15. This is an anonymous Yiddish tale known to the author, provenance unknown. For a similar version, see Ausubel, *Treasury of Jewish Folklore,* pp. 506–7. The concept of the soul being judged in the hereafter is common to many cultures. The ancient Egyptians, for instance, weighed the heart of the deceased—and his sins with it—against the feather of Truth; sinners who failed the test were then doomed to total extinction.

    An applicable motif is Q172.2. "Admittance to heaven for single act of charity."
16. Known to the author, original provenance unknown. See also Ausubel, *Treasury of Jewish Folklore,* p. 109. Judaism has scant patience with the self-righteous or the braggart.
17. Known to the author, who has also heard some non-Jewish versions of this Yiddish folktale, all with the same basic punchline.

    An applicable motif is V410. "Charity rewarded." The tale type is 750B, Hospitality Rewarded.
18. This is a Yiddish folktale from Eastern Europe, specific provenance unknown, quoted by Ausubel, *Treasury of Jewish Folklore,* p. 82.
19. Collected by Musye Mayzls from A. Akives of Litin, Poland, in 1936. See Weinreich, *Yiddish Folktales,* pp. 168–69. This tale belongs to a basic "destiny" type, found throughout Europe and the Near East. In the standard form of the tale, a king who learns from a prophesy that his daughter will marry the son of a lowly peasant has the baby carried off and—he thinks—put to death. But the baby is rescued by a childless couple who raise it as their own child. When the child grows up, he proves his worth to the king so thoroughly that the king agrees to marry him to the princess. Only then does the king learn who the young man really is and admits that no man can overcome destiny. One Yiddish version, quoted by Rockland, *Jewish Party Book,* turns the anonymous king into none other than King Solomon. What makes the present tale different from that standard type is the character of the revenge-obsessed merchant, who literally brings about his own downfall.

    Motifs include K1601. "Deceiver falls into his own trap (literally)"; and M371. "Exposure of infant to avoid fulfillment of prophesy."
20. This is a tale from the Talmud. Implicit in this story is the idea that the villagers brought about their own downfall through their lack of proper charity. See also note 13.

    The tale type is 934D, Nothing Happens Without God.
21. Original provenance unknown. See Ausubel, *Treasury of Jewish Folklore,* p. 60.

22. Collected from a Tunisian Jew, name of collector and informant unrecorded. See Sadeh, *Jewish Folktales,* p. 169. Variants on this cautionary tale can be found throughout the Near East. The motif of the dream warning the dreamer towards better behavior is found in every culture and can even be found in the American musical theater, in the song "Sit Down, You're Rockin' the Boat," from Frank Loesser's 1950 musical, *Guys and Dolls.*

Chapter Nine: Humorous Tales

1. Known to the author. This is a very well-known folk joke among American Jews; almost everyone seems to know it in one form or another. The joke's origin is almost certainly Eastern Europe.
2. Collected by the author from her mother, who in turn learned it from her mother, a Russian Jewish immigrant. This wry joke, with its historical background and all the weight of sorrow behind it shows the three unpleasant choices faced by many a Spanish Jewish family during the time of the Inquisition: convert, flee, or die. Although this is a fairly old version, with its reference to the Spanish Inquisition, other versions of this folk joke were known in the late Middle Ages—where the convert wasn't always specifically Jewish—and have spread fairly widely throughout Western Europe and across the United States. A modern parallel (dating to the days before Catholics were permitted to eat meat on Fridays) tells the same story about an American Jew who voluntarily converts to Catholicism, yet can't give up the pleasures of a good steak on Friday night. This modern variant is a rather ambiguous joke, which can hold elements of either anti-Catholicism or anti-Semitism, depending on who is doing the telling. See Ronald L. Baker, *Jokelore: Humorous Folktales from Indiana* (Bloomington: Indiana University Press, 1986), pp. 148–55 for a similar collection of ambiguous folk jokes; the introduction to this section, showing the persistence of Jewish stereotypes in Midwestern humor, is particularly important.
3. When the author first heard this story, it was told by a New York Jew sometime in the 1970s. The setting was the Lower East Side of New York—the home of a good many turn-of-the-century Jewish immigrants—and the fish seller and his customers spoke Yiddish, but this folk joke about the dangers of too much free advice has also been found in one form or another all the way across Eastern Europe and America. See Ausubel, *Treasury of Jewish Folklore,* pp. 347–48, for a variant set in the Bronx.
4. Known to the author. This is a very popular little fable, still very much in circulation both in the United States and in the Near East. Though there are minor variations—sometimes the animal in question is a camel in-

stead of a donkey—the basic plot remains remarkably constant. See Weinreich, *Yiddish Folktales,* pp. 19–20, for a version collected from a Polish Jewish immigrant. This story is also included in collections of Aesop's Fables. See, for example, *The Fables of Aesop, with Designs on Wood by Thomas Bewick* (New York: Paddington Press, 1975), "The Miller, His Son, and Their Ass," pp. 305–6.

5. Known to the author. This is, perhaps, one of the best-known Jewish folk jokes in North America, told by both Jews and gentiles alike. It remains popular today, although an argument can be made that it only serves to reinforce the unpleasant stereotype of the Jew as grasping merchant. See note 2.
6. Known to the author. Sarcasm is often slyly expressed through the use of ironic logic in Jewish humor.
7. Known to the author. For a very similar version collected by an unnamed collector from Mikhl Zaydelov, a Russian Jew, no date given, see Weinreich, *Yiddish Folktales,* p. 210. This is a widely travelled joke; in various Jewish and non-Jewish versions, the guilty cat devours fish or goose fat. A very similar non-Jewish version from Iran differs only in that the guilty cat has eaten its weight in meat instead of butter. See Alice Geer Kelsey, *Once the Mullah: Persian Folk Tales* (New York, London, Toronto: Longmans, Green and Co., 1954), pp. 8–14.
8. Known to the author. This wry Yiddish folk joke in which things really *can* always get worse is fairly widespread; the author has heard a non-Jewish version set in America. See also Spalding, *Encyclopedia of Jewish Humor,* p. 223.
9. Known to the author. See also ibid., p. 222. This joke is also often told—without the specifically Jewish character of the *shammes*—by non-Jews in America. It belongs to the class of slightly "sick" folk joke in which that most delicate of tasks, advising someone of a death in the family, is mishandled. In another non-Jewish story told in America and probably originally from Great Britain, a man begins bluntly telling his brother about their cat's death, only to be told to try a little more delicacy. So he starts off with, "The cat's on the roof," and goes on to give every detail of how the cat slipped, how the dog caught her, and so on, up to the end. When asked how their mother is doing, the man begins, very carefully, "Well, she's on the roof now . . ."
10. Known to the author. See also Ausubel, *Treasury of Jewish Folklore,* p. 398.
11. Alternately, the punchline might be: "All right, so life *isn't* like a glass of tea with sugar!" The author has heard this folk joke told both ways. It is equally popular among New York City Jews in Yiddish or English versions.

12. Known to the author. This wry little commentary on writers and critics nicely transcends cultural backgrounds. For a similar version, see William Novak and Moshe Waldoks, *The Big Book of Jewish Humor* (New York: HarperPerennial, 1990), p. 6.
13. Known to the author. See also ibid., p. 6. This is a relatively modern folk joke, found more in the United States than abroad, and shows the distinctly Jewish method of making a question serve as an answer. See also notes 14 and 17.
14. Known to the author. No one can argue with the simple logic here.
15. Collected from the author's mother. Rather than spoil a perfectly good story with an instant solution, a good Jewish joke will often go through several convoluted, but perfectly reasonable, steps in logic.
16. Known to the author. See note 15. This is obviously a first cousin of "The Dog" folk joke.
17. Known to the author. This is another very typically Jewish joke, self-parodying that habit of speech in which a positive statement will often be made in the form of a question. For example: "Do you know him?" "He's my cousin, how should I not know him?" See also notes 13 and 14.
18. Known to the author, who has variously heard that herring described as being purple or green. The punchline, with its slightly surrealist air, always remains the same. Sometimes this folk joke is attached to the wise men of Chelm, who are puzzled by the unsolvable riddle. See Novak and Waldoks, *Big Book of Jewish Humor,* p. 24.
19. Known to the author. This tale is also sometimes attached to the wise men of Chelm.
20. Known to the author. See also Spalding, *Encyclopedia of Jewish Humor,* p. 134. No collection of folklore would be complete without one "shaggy dog" story. Tales in which animals or even inanimate objects suddenly acquire the ability to speak abound in folklore, often with a matter-of-fact put-down by an unimpressed human as a punchline. Sometimes the animal itself is the cynic, as in the well-traveled American folk joke about a man trying desperately to get a talent agent to believe that the man's dog can talk. It's only after the man is unceremoniously tossed out that the dog comments dryly, "Who ever heard of a talking dog?"

    The tale type is 1705, Talking Horse and Dog.
21. Known to the author. Although this joke pokes gentle fun at the type of Talmudic scholar who over-analyzes every issue, it is one of a whole subgenre of similar folk jokes. One non-Jewish folk joke known to the author has a traveler analyze at length the trip he is going to take, the type of transportation he is going to use, and so on, making as many choices as the teller's audience will endure, until the plane in which he finally decides to fly starts to crash. He calls out to St. Francis, only to hear an

angelic voice force him to make one last choice: "St. Francis of Assisi or St. Francis Xavier?"

22. Collected by A. Litwin from B. Brukelman, who heard the story in the *yeshiva* (Jewish day school) of Novograd-Vilenske in the Soviet Union, no date. See Weinreich, *Yiddish Folktales,* p. 235. As with the previous joke, this is a parody on the overly analytical.
23. Known to the author. See also Ausubel, *Treasury of Jewish Folklore,* p. 371. This trickster theme of escape through reverse psychology has its parallels throughout world folklore. The variant perhaps most familiar to American readers is the African-American tale of the captured Brer Rabbit escaping by begging not to be thrown into the briar patch when that rabbit sanctuary is exactly where he wants to be.

    An applicable motif is K584. "Throwing the thief over the fence."
24. From the Midrash. A common feature of tricksters is the conning of a supposed superior—in this case, a haughty Greek during the time of the Greek occupation of Israel—out of money by pretending to take quite literally a not-too carefully worded order.

    Motifs include J2461.1 "Literal following of instructions about actions"; and K100. "Deceptive bargain." The tale type is 1539, Cleverness and Gullibility.
25. Known to the author. The fellow in this Yiddish folk joke demonstrates perfectly the definition of *chutzpah,* that quintessentially Jewish form of colossal gall.
26. Known to the author. Here is another Yiddish example of both *chutzpah* and incredibly convoluted logic.
27. Known to the author, who first heard this "biter bite" folk joke, in which *chutzpah,* for a change, does *not* carry the day, in New York, possibly in the 1970s.
28. Original source unknown. For more about the possible history of Hershele, see Novak and Waldos, *Big Book of Jewish Humor,* pp. 25–26.

    An applicable motif is A521. "Culture hero as dupe or trickster."
29. Known to the author in both Jewish and non-Jewish variants. This is a well-known American and European folk joke that has become attached to the Hershele canon.

    Motifs are A521. "Culture hero as dupe or trickster"; and X900. "Humor of lies or exaggerations."
30. Collected from the author's mother. This is another well-known folk joke that isn't always attached to the Hershele cycle. "Oy" is an all-purpose Jewish Yiddish exclamation, used as everything from a cry of dismay to a yelp of surprise to a shout of delight. It can be a single word or part of a chorus, "oy, oy, oy!" for extra emphasis. In this case, of course, the meaning is a sarcastic "Alas!" For a look at the many shadings of "oy," see

Leo Rosten, *The Joys of Yiddish* (New York: Pocket Books, 1970), pp. 277–79.

In a mirror image folk joke told in the United States, a diner in a restaurant that boasts it will serve any type of meat requests a steak from an expensive animal—in some versions an elephant—only to be told by the waiter, "I'm sorry, sir. We can't kill a whole elephant for one small steak."

Motifs include A521. "Culture hero as dupe or trickster"; and X1020. "Exaggerations."

31. Known to the author, original source unknown.

    An applicable motif is A521. "Culture hero as dupe or trickster."

32. Known to the author. See also Novak and Waldoks, *Big Book of Jewish Humor,* pp. 27–28. This Yiddish folktale, with its blank canvas and its pretend painting that only the elite can see, is first cousin to the tale of "The Emperor's New Clothes."

    An applicable motif is A521. "Culture hero as dupe or trickster."

33. See Shtutshkof, *Yidisher Shprakh.* Chelm is, or was, a perfectly real Polish town, with perfectly normal people in it. It also is the site of one variant of the golem theme (see chapter 6, note 16). How Chelm gained a whole cycle of foolish-folk folktales about it is one of the mysteries of folklore.

    The Wise Men of Chelm, the folkloric Chelm, that is, are not alone in their silliness; ninny tales have always been exceedingly popular, and similar stories can be found all over the world. Almost every child is familiar with tales about the Germanic fools who sit and weep over the axe that *might* fall someday and hit some hypothetical offspring or about the English sillies who are sure they have lost one of their party because each time they try to count themselves, they forget to include the person doing the counting.

    The idea of a whole town of silly folk is not unique to Chelm. The wise men of Chelm have their counterparts in England in the Wise Men of Gotham, who have been noted for their silly deeds—such as trying to trap a cuckoo behind walls, never noticing there is no roof—for centuries. Their antics were first written down in *The Foles of Gotyam* in 1450, and can be found in a modern adaptation by Malcolm Carrick in *The Wise Men of Gotham* (New York: Viking, 1975).

    An applicable motif for the Wise Men of Chelm tales is J1703. "Town (country) of fools."

34. Known to the author. The idea that bread always falls butter-side down is well-known in America too, as one of Murphy's Laws.
35. Known to the author. See also Novak and Waldoks, *Big Book of Jewish Humor,* p. 24.
36. Known to the author. See also ibid.

37. Ausubel, *Treasury of Jewish Folklore,* pp. 326–27. One point to be noted about the wise men of Chelm is that they are eternally optimistic. No matter how far awry their plans may go, they continue to cheerfully make new ones.
38. Known to the author. It is not so much that the people of Chelm are naive; they simply see life from a very different angle.
39. Known to the author. See also Novak and Waldoks, *Big Book of Jewish Humor,* p. 23. A common—and just as weirdly illogical—superstition in the United States is that if you carry an umbrella, it will not rain!
40. Collected by N. Prilutski from an anonymous informant from Lublin, Poland, no date given. See Weinreich, *Yiddish Folktales,* p. 227. This is a classic "ninny" tale of the sort popular worldwide; in such a tale a stranger attempts to help foolish people, only to find they don't *quite* get the point of his advice.

    An applicable motif is J1810. "Physical phenomena misunderstood."
41. Known to the author. See also Novak and Waldoks, *Big Book of Jewish Humor,* p. 25.
42. Known to the author.

    An applicable motif is J1810. "Physical phenomena misunderstood."
43. Collected by T. S. Kantor, circa 1937, from an anonymous Russian Jewish informant. See Weinreich, *Yiddish Folktales,* p. 227. The Chelmites' ignorance of cats is reminiscent of that of the savage folk in chapter 8, note 14.

    Motifs include F708.1. "Country without cats"; N411.1. "Whittington's cat"; J1900. "Absurd disregard or ignorance of animal's nature or habits"; and J2101. "Getting rid of the cat."
44. Known to the author.

    An applicable motif is J1810. "Physical phenomena misunderstood."
45. Known to the author. This "ninny" tale has been frequently retold as a silly story for children in the United States.

    Motifs include J1791. "Reflection in water thought to be the original of thing reflected"; and J1810. "Physical phenomena misunderstood."
46. Known to the author. See also Weinreich, *Yiddish Folktales,* p. 228, for a version collected by Benyomin Volf Segel (pen name of B. V. Shiper) from an anonymous informant from Galicia, Poland, no date recorded.

    Motifs include J1810. "Physical phenomena misunderstood"; and J1820. "Inappropriate action from misunderstanding."
47. Known to the author. See also Spalding, *Encyclopedia of Jewish Humor,* pp. 111–12.

    An appropriate motif would be the catch-all J2160. "Other short-sighted acts."
48. Known to the author. See also ibid., p. 113. This tale is a fine example of both the Chelmite's type of surrealist logic and his eternal optimism.

    An appropriate motif is J1810. "Physical phenomena misunderstood."

49. Known to the author. This is another popular ninny tale that has turned up in Europe and the United States as a non-Jewish joke as well.

    Motifs include J1810. "Physical phenomena misunderstood"; and J1934. "A hole to throw the earth in."
50. Known to the author. This is one of the classic jokes on anti-Semitism and one of the most graceful examples of the Jewish gift for turning an insult back upon the would-be insulter. Although most versions are attached to Mendelssohn's name, the joke has also been updated to Czarist Russia and Nazi Germany. As pointed out in Novak and Waldos, *Big Book of Jewish Humor,* jokes about anti-Semitism are, sadly, highly adaptable to many different times and places.
51. Known to the author. Versions of this bitter folk joke involve the Nazis in place of the Czarist soldiers.
52. Collected by the author in the 1980s from an anonymous Russian emigree. Some versions update this joke to Soviet times, when the drowning man bad-mouths Stalin instead.
53. Known to the author. See also Novak and Waldos, *Big Book of Jewish Humor,* p. 83. Versions of this story turn the officer from a Russian to a Nazi.
54. Collected by the author in the 1980s from the same Russian emigree as in note 52. The informant knew both this version, which is also quoted by Ausubel, *Treasury of Jewish Folklore,* p. 17, and one which substituted Cossacks for Nazis.
55. Known to the author. There are many variations on this bitterly ironic joke, all of them involving the accidental saving of Hitler by a Jew or a member of another persecuted group. Some non-Jewish versions set in the South in the United States involve the rescuing of a white bigot by a black man. Prejudice, and jokes against it, know no boundaries.
56. Known to the author. See also Ausubel, *Treasury of Jewish Folklore,* pp. 442–43.
57. Collected by the author from Canadian writer S. M. Stirling, who heard the story in the 1980s from a Russian Jewish immigrant in Toronto. For a similar version, see Novak and Waldoks, *Big Book of Jewish Humor,* p. 76.
58. Known to the author. Has this sort of joke already become a thing of the past? Only time will tell, though the recent rise of anti-Semitism in Moscow bodes ill for the future of Jews remaining there.
59. Known to the author. This is a well-known American Jewish folk joke, expressing the Jewish fear that the American way of life may be so seductive that Jews will assimilate too thoroughly—will, in effect, stop being Jews.
60. Collected from the author's mother, who heard this folk joke frequently told in New York City during the latter years of World War II.

61. Spalding, *Encyclopedia of Jewish Humor,* p. 203. This is, sadly, not that outdated a joke. It is now illegal to discriminate against any orderly paying customer in a New York City restaurant. But as late as the early 1970s, a Jew who looked too "ethnic" or who had too blatantly a Semitic name sometimes still ran into invisible "no Jews allowed" signs in certain restaurants or hiring difficulties in some offices.
62. Known to the author. This is a fairly well-known joke among Jewish-Americans. The Jews have always been able to laugh at their own foibles, even to the point of mocking their own fears about anti-Semitism.
63. Known to the author. This is another well-known folk joke among Jewish-Americans. See, for example, Novak and Waldoks, *Big Book of Jewish Humor,* p. 85, and Richard M. Dorson, "Jewish-American Dialect Stories on Tape," in *Studies in Biblical and Jewish Folklore,* edited by Raphael Patai, Francis Lee Utley, and Dov Noy (Bloomington: Indiana University Press, 1960), pp. 122–24, for similar versions.
64. Known to the author. See also Ausubel, *Treasury of Jewish Folklore,* p. 426. This tale, parodying the Jewish tendency towards looking at every event from the angle of how it will effect the Jews, has been updated over the years to include more modern baseball players. In some versions football is substituted for baseball. See, for example, Dorson, "Dialect Stories on Tape," p. 156.
65. Known to the author. This is another widely known self-parodying Jewish-American jest.
66. This is a very popular Jewish folk joke, and has been heard by the author in one variation or another in almost every part of New York City.
67. Known to the author. Here is another very popular Jewish folk joke, playing off the over-sophisticated voice of the British secretary against the unpretentious language of the down-to-earth housewife. The joke is so well-known that the punchline has become a catch phrase in the author's family!
68. Known to the author. See also Novak and Waldoks, *Big Book of Jewish Humor,* p. 94, for a similar version. "Oy vey" (also frequently spelled "oy vay") means, more or less, "oh, pain." Tales of pretentious folk getting their comeuppance abound in folklore. See, for example, "The Master of All Masters," in Jacobs, *English Fairy Tales,* pp. 220–21, in which a man's pretentious language almost results in his house burning down.
69. Known to the author, who originally heard it from her mother. See also Ausubel, *Treasury of Jewish Folklore,* p. 434, for a version set in Brooklyn. This is another well-known folk joke particularly popular in New York City.
70. Some of the chosen expressions might be the inquisitive "Nu?" which is as common in Jewish-American usage as "oy," and which can not only ask, "So?" but imply, "So what else would you expect?" "Nu" is so quint-

essentially Jewish that it can be used to ask, "Are you Jewish?" See Rosten, *Joys of Yiddish,* pp. 271–73, for more on "nu" and its many uses. Another volume-in-a-word is the supremely contemptuous "Eh!" or "Feh!" which implies that the person or situation being criticized is almost beneath notice. This gift of saying much with only a word or two starts young; when a man decided to run naked through a crowded convention hall, the author heard an eight-year-old girl of her acquaintance sum him up with a dismissing wave of the hand and a bored, "Eh!"

71. This is a popular Jewish folk joke known to the author, and to many New York City Jews. See also ibid., p. 6, in which Rosten uses a similar variant to illustrate one of the possible meanings of the Yiddish "aha," which can be used for any situation from surprise to triumph. This joke is usually set in New York's Lower East Side, with its high population of Yiddish-speaking Jews. It is also an example of convoluted logic at its finest; to actually ask for a spoon would ruin the chance to make that one-word philosophical point. The proper pronunciation, incidentally, is "ah-HA!"
72. Both versions are known to the author.
73. Known to the author. This joke loses a good deal by being written down, rather than being told orally. The "eh-eh," of course, should be said with a "so-so" intonation; the other pronunciations should be obvious. For a very similar version, see Spalding, *Encyclopedia of Jewish Humor,* pp. 294–95.
74. Known to the author—and to a great many Jewish comedians! See also Alan Dundes, "The J.A.P. and the J.A.M. in American Jokelore," *Journal of American Folklore,* 98, no. 390 (1985): 457. One of the traits of the folkloric Jewish-American Mother is the impossibility of an offspring ever managing to satisfy her.
75. Quoted by Dundes, "The J.A.P. and the J.A.M.," p. 458; he also cites variations on this theme. Another characteristic of the Jewish-American Mother is her obsession with seeing her offspring well-fed.
76. Known to the author. Aside from including a neat Yiddish pun, this folk joke also stresses the Jewish-American Mother's insistence that her child eat well.
77. Known to the author. See Dundes, "The J.A.P. and the J.A.M.," p. 459, for a version learned from his mother. Two of the main concerns of the Jewish-American Mother are to see her daughter married to someone in a respectable, well-paying profession, traditionally a doctor, and for her son to keep in close touch.
78. Known to the author. For a larger selection of Jewish-American Princess jokes, see Dundes, "The J.A.P. and the J.A.M." Jewish-American Princess jokes are widespread in the United States, and can even be discovered on greeting cards and books of paper dolls. See, for example, the tongue-in-cheek *The Official J.A.P. Handbook* by Anna Sequoia and Patty Brown

(New York: New American Library, 1982) and the equally tongue-in-cheek *The Official J.A.P. Paper Doll Book,* by Maude Thickett (New York: New American Library, 1983). A very recent and interesting folklore phenomenon that has been occuring in America only in the last year or so is the replacement of the J.A.P. in some jokes with the more generic, if equally offensive, "dumb blonde."

79. These are folk jokes of very modern vintage indeed, dating from only the last year up to the 1991 Desert Storm campaign. See Blanche Knott, *Truly Tasteless Military Jokes* (New York: St. Martin's Paperbacks, 1991). The "GI J.A.P." joke refers, of course, to the GI Joe military dolls popular (traditionally among boys) in the United States.

Chapter Ten: A Sampling of Proverbs and Riddles

1. From the Talmud.
2. Ibid. Compare the Mexican-American "There are no roses without thorns." See John O. West, ed., *Mexican-American Folklore* (Little Rock, Ark.: August House, 1988), p. 44.
3. From the Talmud.
4. Ibid. Compare with the Latin motto *"In vino veritas."*
5. Ibid. Both English and German speakers might say instead, "The apple doesn't fall far from the tree."
6. Ibid.
7. Ibid.
8. Ibid. Or, as English-speaking people say, "Empty barrels make the most noise."
9. Ibid. Compare with the familiar "Too many cooks spoil the broth."
10. Ibid.
11. Ibid. Compare with the German "Talk is silver, silence golden." See Mac E. Barrick, ed., *German-American Folklore* (Little Rock, Ark.: August House, 1987), p. 44.
12. Proverbs, XIV, 20. This proverb of Solomon expresses a truism found in a good many cultures, from Sanskrit to Latin to English. Compare such variants as the ancient Greek "Everybody honors the rich, but despises the poor" and the Mexican-American "Very few friends has he with nothing to give."
13. A proverb of Solomon, Proverbs, XIV, 10. Also: "A wise son maketh a glad father; but a foolish man despiseth his mother" (Proverbs, XV, 20).
14. Proverbs, XV, 1.
15. From the Talmud.
16. Ibid. Or, as St. Ambrose (340–97) put it, "When you are at Rome, live in the Roman style." The modern English equivalent is, "When in Rome, do as the Romans do."

17. Ibid.
18. Ibid. No, this proverb did not originate with Shakespeare!
19. Known to the author. Also: "If they give, take, if they take, yell for help!" A Russian version known in the author's family says, "If they give, take, if they beat, run!"
20. Known to the author. Compare this Yiddish proverb with the New England "What goes around, comes around."
21. Known to the author. Compare with note 11.
22. The author has heard this originally Yiddish proverb quoted in English by New York City Jews. The Russians say, "If you don't grease, you don't ride." See Simeon Aller, *The Russians Had a Word for It* (Los Angeles: Ward Richie Press, 1963), p. 2.
23. Known to the author.
24. A Yiddish proverb, origin unknown. A Russian proverb adds, "The naked fear no robber." See Aller, *Russians Had a Word for It,* p. 138.
25. Known to the author. The same sentiment is expressed by the Germans: "Small thieves are hung, big ones go free." See Barrick, *German-American Folklore,* p. 38.
26. A Yiddish proverb, source unknown. English-speaking peoples say, "Time heals all wounds."
27. A Yiddish proverb, source unknown. Compare with the New England "Too smart for his own good."
28. Known to the author.
29. Known to the author, who has heard the same sentiment expressed in Yiddish and English in America.
30. Known to the author. Also: "If one person says you have the ears of an ass, pay no attention; if two say so, better buy a saddle."
31. Known to the author.
32. Known to the author's family as "Never spit in the well; you may have to drink from it some day." Compare with the Mexican-American "Don't spit at the sky because it will fall on your face." See Mark Glazer, *Flour from Another Sack: A Collection of Folklore from the Rio Grande Valley of Texas* (Edinburg, Texas: Pan American University, 1982).
33. A Yiddish proverb, source unknown.
34. Known to the author. Also: "When a thief kisses you, count your teeth."
35. A Yiddish proverb, source unknown, known in this country as one of Murphy's Laws!
36. Known to the author.
37. Known to the author.
38. Known to the author. The Russians say this too.
39. A Yiddish proverb, source unknown.
40. A Yiddish proverb, source unknown. Compare to an American saying: "Stupidity is contagious."

41. Known to the author.
42. A Yiddish proverb, source unknown. Also familiar in America as "Cheap is dear."
43. Known to the author. A universal sentiment, though Americans combine death and taxes as two inevitabilities.
44. Known to the author. Also: "The world is small and brings all together." Compare with the American "It's a small world after all."
45. The Hebrew original was collected in Israel, collector and informant unknown, no date given. See Carl Withers and Sula Bennet, eds., *Riddles of Many Lands* (New York: Abelard-Schuman, 1956), p. 101.
46. The Hebrew original was collected in Israel, collector and informant unknown, no date given. See ibid., p.101. See also note 47.
47. The Hebrew original was collected in Israel, collector and informant unknown, no date given. Religious riddles such as this one and the one above, meant to gently test the hearer's knowledge of Judaism, are not uncommon in Jewish folklore. See ibid., p. 102.
48. This Yiddish riddle, source unknown, reflects the traditional Jewish respect for learning. An Anglo-Saxon book riddle is similar but more elaborate, emphasizing the elegance of the book's binding rather than the wisdom of its contents. See Michael Alexander, *The Earliest English Poems* (Baltimore: Penguin Books, 1966), p. 96.
49. Known to the author. This type of "gotcha" puzzle, in which a seemingly unsolvable problem is resolved with a tricky yet logical ending, is common throughout the world. The author remembers one that begins, "You are the bus driver," and proceeds through a long and convoluted description of passengers and their stops to ask, "what color are the bus driver's eyes?" The answer, of course, since "you are the bus driver," is obvious!
50. Known to the author. This riddle is found in various forms throughout the world.
51. The author remembers hearing this one and a variant that was told about an egg.
52. Known to the author. This is another "gotcha" joke.
53. Known to the author. This riddle is known in almost identical versions in every country familiar with onions!
54. Known to the author. This is not so much a "gotcha" joke as it is a little test in logic.
55. Known to the author. Here is yet another riddle known in similar forms around the world.
56. This, and several other versions, known to the author. This problem in logic can be found in various versions throughout the world. In place of the merchants and thieves, variants include wolves and sheep or foxes and geese, all of which must be ferried safely across a lake or river. This

Yiddish version must surely have prompted someone to ask why, when all three thieves were across the lake and all three merchants were not, the thieves didn't live up to their nature and steal the boat?

An applicable motif is H506.3. "Test of resourcefulness: carrying wolf, goat and cabbage across stream."

BIBLIOGRAPHY

◇ ◇ ◇

PART 1: LIFE CYCLES

Diamant, Anita. *The New Jewish Wedding.* New York: Simon & Schuster, Summit Books, 1985.

———. *The Jewish Baby Book.* New York: Simon & Schuster, Summit Books, 1988.

———. *Living a Jewish Life: Jewish Traditions, Customs and Values for Today's Families.* New York: HarperCollins, HarperPerennial, 1991.

Donin, Rabbi Hayim Halevy. *To Be a Jew.* New York: Basic Books, 1972.

Dresner, Samuel H. *The Jewish Dietary Laws.* New York: Burning Bush Press, 1955.

Edidin, Ben M. *Jewish Customs and Ceremonies.* New York: Hebrew Publishing Company, 1978.

Eisenberg, Hattie. *Bar Mitzvah with Ease.* Garden City, N.Y.: Doubleday & Co., 1966.

Fisch, Harold, trans. *The Holy Scriptures.* Jerusalem: Koren, 1969.

Gaster, Theodore H. *Purim and Hanukkah in Custom and Tradition.* Boston: Beacon Press, 1950.

———. *Thespis.* Boston: Beacon Press, 1950.

———. *Festivals of the Jewish Year.* New York: William Morrow & Co., 1952.

———. *Passover: Its History and Traditions.* Boston: Beacon Press, 1962.

Goldberg, Rabbi David. *Holidays for American Judaism.* New York: Bookman Associates, 1954.

Goodman, Philip, ed. *Purim Anthology.* Philadelphia: Jewish Publications Society, 1949.

———. *Passover Anthology.* Philadelphia: Jewish Publications Society, 1961.

———. *Rosh Hashanah Anthology.* Philadelphia: Jewish Publications Society, 1970.

———. *Yom Kippur Anthology.* Philadelphia: Jewish Publications Society, 1971.

———. *Shavuot Anthology.* Philadelphia: Jewish Publications Society, 1975.

———. *Hanukkah Anthology.* Philadelphia: Jewish Publications Society, 1976.

Greenberg, Blu. *How to Run a Traditional Jewish Household.* New York: Simon & Schuster, 1983.

Greenberg, Rabbi Irving. *The Jewish Way: Living the Holidays.* New York: Simon & Schuster, Summit Books, 1988.

Haran, Menahem. "Seething a Kid in Its Mother's Milk," *Journal of Jewish Studies* 30, no. 1 (Spring 1979): 23–35.

Heschel, Abraham Joshua. *The Sabbath: Its Meaning for Modern Man.* New York: Farrar, Straus and Giroux, 1951.

Himmelstein, Rabbi Dr. Shmuel. *The Jewish Primer.* New York: Facts on File, 1990.

The Holy Scriptures According to the Masoretic Text. Philadelphia: Jewish Publication Society of America, 1955.

The Jewish Encyclopedia. 12 vols. New York: Funk and Wagnalls, 1912.

Kertzer, Rabbi Morris N. *What Is a Jew?* New York: Bloch Publishing Co., 1973.

Knobel, Peter S., ed. *Gates of the Seasons: A Guide to the Jewish Year.* New York: Central Conference of American Rabbis, 1983.

Kolatch, Alfred J. *The Jewish Book of Why.* Middle Village, N.Y.: Jonathan David Publishers, 1981.

———. *The Second Jewish Book of Why.* Middle Village, N.Y.: Jonathan David Publishers, 1985.

Kolb, Sylvia and John, eds. *A Treasury of Folk Songs.* New York: Bantam Books, 1954.

Lamm, Maurice. *The Jewish Way in Death and Mourning.* New York: Jonathan David Publishers, 1969.

———. *The Jewish Way in Love and Marriage.* San Francisco: Harper & Row, 1980.

Latner, Helen. *The Book of Modern Jewish Etiquette: A Guide to All Occasions.* New York: Schocken Books, 1981.

Lauterbach, Jacob Z. "The Ceremony of Breaking a Glass at Weddings," *Hebrew Union College Annual* 2 (1925): 351–80.

Levi, Shonie B., and Sylvia R. Epstein. *The Bar/Bat Mitzvah Planbook.* New York: Stein and Day, 1982.

Maslin, Simeon J. *Gates of Mitzvah: A Guide To the Jewish Life Cycle.* New York: Central Conference of American Rabbis, 1979.

Morgenstein, Julian. *Rites of Birth, Marriage, Death and Kindred Occasions Among the Semites.* Cincinnati: Hebrew Union College Press, 1966.

Percy, Thomas. *Reliques of Ancient English Poetry.* London: George Routledge and Sons, n.d.

Power, Patrick C. *Sex and Marriage in Ancient Ireland.* Dublin: Mercier Press, 1976.

Rockland, Mae Shafter. *The Jewish Party Book.* New York: Schocken Books, 1978.

Rottenberg, Lilly S., and Ruth R. Selding. *The Jewish Wedding Book.* New York: Schocken Books, 1967.

Schauss, Hayyim. *The Jewish Festivals.* New York: Schocken Books, 1962.

Sherman, Josepha. *Indian Tribes of North America.* New York: Portland House, 1990.

Strassfield, Michael. *The Jewish Holidays: A Guide and Commentary.* New York: Harper & Row, 1985.

The Torah: The Five Books of Moses. Philadelphia: The Jewish Publication Society of America, 1962.

Twersky, Isador, ed. *A Maimonides Reader.* New York: Behrman House, 1972.

Van Gennep, Arnold. *The Rites of Passage.* Chicago: University of Chicago Press, 1960.

Weinberg, Sheila Peltz. "Kashrut: How Do We Eat?" In *The Jewish Family Book,* edited by Sharon Strassfield and Kathy Green. Toronto: Bantam Books, 1981.

PART 2: FOLKLORE

Aesop. *The Fables of Aesop, with Designs on Wood by Thomas Beswick.* New York: Two Contintents Publishing Group, Paddington Press, 1975.

Afanas'ev, Aleksandr. *Russian Fairy Tales.* New York: Pantheon Books, 1945 and 1973.

Alexander, Michael, trans. *The Earliest English Poems.* Baltimore: Penguin Books, 1966.

Aller, Simeon, trans. *The Russians Said It First: A Heritage of Proverbs.* Los Angeles: Ward Richie Press, 1963.

Asbjornsen, Peter Christen, and Jorgen Moe. *Norwegian Folktales Selected from the Collection of Peter Christen Asbjornsen and Jorgen Moe.* Translated by Pat Shaw and Carl Norman. New York: Pantheon Books, 1960.

Ausubel, Nathan, ed. *A Treasury of Jewish Folklore.* New York: Crown Publishers, 1948.

———. *A Treasury of Jewish Humor.* New York: Doubleday & Co., 1951.

The Babylonian Talmud. Translated by Rabbi Dr. I. Epstein. 36 vols. London: Soncino Press, 1935–52.

The Babylonian Talmud. Translated by Michael Rodkinson. New York: New Talmud Publishing Company, 1900.

Baker, Ronald L. *Jokelore: Humorous Folktales from Indiana.* Bloomington: Indiana University Press, 1986.

Barclay, Joseph, S.L. Macgregor Mathers, and Mrs. Henry Lucas, trans. *Hebrew Literature.* New York: Colonial Press, 1901.

Barash, Asher. *A Golden Treasury of Jewish Tales.* New York: Dodd, Mead & Company, 1966.

Barrick, Mac E. *German-American Folklore.* Little Rock, Ark.: August House, 1987.

Basset, Rene, and Chauncey C. Starkweather. "Popular Tales of the Berbers," *Moorish Literature.* New York: Colonial Press, 1901.

Ben-Amos, Dan. "The 'Myth' of Jewish Humor," *Western Folklore,* no. 32 (1973): 112–31.

Bilski, Emily D. *Golem! Danger, Deliverance and Art.* New York: Jewish Museum, 1988.

Bin Gorion, Micha Joseph, ed. *Mimekor Yisrael: Selected Classical Jewish Folktales.* Bloomington: Indiana University Press, 1990.

Birnbaum, Philip, ed. *The New Treasury of Judaism.* New York: Sanhedrin Press, 1977.

Bloch, Chayim. *The Golem: Mystical Tales From the Ghetto of Prague.* Translated by Harry Schneiderman. New York: Rudolf Steiner Publications, 1972.

Breslauer, S. Daniel. "The Ethics of *Giglgul,*" *Judaism* 32, no. 2 (Spring 1983): 230–35.

Briggs, Katherine M., and Ruth L. Tongue. *Folktales of England.* Chicago: University of Chicago Press, 1959.

Browne, Lewis, ed. *The Wisdom of Israel.* New York: Modern Library, 1945.

Buber, Martin. *The Legend of the Baal-Shem.* Translated by Maurice Friedman. New York: Harper & Brothers, 1955.

Carrick, Malcolm. *The Wise Men of Gotham.* New York: Viking Press, 1975.

Clarkson, Atelia, and Gilbert B. Cross, eds. *World Folktales.* New York: Charles Scribner's Sons, 1980.

Courtlander, Harold, ed. *Ride with the Sun: Folk Tales and Stories from All Countries of the United Nations.* New York: McGraw Hill, 1955.

Czarnomiska, Elizabeth, ed. *The Authentic Literature of Israel.* 2 vols. New York: Macmillan Company, 1924.

Dorson, Richard M. "Jewish-American Dialect Stories on Tape." In *Studies in Biblical and Jewish Folklore,* edited by Raphael Patai, Frances Lee Utley, and Dov Noy. Bloomington: Indiana University Press, 1960.

———. *American Folklore.* Chicago: University of Chicago Press, 1977.

Dundes, Alan. "The J.A.P. and the J.A.M. in American Jokelore," *Journal of American Folklore* 98, no. 390 (1985): 456–75.

Evans-Watts, Walter Yeeling. *The Fairy Faith in Celtic Countries.* University Press, 1966.

"Folklore," vol. 4, pp. 348–49, *The Universal Jewish Encyclopedia in 10 Volumes.* Edited by Isaac Landman. New York: Universal Jewish Encyclopedia Company, 1948.

Frankel, Ellen, ed. *The Classic Tales: 4000 Years of Jewish Lore.* Northvale, N.J.: Jason Aronson, 1989.

Frazier, Sir James George. *The New Golden Bough.* Edited by Theodor H. Gaster. New York: Criterion Press, 1959.

———. *The Golden Bough.* One volume abridgement. New York: Macmillan Company, 1960.

Gaster, Moses. *The Exempla of the Rabbis: Being a Collection of Exampla, Apologues and Tales Culled from Hebrew Manuscripts and Rare Hebrew Books.* London: Asia Publishing Co., 1924.

Gaster, Theodor H. *The Oldest Stories in the World.* Boston: Beacon Press, 1952.

Gershator, Phillis. *Honi and the Magic Circle.* Philadelphia: Jewish Publication Society of America, 1979.

Ginzberg, Louis, ed. *The Legends of the Jews.* 7 vols. Philadelphia: Jewish Publication Society of America, 1909–46.

———. *Legends of the Bible.* New York: Simon & Schuster, 1956.

Glazer, Mark, ed. *Flour from Another Sack: A Collection of Folklore from the Lower Rio Grande Valley of Texas.* Edinburg, Tex.: Pan American University, 1982.

Goldstein, David, ed. *Jewish Legends.* Library of the World's Myths and

Legends. New York: Peter Bedrick Books, 1987. Originally published as *Jewish Folklore and Legend* (London: Newnes Books, 1980).

Grimm, Jacob and Wilhelm. *The Complete Fairy Tales of the Brothers Grimm.* Translated by Jack Zipes. New York: Bantam Books, 1967.

Harris, Ethel. *The King and the Flea and Other Tales.* Oakville, N.Y., and London: Mosaic Press, 1990.

Harris, M. H., trans. *Hebraic Literature.* New York: Tudor Publishing Co., 1941.

Howey, M. Oldfield. *The Horse in Magic and Myth.* New York: Castle Books, 1958.

Ish-Kishor, Judith. *Tales From the Wise Men of Israel.* New York: J. B. Lippincott Company, 1962.

Ish-Kishor, Sulamith. *The Master of Miracle: A New Novel of the Golem.* New York: Pantheon Books, 1963.

Jacobs, Joseph. *More Celtic Fairy Tales.* New York: David Nutt, 1894. Reprint. New York: Dover Publications, 1968.

———. *More English Fairy Tales.* New York: G. P. Putnam's Sons and David Nutt, 1894. Reprint. New York: Dover Publications, 1967.

———. *English Fairy Tales.* New York: G. P. Putnam's Sons and David Nutt, 1898. Reprint. New York: Dover Publications, 1967.

———. *European Folk and Fairy Tales.* New York: G. P. Putnam's Sons, 1916.

Kelsey, Alice Geer. *Once the Mullah: Persian Folk Tales.* New York, London, and Toronto: Longmans, Green and Co., 1954.

Knott, Blanch. *Blanche Knott's Truly Tasteless Military Jokes.* New York: St. Martin's Press, St. Martin's Paperbacks, 1991.

Knox, Israel. "The Wise Men of Helm," *Judaism* 29, no. 2 (Spring 1980): 186–96.

Kumove, Shirley. *Words Like Arrows: A Collection of Yiddish Folk Sayings.* Toronto: University of Toronto Press, 1984; New York: Schocken Books, 1985.

Lehrman, S. M. *The World of the Midrash.* New York: Thomas Yoseloff, 1961.

Levin, Meyer. *Classic Hassidic Tales.* New York: Dorset Press, 1956.

McDermott, Beverly Brodsky. *The Golem.* Philadelphia and New York: J. P. Lippincott Company, Caldecott Honor Book, 1976. [A picturebook retelling of the Golem legend.]

Maccoby, Hyam. *The Day God Laughed.* New York: St. Martin's Press, 1978.

Meyrink, Gustav. *The Golem.* Translated by Madge Pemberton. Prague and San Francisco: Mudra, 1972.

Midrash Rabbah in 10 Volumes. Edited by Rabbi Dr. H. Freedman and Maurice Simon. London: Soncino Press, 1961.

Nadich, Judah. *Jewish Legends of the Second Commonwealth.* Philadelphia: Jewish Publication Society of America, 1983.

Nahmad, H. M. *A Portion in Paradise and Other Jewish Folktales.* New York: W. W. Norton and Company, 1970.

Neusner, Jacob. *Invitation to Midrash.* New York: Harper & Row, 1989.

Novak, William, and Mose Waldoks. *The Big Book of Jewish Humor.* New York: HarperCollins, HarperPerennial, 1981.

Noy, Dov, ed. *Folktales of Israel.* Chicago: University of Chicago Press, 1963.

O'Flaherty, Wendy Doniger. *Other People's Myths.* New York: Macmillan Publishing Company, 1988.

Ozaki, Yei Theodora. *Japanese Fairy Tales.* New York: A. L. Burt Company, n.d.

Oring, Elliott. "The People of the Joke: On the Conceptualization of a Jewish Humor," *Western Folklore* 42, no. 4, (October 1983): 261–71.

Patai, Raphael, ed. *Gates to the Old City: A Book of Jewish Legends.* New York: Avon Books, 1980.

———. *On Jewish Folklore.* Detroit: Wayne University Press, 1983.

Pritchard, James B., ed. *The Ancient Near East: An Anthology of Texts and Pictures.* 2 vols. Princeton: Princeton University Press, 1958.

Rappoport, Dr. Angelo S. *The Folklore of the Jews.* London: Soncino Press, 1937.

———. *Myth and Legend of Ancient Israel.* 3 vols. New York: Ktav Publishing House, 1966.

Rhys, John. *Celtic Folklore: Welsh and Manx.* 2 vols. Oxford: Oxford University Press, 1901; London: Wildwood House, 1980.

Riordan, James. *The Sun Maiden and the Crescent Moon: Siberian Folk Tales.* Edinburgh: Canongate Publishing, 1989; New York: Interlink Books, 1989.

Rosten, Leo. *The Joys of Yiddish.* New York: McGraw Hill, 1968; New York: Pocket Books, 1970.

———. *Treasury of Jewish Quotations.* New York: McGraw Hill, 1972.

Rugoff, Milton, ed. *A Harvest of World Folk Tales.* New York: Viking Press, 1949.

Sadeh, Pinhas. *Jewish Folktales.* New York: Doubleday, 1989. Translated by Hillel Halkin. Originally published as *Sefer ha-dimyonot shel ha-Yeshudim* (Tel-Aviv: Schocken Publishing House, 1983).

Schram, Peninnah. *Jewish Stories One Generation Tells Another.* Northvale, N.J.: Jason Aronson, 1989.

Schwartz, Howard. *Elijah's Violin and Other Jewish Fairy Tales.* New York: Harper Colophon Books, 1985.

———. "Jewish Tales of the Supernatural," *Judaism* 36, no. 3 (Summer 1987).

———. *Lilith's Cave: Jewish Tales of the Supernatural.* New York: Harper & Row, 1988.

———. *Miriam's Tambourine: Jewish Folktales from Around the World.* Oxford: Oxford University Press, 1988.

Sequoia, Anna, and Patty Brown. *The Offiical J.A.P. Handbook.* New York: New American Library, 1982.

Shtutshkof, Nokhem. *Der Oyster Fun Der Yidisher Shprakh.* New York: Yiddish Scientific Institute-YIVO, 1950.

Simon, Solomon. *The Wandering Beggar.* New York: Behrman House, 1942.

———. *The Wise Men of Helm and Their Merry Tales.* New York: Behrman House, 1955.

———. *More Wise Men of Helm and Their Merry Tales.* New York: Behrman House, 1965.

Spalding, Henry D. *Encyclopedia of Jewish Humor from Biblical Times to the Modern Age.* New York: Jonathan David Publishers, 1989.

Steinsaltz, Adin. *The Essential Talmud.* Translated by Chaya Galai. New York: Basic Books, 1976.

Studies in Jewish Folklore: Proceedings of a Regional Conference of the Association for Jewish Studies Held at the Spertus College of Judaica, Chicago, May 1–3, 1977. Cambridge, Mass.: Association for Jewish Studies, 1980.

The Talmud of the Land of Israel. Translated by Tzvee Zahavy. Chicago: University of Chicago Press, 1989.

Theal, George McCall. *Kaffir Folk-Lore.* London: S. Sonnenschein, Le Bas & Lowrey, 1886; Westport, Conn.: Negro Universities Press, 1970.

Thickett, Maude. *The Official J.A.P. Paper Doll Book.* New York: New American Library, 1983.

Thompson, Stith. *The Types of the Folk-Tale:* Antti Aarne's *Verzeichnis der Marchentypen* translated and enlarged. FF Communications No. 74, Helsinki, 1928.

———. *Motif-Index of Folk-Literature:* a classification of narrative elements in folktales, ballads, myths, fables, mediaeval romances, exempla, fabliaux, jest-books, and local legends. 6 vols. Bloomington: Indiana University Press, 1932–36.

———. *The Folktale.* New York: Holt, Rinehart and Winston, 1946; Berkeley and Los Angeles: University of California Press, 1977.

Trachtenberg, Joshua. *Jewish Magic and Superstition: A Study in Folk Religion.* New York: Atheneum Publishers, 1970.

Weinreich, Beatrice Silverman, ed. *Yiddish Folktales.* Translated by Leonard Wolf. New York: Pantheon Books and YIVO Institute for Jewish Research, 1988.

West, John O. *Mexican-American Folklore.* Little Rock, Ark.: August House, 1988.

Withers, Carl, and Sula Benet. *Riddles of Many Lands.* New York: Abelard-Schulman, 1956.

The World's Best Yiddish Dirty Jokes. Secaucus, N.J.: Citadel Press, 1984.

Yolen, Jane, ed. *Favorite Folktales from Around the World.* New York: Pantheon Books, 1986.

Zheleznova, Irina, ed. and trans. *Folk Tales from Russian Lands.* New York: Dover Publications, 1969. Originally published as *A Mountain of Gems: Fairy-Tales of the Peoples of the Soviet Land* (Moscow: Foreign Languages Publishing House, 1963).